Counterclockwise

Counterclockwise

A Novel

MICHAEL G. HICKEY

NCP
Northchester Press
northchesterpress.com

Published in the United States by Northchester Press

This book is a work of fiction. Names, characters, businesses, organizations, places, events and incidents are either the product of the author's imagination or are used fictitiously.

The Cataloging-in-Publication Data is on file with the Library of Congress

ISBN: 978-1-47745-866-00

Design: Sonya Unrein

NORTHCHESTERPRESS.COM

Printed in the United States of America

Acknowledgments

Thank you especially to my family Mona, Nathan, and T.J., as well as teachers and students—past, present, and future —including Robert C.S. Downs, Robert Houston, Maura Stanton, Chris O'Dell, and David Shields. Also, I owe a special debt of gratitude to the many readers and editors who unselfishly gave their valuable time to read drafts, without which this book in its final form would not be possible.

Clocks slay time . . . time is dead as long as it is being clicked off by little wheels; only when the clock stops does time come to life.

—William Faulkner

for Elaine

PART I: FRIDAY

1. Premonition

Jasper Trueblood poured two fingers of Kahlua into his morning coffee, then lifted the bottle up to the ambient light cast from the kitchen to see how much was left. A couple drops slipped over the lip of the cup and onto the *Arizona Daily Star*. It was May 9, 1980, his twenty-first birthday, a day he had once eagerly anticipated. "Happy fucking birthday to me," he said. Jasper had just turned twenty-one and felt like he was dying of old age. He knew exactly where he was, yet was absolutely lost.

Finally legal. No more fake IDs or friends with older brothers who could buy booze at a mom-and-pop store out on the old county road. Today, Jasper could walk into any bar or, for that matter, conduct any business transaction as a full-fledged adult. It should have been a time for reverie and celebration but there would be no tickertape, confetti, or blondes bouncing out of cakes, just the post-piñata holding pattern that had become his life. It may have been Jasper's birthday, but the only thing distinguishing this day from any other was that if his old man were ever going to show up, this would be the day he'd do it, the one party his father might be willing to crash.

Jasper had been in Tucson for almost a year and found it to be the kind of place where locals stared down strangers and looked the other way from people they knew. He had heard it was still legal to walk around with a gun and holster in plain sight like the old days of John Wayne. There were plenty of cowboys and quasi-cowboys who wore Stetsons, lizard-skin boots, and listened to country western music heavy on the slide guitar, but there didn't seem to be much of the Wild West left in this old desert. Amidst the Santa Catalina Mountains and severe water shortage stood the saguaro cacti, arms raised in supplication, praying for the souls of yuppie urban raiders who were desecrating the land with housing developments and strip malls for the aspiring middle class. Mother Nature was being raped in Tucson just as she had been up north in Phoenix, which had already succumbed to the furtive political desire to replicate L.A. It wouldn't be long before the hundred miles between Tucson and Phoenix would be consumed entirely by apartment complexes, condominiums, and billboards proclaiming, "Arizona, your time has come!"

Jasper often thought that outwardly Tucson was an unlikely destination for a good Catholic boy like himself, he who had never strayed far from the friendly confines of the Midwest. Nonetheless, this was where he had landed, Tucson—the last leg of his escape. Perhaps, he thought, the isolation and commensurate solitude of the Sonoran desert was the perfect symbol for survival, for liberation from his past.

Eleven months earlier, Jasper had extricated himself from his father and 235 Magellan Drive—a brick house in the suburbs of southern Illinois—by talking the old man into signing a student loan application. His father had been uncharacteristically compliant, still under the spell of grief and prescription nerve pills. Ever since Jasper's mother surrendered to cancer in February of

1978, his father had been caught in a death spiral. He'd become a phantom. He went to church, prayer meetings, and read the Bible in his room while watching Jesus TV on his little black-and-white. Jasper understood his sorrow and pain only too well. He missed his mother like a farmer missed the rain in a drought. It was the only thing he and the old man had left in common. Sadness. Without so much as saying goodbye, Jasper packed a duffle bag and hopped a Greyhound bus with screechy air brakes. He embarked on a rainy Tuesday night, the trip to Tucson would take two days, and other than a dormitory at the University of Arizona, Jasper didn't know where he was going, only what he was leaving behind. By the second day of the trek, his socks felt like they were welded on and he finally peeled them off. He arrived in Tucson, shading his eyes from the afternoon sun. The mountains were spectacular, as were the palm trees and scantily-clad coeds. He took a taxi to a cheap motel near campus where he would hole up for a few days before school started, writing poetry and walking the streets until the dormitory opened for business. It was during this time that Jasper's most prodigious creative act to date revealed itself. He decided to change his name.

Jasper went to the municipal court downtown, filled out the perfunctory paperwork, and for two hundred and fifteen dollars legally changed his name from Junior McPherson to Jasper Trueblood, a name he'd found in the phone book. He figured his father, Robert McPherson, deeply immersed in spiritual flogging, would eventually become aware of Jasper's departure and look for him. The name change would throw him off-course. And for the first few months of Jasper's emancipation, that appeared to be true. He stopped wondering if the old man were searching for him anymore. But in the last few days, Jasper had been having what he described to his boss, Tony, as premonitions. In these moments, all the clocks in all the world seemed to stop but time seemed to come alive, which made no sense if you thought about it, but it was how it felt. Time became relevant. Jasper closed his eyes and imagined a face-to-face meeting with Robert McPherson, the discomfort of which generated a buzzing in the marrow of Jasper's bones.

He finished his coffee, what was left of the Kahlua, and stepped in the shower trying to remember his father's face: the salt-and-pepper comb-over, the scar on his right eyebrow from a welding accident in the Navy, and the paunch gut from an insatiable appetite for Tootsie Rolls. Jasper wondered if the old man's aging process had accelerated in the last eleven months, like those pictures of Jimmy Carter before and after.

While he was shampooing, Jasper inexplicably felt his father's presence in the soap, the suds, every rivulet of water . . . like he was in the room and penetrating the entire blueprint of Jasper's DNA. Jasper had to peek outside the shower curtain just to be sure the old man wasn't standing there. This sense of foreboding even had its own aroma, something akin to the scent of an impending thunderstorm. Increasingly, Jasper had been having visceral moments of prescience in which he could hear the following percussive exchange vibrate in both eardrums.

Hello, Son.
Leave me alone.
Why don't you come home, Son?
Why don't you go to hell?

The old man's voice would be smoky and low-toned, seductive, like a hostage negotiator. Jasper could close his eyes and hear the way Robert McPherson would pause for emphasis and lower his inflection to a near-whisper then, without warning, erupt into some ear-splitting invective about the crisis du jour. But after Jasper's mother had died, Robert McPherson was mostly a ghost. He no longer lost his temper over utility bills, parking tickets, or the missing *TV Guide*. He no longer bemoaned the dirty floor or the absence of dinner on the table at the prescribed hour, nor did he bother to deride his only child. He barely made eye contact, and when he did, Jasper noticed a lack of awareness. There was no light in his father's eyes. Before her death, the old man's application of corporal punishment had ascended new heights. In the past, he had beaten Jasper in the bathtub with a belt, kicked him down a flight of stairs, spit in his face, and chased him around the churchyard across the street in his boxer shorts. Robert McPherson could be accused of many things, yet wasn't guilty of the greatest crime of all—sparing the rod and spoiling the child. But that was the old, pre-shadow Robert McPherson. Now he had no anger left. Or maybe it was that he had no energy. Jasper imagined his father learning about the name change. The scar on his eyebrow would twitch, his lower lip would tremble, and the purple vein in his forehead would pulsate.

As he pulled on his jeans, Jasper caught a glimpse of himself in the mirror and reflected on his first twenty-one years. There were the sixties: 'Nam, Nixon, sex, drugs, rock 'n' roll, but by the end of the decade, tuning in, turning on, and dropping out had lost much of its appeal. Then came the seventies: mood rings, pet rocks, and discotheques. The hippies-become-yuppies of the so-called "me" generation worked lots of overtime so they could retire by fifty, wear designer jeans, and go on scavenger hunts to find their inner children. They stopped dropping acid and started snorting coke. In time, just about anyone could work their way up to low-self esteem. And what did the eighties have in store? It was still too soon to tell but so far, the economy was in shambles, a bad actor was running for president, and all anyone seemed to talk about was who shot a fictional television character named J. R.

Jasper looked in the mirror. In the steamy reflection was a grown-up Huck Finn with a farmer's tan, a boyish cowlick, eyes the color of jade marbles, and an extra twenty pounds around the waist. He sucked in and flexed his biceps, but when he exhaled, the flab capitulated to gravity. "Happy fat ass birthday," he said.

As he snapped the buttons of his western shirt, he tried to recall a dream he had had the night before about a woman with dark hair and a familiar face.

The phone rang twice and stopped. This was his boss calling from the market, a signal to pick up the pace. Life, his boss was fond of saying, was all about punctuality. *Learn your lines, show up on time, and the rest'll take care of itself.*

Jasper believed dreams were the pilot light for his poetry, the flicker and flame of his subconscious where all the ideas hid, the foundation for his art. Dreams were the vehicles he used to explore the vistas of the brain humans didn't typically use, dusty old synapses like Christmas lights left in the basement. Although he didn't tell people this, he believed that through poetry he would one day win all the prestigious literary awards, get his picture in the paper, and at last become somebody. What Jasper lacked in talent he compensated for in ambition. While tying his tennis shoes, he finally placed the face of his dream girl.

It had been months since he'd reflected on their chance encounter at his old community college back in Illinois. The cafeteria had been nearly empty that day. In addition to repeating a math class, Jasper had been employed as a work-study custodian: sweeping halls, painting walls, and cutting grass on a riding lawn mower. He'd been eating lunch when Faith—her name was *Faith*—asked if she could join him. He could still recall her cheeks dappled with freckles and twists of walnut hair cascading to the middle of her back. Next to her worn leather book bag was her lunch, fruit cocktail and a can of Fresca. She was optimism personified. "You have the prettiest hazel eyes," she had said.

As it turned out, Faith had been poised to transfer to the University of Arizona, where palm trees and eighty-degree-winters created an academic paradise, especially for people familiar with the wind chill factor of the Midwest. Faith's impending desert adventure illuminated her incandescent smile.

"The beauty of it all is that I don't have a dime to my name," she explained. "I'm doing it all with student loans." She chronicled with considerable zeal how Jimmy Carter was handing out student loans like religious tracts at a Billy Graham Crusade, and she couldn't wait to liberate herself from her nagging parents and annoying ex-boyfriend.

Faith's proclamation and well-orchestrated plan to escape her life was enticing. It planted itself in Jasper's mind and germinated for weeks, and eventually became the ticket away from the melancholy he and his father shared.

Whatever happened to Faith? he wondered.

By the time Jasper's Greyhound bus glided into Tucson, his appetite for academe had waned. He went through the ritual of registration but his energy was severely depleted, the bouncy coeds were a constant distraction, and a few of the guys in the dorm liked to stay up late drinking tequila.

He had liked his writing class, but the other courses were torturous exercises in mental masturbation. He didn't want to become an authority on Chaucer, learn a foreign language, or memorize entire pages of ancient poems written in Olde English. He was flabbergasted to learn that some of the so-called famous poems in his anthology were penned by authors listed as ANONYMOUS. The profs didn't even know who wrote the damn things! It wasn't long before Jasper's train had jumped the tracks. He was fortunate to have landed a job at the first place he applied, Thyme Market, a gourmet store near campus. He had exited his old life two thousand miles away and reinvented himself in a desert grocery store, and he owed it all to Faith and that fateful day in the cafeteria.

Violence & Paranoia

She chases him
out the front door
hot yellow grass, August pavement
she squeezes the trigger
the first shot hits his neck
the next five drench his shirt
he screams once for each
she smiles
the water is ice cold.

This was a poem Jasper had written the night before. He imagined reading it for an audience who would be understandably horrified by the implied violence until they realized the weapon was a water gun. Then Jasper would pull out a real water gun from his coat pocket and squirt them. It was an idea still in progress.

He checked the clock and snatched his keys off the dresser when the phone rang again. He picked it up. "I know I'm late, Boss. I'm walking out the front door even as we speak."

There was a pause on the other line and then, demurely, "Junior, is that you?"

"Who is this?" But as soon as Jasper uttered the words, it hit him. Who else would call him *Junior*? "I knew you were going to call," Jasper said soberly. "I had a premonition."

"Junior, is that you?" There was a fissure in the timbre of Robert McPherson's barely audible voice.

"Yes."

"Son, I want to talk to you. First off, I want to wish you a happy birthday."

Jasper rubbed his forehead and covered the mouthpiece with his hand. "Shit," he said aloud. He glanced at the clock. Nausea swept through his central nervous system. Until the past few days, he'd nearly convinced himself he no longer had a father.

"Junior, say something."

"How did you get this number?"

There was an anxious laugh. "It wasn't easy. I'd like to talk to you, Son. It's been a long time."

"How did you get this number?"

"I hired a private investigator. I thought you might be kidnapped or something. Like those hostages in Iran. I called the police, the sheriff, the FBI. I've been looking all over. How come you changed your name?"

"I'm late for work. I have to hang up."

"Junior," there was a prolonged pause, "we have to talk. There are things you need to know."

"Don't call me *Junior*. That's not my name anymore."

"Let me come see you."

Jasper laughed. "Don't even think about it."

"Listen, Junior, I failed as a father. But as bad as I was, there was food on the table and a roof over your head. That's more than my old man ever gave me. Oughta be worth something."

Jasper's jaw quivered. "Look, if you're calling because you're feeling guilty for treating my mother like shit even when she was dying of cancer, it's too late. She's dead. She ain't comin' back. There ain't no turnin' back the clock. I have no sympathy for you or me or anyone else."

"When's the last time you went to church?"

"You gotta be kidding. You called to calibrate my moral compass? It's a little late for preaching, don't you think?" Jasper laughed again.

"How about a little *respect*? Is that too much to ask? You didn't have the common courtesy to tell me you were leaving, didn't have the decency to drop me a line. My wife dies of cancer, my kid jumps ship. Put yourself in my shoes."

"After her funeral, you told me it was time I learned how to survive on my own. That's what I'm doing. I'm *surviving*."

"Think of your mother. Would she approve of this attitude?"

"You think of her," Jasper said. "You killed her."

A silence hung between them as twisted and tangled as the telephone cord.

Jasper checked the guitar-shaped clock on the wall. His bellicose boss was going to be livid.

"That's not fair," his father's voice was now a whisper.

"She was sick for a long time. You could've redeemed yourself. You could've consoled her. You could have held her. But instead, you became an even bigger prick. You wouldn't even clean out the fucking puke bucket after her chemotherapy." Jasper heard his father cry, a strange kind of crying, too, like a baby who cries himself to sleep and continues to whimper in his dreams. Jasper resisted the temptation to quote one of Robert McPherson's favorite old bromides: big boys don't cry.

"I was going through some serious shit, Junior. There are a lot of circumstances you don't know about. Let your old man fly out and see you. Just for a weekend."

"When I think of you, I think of her. When I think of her, I can hear the wind blow through my soul. That's why I can't see you. Now do you understand? I have to go to work." Jasper started to hang up the phone.

"*Don't!*" his father shrieked. "Don't hang up. Look, I never asked you for anything before, but I'm asking you now. Tell me about school. I want to know about your school. That's the least you can do considering you practically stole my signature to get there."

"Fuck school. I quit school. Listen, I'm late. I have a job. I gotta go."

"I'll call when you get home."

"If you ever call me again, I'll get an unlisted number."

"Junior . . . please. I loved her. In my own way, I really did."
Jasper looked disgustedly at the dark receiver. "You never
loved anyone. Not even yourself."

There was another pause. "At least I never hit her."
Jasper laughed. "You're so full of shit. You slapped her in the
face that one morning right before church."

"With an open hand."

"That's how you justify it? Open hand, not closed fist? Do you
even have an inkling of how fucked up that sounds? Listen, I
gotta cruise. I'm running late. I've been very busy . . . *surviving.*"

"I need to talk to you. I won't subject you to excuses or apologies. This is more like a business trip. There are things you
should know about your life. God's forgiven me. You should try
to do the same."

Jasper held the receiver away from his chest and then dropped
it abruptly into its cradle before he could change his mind. His
heart was tap dancing inside his ribcage. "Perfect," Jasper said.
"That's just perfect. I knew he was gonna call."

Then he ran the three blocks to Thyme Market. Breathless
and still in shock, he was eighteen minutes late.

"Good morning, Mrs. Fergus," he said, panting at the front
door.

"Low-fat cottage cheese. Low-fat cottage cheese. How many
times do I have to tell you? Jesus Christ!" The woman pulled
her plump derriere over an antique bicycle the way a hen set-
tles itself over an egg. "Now I have to ride all the way down to
the Twelfth Street Meat Market just for goddamn low-fat cottage cheese. I told that pig ten times," she said motioning toward Tony, the owner, who was working the cash register. "He
doesn't care. He couldn't care less." The bike angrily wiggled
away down the sidewalk.

Jasper rubbed his eyes. "Hello Boss, sorry I'm late."

Tony, in a blood-stained apron, was inserting a new receipt

tape into the cash register. "One of these days you'll be early and I'll go into cardiac arrest. You owe me twenty minutes. What took you so long?"

"I got a phone call from back home. I'm sorry. Today's my birthday. I'll make up the twenty minutes at lunch. It won't happen again. Promise."

"Happy birthday and invest in a damn alarm clock. I need somebody I can depend on. You've told me that story three times in the last month. I've been talking with Pam about making you manager, but every time we're about to invest in you, you come to work twenty minutes late." He removed the big bills from the register and locked them in the floor safe. "It's all yours."

Jasper tossed his faded St. Louis Cardinal cap behind the cigarette display, hoping like hell the old man didn't have his work number. At least *I never hit her.* That was a good one. He hoped it wasn't going to be a day of cottage cheese fanatics. Ninety-eight percent of the clientele were cool, considering the gourmet prices. But the other two percent evened the score. They were dirty, rude, mentally unstable, prone toward shoplifting, and despite the brevity of his employment at Thyme Market, Jasper's esteem for the general public had taken a nosedive.

The morning lumbered along, distracting him if only intermittently from dear old dad's wake-up call. On Fridays, most of the delivery men came in to leave ample supplies for the weekend. Every time the old man's voice crept back into Jasper's consciousness, he tried to soothe his discomfort with thoughts of his sometimes-girlfriend, Lani. Sweet, elusive, poetry-loving Lani. Brilliant, ebullient, curvaceous—a brunette bombshell with brains. Every time he heard his father's voice, he'd repeat this mantra: *Lani Sablan from the island of Guam.* He'd call later to see if she had plans after he got off work. Lani could make him forget. Lani could make anyone forget anything.

"See ya later, gorgeous," Jasper said, regaining his composure. The distinguished gray-haired woman turned and winked. Jasper knew how far he could go. He called the school girls *ladies* and the older women *girls*. It seemed to work. He figured females who thought about love thought he must be a fine young lover because he was such a deft flirt, but behind his outgoing veneer Jasper knew he was poverty-stricken, overweight, and a college dropout—not much of a catch. He wasn't sure what Lani saw in him other than her penchant for poetry. That was his only in.

Thyme Market was a curious landmark located near the edge of downtown on Third Street and Third Avenue, a point of demarcation that divided the middle class from the downtrodden and impoverished. Most everything to the north was high-rise condos with manicured lawns. Most everything to the south was slums, barrios, and litter-strewn pocket parks sprinkled with transients. Jasper noticed the vagrants thrived on variety: one green sock, one red sock, one tennis shoe, one bare foot. The ones in fatigues were Vietnam vets. During the war, the enemy had been hidden in trees. Now everyone was the enemy—life was the enemy!—and it was hiding everywhere. The non-vets were derelicts of more personal wars, Jasper guessed, and the most deranged, like King Rat and the Rubber Band Man, were psychotic and physically disfigured. They were the ones to watch. Jasper could see why Tony didn't want them around.

There were others: Man-Woman, the Human Ant, Iris the Virus, and the Lady with the Glass Eye. They were strange, but not dangerous. Their money was as good as anybody's. Man-Woman, for example, was androgynous; thick black hair covered her arms, face, and knuckles, and her hands were bigger than Jasper's. At first she scared him, but turned out to be just another Bible-thumper and other than her beard, no different than any other Jesus freak. It was the dangerous ones whom Tony didn't like. All they bought were quarts of Budweiser and even if it were a hundred quarts a day, it was dirty money scaring away decent customers. Their M.O. was to take a food stamp, equal in legal tender to one dollar, and buy the cheapest item in the store, usually gum or candy. The clerk would subsequently give the customer change, and this practice was repeated day after day, store after store. The transients' occupation had become converting food stamps into beer money. They were entrepreneurs of the welfare state. Just let them buy the beer with food stamps and save everyone a lot of time, Jasper thought.

It was almost noon. He wanted to find the boss so he could eat lunch and call Lani, but a long-haired health fanatic with a pound of plums and a bunch of grapes went into a long song and dance about some old Mexican who had given him a sacred necklace capable of warding off evil spirits, which the long-haired health fanatic sported proudly around his neck. It looked suspiciously to Jasper like an avocado pit on a piece of string. The health fanatic explained that his long hair had been the inspiration for the old Mexican's generosity, apparently reminding the gentleman of a medicine man he once knew in Chihuahua.

As soon as Jasper sensed an opening, he interrupted. "Look, I have to find the boss, but take it easy all right? Eat some plums, will ya?" He smiled.

The long-haired health fanatic smiled back heartily, genuinely, and wished Jasper a *really nice day*. Jasper high-tailed it back to the deli wondering if the guy was gay.

"Hey Boss, can I make myself a sandwich?"

Tony was behind the counter, taking lunch orders and making occasional passes at his shapely and efficient blonde wife, Pam, who ran the deli with military precision. She didn't appreciate Tony's public displays of affection. "You owe me twenty minutes," Tony said to Jasper.

"I know."

"Be on time from now on. How old are you today?"

"The big two-one."

"When I was twenty-one, I already had two kids. Any of the undesirables been around today?"

"King Rat earlier, out back by the trash."

"Did you run him off?"

"Yeah. I told him to hang out at the Twelfth Street Meat Market, but I think he likes it here. I guess we have better shit in our Dumpster."

Tony took over the front register, checking the store mirrors. A large white ball resembling a deep sea diver's helmet hung from the ceiling in the middle of the store. It contained six camera eyes intended to search out shoplifters and although none of the eyes technically worked, a red blinking light served as a steady beacon against crime. Tony depended on the contraption for intimidation. The mirrors were his real friends.

Jasper tried to call, but Lani must have gone to school or the pool. No one ever answered at Lani's anymore. Pam was busy with the lunch crowd so Jasper made his own sandwich.

As he sat on the picnic bench behind the store, he thought about Robert McPherson. He'd been pretty hard on old Bob. He also imagined Lani with her newest frat rat, the one with the yellow Porsche he'd seen her with the other day outside the sorority house. What was his name? Jasper could never remember their names. For a couple months Jasper had a used motorcycle, an old 350 Honda, and he and Lani went for rides in the desert. She claimed to love the wind in her hair and all, said it made her feel *zoomy*. But the bike had a blown piston and clearly Lani was quite comfortable, thank you very much, with immense wealth in general and yellow Porsches in particular.

After lunch, Jasper returned to the register thirty minutes early. He was back on the boss's good side. "Pam's closing the deli now and we're going shopping," Tony said. "Can you handle it?"

"Sure thing, Boss."

"Seriously? Because if you can't, I'll get someone in here who can. Happy birthday and everything, but this is my life. This store is my life. Don't let anything happen to it."

Jasper nodded. "Promise."

"Did you bring your keys?"

Jasper dug them out of his pocket and jingled them in the air. "I sleep with them under my pillow at night and wish for a raise."

"Make sure you lock both doors after you clean up," Tony said. "And remember to lock the safe and change the sign, too."

"Don't worry, it's under control. Look, I'm sorry I was late. Right as I was walking out the door my old man called me. Remember how I told you I hadn't spoken with him? Remember how I told you the other day I had a feeling he was gonna call?"

"So how did it go?"

"Not well."

Tony lightly grabbed Jasper's shoulder. "Hey, Pam's waiting in the truck and I gotta run, but I wanna hear more about this later, OK?"

* * *

Jasper liked working alone. He enjoyed making small business decisions, even if they were just like check approval or how much merlot to order. The autonomy, albeit not earth-shaking, gave him a sense of respect, integrity. Robert McPherson once said he hated spoiled children more than God hated Satan. Jasper had always wondered exactly what that meant.

It was hard to believe he was even his father's son. They weren't just different, they were diametric opposites. Robert McPherson was left-brain mechanical, loved to take things apart and put them back together. He was ex-Navy, a loner, and had practically no regard for politics, sports, or the arts. Jasper, conversely, couldn't fix a car to save his life and was damn proud of it. He lived for poetry and the St. Louis Cardinals. Also, unlike his father, he easily made friends with total strangers, a trait inherited from his mother. Jasper missed his mother so much that lately, he'd become lonely enough to consider joining a club or belonging to an organization. He missed his friends back home. He missed Faith, the girl in his dream.

Even before Robert McPherson's wake-up call, forgetting about his other life hadn't been working so well. As much as he hated to admit it, Jasper had been catching himself wondering how the old man was holding up. At times, Jasper got to feeling guilty about his vanishing act. And he realized that changing his name hadn't changed anything. The pain was still percolating like a not-so-dormant volcano.

"It's going to rain tomorrow," a customer announced. His khaki shorts and pith helmet gave him the appearance of a mail carrier.

Jasper poked his head outside the door. It was oppressively hot, still several weeks away from the monsoon season, and waves of heat rose from the city streets. It was well over a hundred degrees, and the blistering sun stood high in a blue cloudless sky. "What makes you say that?"

"The leaves."

"The leaves are going to rain?"

"No. The backs of the leaves are white."

"Doesn't sound very scientific," Jasper said.

The mailman look-alike chuckled. "I grew up on a farm in Vermont. When the leaves turn white and the cows sit on the ground, you know the rain is coming. It's not science, it's nature. There's a big difference."

Nice sentiment, Jasper thought, whatever the hell it meant.

The mailman purchased a bottle of expensive French wine and exited as two university girls entered. Jasper had been working up the courage to ask out the one with the big brown eyes but figured anyone with peepers like that had to have a linebacker-boyfriend lurking nearby. Her companion headed back to the frozen foods section and just as Jasper was left alone with Brown Eyes, trying not to ogle her directly, an angular man ambled in the store. He had a long black beard streaked gray and white, a white robe hanging from his shoulder blades, and a length of rope knotted around his waist that held everything intact. He looked like he had just stepped out of the New Testament. Jasper's mouth hung open, and Brown Eyes was staring too.

"Are you aware that Jesus loves you?" the emaciated patron asked.

"Yes," Jasper said. "I mean, I've always suspected it."

"In that case, would you care to break bread in the name of our Lord and Savior?"

"I would," Jasper said, "but the owner wouldn't and it's his bread. Sorry."

"I don't beg charity, brother," he said. "I am prepared to perform a task. Perhaps I can sweep?"

"Look, not today. OK?"

"Don't be sorry," the man said. "Rejoice. Jesus loves you."

The biblical beggar left and Jasper felt embarrassed and not like rejoicing at all because Brown Eyes flashed him a condescending sneer and took off with her friend like he was supposed to give away the store or something.

Later, as Jasper paged through a *Playboy*, which was strictly forbidden on the job, he wondered what it would cost to have his phone number unlisted. Still, a private eye could probably find him anywhere. The after-work rush hit. Fridays were paydays for most working folk, and a stack of twenties collected along with personal checks for cigarettes, foreign beer, and other weekend necessities. The line was six deep, but this didn't concern Jasper who, even blindfolded, believed he operated his register faster than any of those over-paid chain store clerks.

"Seven-fifty."

The woman laid out a five, two ones, and two quarters. Jasper bagged her groceries. "I need another nickel."

"You said seven-fifty."

"I'm sorry. I should've charged five more cents on tax. It's seven dollars and fifty-five cents."

"What?"

"I should have charged you five more cents on tax."

"But you said seven-fifty."

Jasper sighed. The woman was an attractive redhead in her thirties and usually quite pleasant. People in line began to take notice. "Forget it," Jasper said. "Never mind."

"What?"

"Forget it. My mistake. Sorry."

The woman dug in. She was going nowhere. "Are you trying to insult me? Are you trying to make a fool out of me?"

Wouldn't take much, Jasper thought. "No. just a clerical error, all right? My fault. I'm sorry." He resented having to apologize to strangers for a living.

"You're trying to make an idiot out of me."

"Here." Jasper tossed a nickel on the counter. "Geez, I'm sorry I brought it up. We won't go broke either way. Let's make it seven forty-five. Have a nickel and a nice day. Next?"

The woman picked up the nickel and flipped it on the floor. "The owner's going to hear about this. You're a real asshole," she said.

Jasper turned toward the line of customers that now extended halfway down the aisle. All eyes were on him. "Next please."

A well-dressed black man he knew from the prosecuting attorney's office stepped up to the register, grinning. "Friend of yours?"

Jasper smiled back.

The steady stream of humanity made the rest of the day pass quickly and five minutes before lock-up, Jasper covered the produce section with plastic and swept the floor. Just before he went to lock the front door and switch the sign to CLOSED, Mrs. Landish plodded in. Mrs. Mildred Landish, a.k.a. Mrs. Outlandish, was a retired seamstress from the old country whose bony, slender jaws and pointed chin made her look like a stork. She had a new problem every day, usually related to her health or her son. She was a spry old gal and Jasper admired her spunk, but not five minutes before closing. Not when there was still the remote chance of tracking down Lani on his twenty-first birthday.

"Hello, hello. Can you help me? I need help today, sonny boy."

"Yes, Mildred, I'll help, but . . . " Jasper was poised with a reprimand, but the faraway look in her eyes suggested it would only precipitate further delay. "You must try to come earlier."

"What time is it?" She squinted, her wrinkles forming a faint smile.

"I'm supposed to lock up in two minutes."

"I fell asleep because of the heat, and my son forgot to wake me up, and I forgot to tell him—"

"That's all well and good," Jasper interrupted. "Let's take care of your order." He had to stay on top of her or she'd set up camp. He locked the front doors.

"I don't like this," she said. "I don't like this at all. It's bad when you hurry. When you hurry, you make mistakes."

My whole life is a mistake, Jasper thought. "I won't hurry, but the store is technically closed."

"All right, all right." She fished a grocery list from a beaded coin purse. "I need only cheese, cookies, and tea."

He led her to the deli, her legs a network of varicose veins supported by a twisted wooden cane.

"Here are the cheeses," he said, pointing to the glass deli case where portions of cheese were displayed with a diminutive name tag.

"I can't read those little flags, sweetie. My eyes can't see that small. My son sees clear as day."

Jasper sounded off the names. "Domestic Swiss, Swedish Ambrosia, Canadian Black Diamond . . ."

"What about a diamond?"

He ignored her and continued. "Brie, Gorgonzola, Oregon Tillamook. Are you with me?"

"I don't know what those are. They're all different."

"You don't really want any cheese, do you?"

"No, because you hurry so fast I can't think. I want cookies and tea."

Jasper led her to the confections aisle and recited the name of each kind of cookie on the shelf, absent of the trademark conviviality that customers had come to expect of their neighborhood grocer with the personal touch. "Butterfingers, chocolate chip, coconut swirl . . ."

Mildred scratched the sparse patch of hair on her head then rubbed her chin in frustration. "Let's find tea then cookies. My doctor says to drink tea. Too hot to boil anything today, so tonight when the sun goes down I must drink tea."

"Jasmine, peppermint, spearmint, chamomile, Red Zinger—"

"Red who?" With a grimace, Mildred waved her baggy arm. "When you hurry, I can't think straight. What do they taste like?"

"I don't know. I don't drink tea. I don't know what any of them taste like."

"But you should know because people will ask you. People will always ask you what something tastes like. You should know that."

Jasper employed a new strategy. The silent treatment.

"My sweet, impatient young boy, see what happens when you hurry? Now I leave and don't drink tea. I go home. The doctor says I need tea to circulate my blood."

"I'm sorry, Mildred. Can we circulate your blood tomorrow? Come in earlier and take all the time you need. Maybe you could bring your son with you. I'll even let you taste-test some cheeses."

"Just let me buy a newspaper." She grabbed the last copy of the *Tucson Citizen* from the rack and felt for a quarter inside her coin purse. "Do you read the newspaper? Everyone should read the newspaper every day, that's what I say. I read my horoscope with a magnifying glass."

Jasper unlatched the front door, let her out, locked it up again, rang out the cash register, and locked the money in the safe. He carried boxes of the more delicate fruits and vegetables back to the beer cooler where they could recover from being bruised by inquisitive fingers all day. Before mopping the floor, he unlocked the back door and lit up the joint he'd saved in his shirt pocket. He sat on a milk crate in the alley, his own private birthday party. Maybe by some miracle Lani would be home. Maybe she would remember it was his birthday. He finished the joint, opened the back door, and dialed her number. No one home. Again.

Jasper mopped the floor, double-checked the safe, turned out the lights, grabbed his cap and a *Playboy,* then let himself out the front and secured the padlock. The burglar alarm used to work but now, like the myopic eyes of the security camera, a red light winked on and off, but the alarm itself was inoperable. Walking away, he noticed he had forgotten to switch the sign to CLOSED.

Oh well.

He went home, stared at the phone, then unplugged it. He lowered the shades just in case there were private eyes peeking through his windows with a telescopic lens. Jasper masturbated to the new *Playboy* centerfold, Miss June, and drank twenty-one shots of Budweiser all lined up in Dixie cups on his coffee table. He fell asleep on the couch watching Johnny Carson. Never in a million years could he have imagined not going out to a bar on his twenty-first birthday. Never in a million years could he have imagined being so alone.

In his dream, his mother was cooking dinner in the kitchen, screaming at a silhouette. When the figure turned around, Jasper was expecting to find his father but instead it was Faith, the mystery girl from his college, crying inconsolably. The dream was lucid, intense. And most disconcerting of all was that some people were calling him *Jasper* and others were calling him *Junior*. Frightening. His mother was always alive in these dreams and dead the minute he woke up. It was a phenomenon that took time to get used to.

2. One Man's Trash

Rock star extraordinaire and lead singer of the Unknowns, Troy Archer, had recently developed a perilous new hobby: slumming. Although he had tried to convince his girlfriend Hilary and Bud, his best friend, that slumming was research for a new solo album, they weren't buying it. Certainly it was not unusual for artists to do field work in order to cultivate and synthesize the imagination; that ethereal endeavor could certainly lead just about anywhere. But Hilary and Bud knew Troy too well. This wasn't research. Something apoplectic and self-destructive was on the horizon.

Hilary Hightower was a long, lean lightning rod of a woman, with dishwater blonde hair and brown walnut eyes. She was headstrong, sardonic, opinionated, 34-26-34, Ivy League educated, and a voracious reader of everything from British literature to Tarot cards. Her father was a retired Cornell physics professor, her mother a former Miss New Jersey. Hilary was also a direct heir to the *Yummy Yogurt* conglomerate on her mother's side, appraised at six hundred and fifty million dollars. She and her mother hadn't spoken since Thanksgiving, 1974.

Among Hilary's greatest assets was her versatility. She was as comfortable cavorting about Monte Carlo in ermine and pearls, eating caviar and drinking champagne, as she was in El Paso behind a bumper pool table and a glass of draft beer. She could chop wood, whip up a meal out of almost anything, recite the names of all thirty-nine presidents in less than sixty seconds, and persuasively debate any subject from religion and politics to literature or the big bang theory. Hilary was a cult of one who liked to start her own rumors, the kind of woman hurricanes were named after, the kind who neutered rock stars. Troy strongly suspected she had already outgrown him.

Bud Black, the yin to Hilary's yang, had been Troy's best friend since seventh grade. He didn't own a razor and hadn't shaved since he returned from Viet Nam a decade earlier. His wild coppery hair curled up at the shoulders, and his reddish-brown mutton chops appeared to be double-teamed in a hostile takeover of Bud's face. His role for the last several years had been in the capacity of caretaker for Troy's sprawling glass ranch in the foothills of the Santa Catalina Mountains. Bud was twice divorced, once before the war and once after, and he was a bona fide, self-taught genius in architecture, engineering, and mechanical gadgetry. Bud could build or fix anything. He had successfully converted Troy's broken down old horse ranch into an oasis even by rock star standards. Troy had to smile at all the new gadgets and gizmos Bud cooked up. Bud's motto was: *it's never too late to become who you might have been.*

That he had survived Nam was heroic enough, but more miraculous was how he had recovered from his bout with what the doctors called "hysterical blindness." He had returned home ninety-eight percent blind due to psychological trauma suffered on the battlefield, ironically, in a cemetery. If he could survive that, he could go on more-or-less unfazed by protesters spitting on him at the airport upon de-boarding.

As for Hilary, Bud couldn't be in the same room with her for longer than ten minutes. Hilary and Bud were Troy's only real friends though they agreed on practically nothing. To push his jungle buttons, as she called them, Hilary referred to Bud as the "Gook Killer," to which Bud responded with "anti-Christ in spiked heels," and so on. But together, they knew Troy completely. He was what they had in common. They were mock parents, mock children, mock family. And the only thing they had agreed on lately was the transparency of Troy's slumming masquerade.

Troy was a songwriting composer of limited skill at best, his only solo album a financial catastrophe back in the early seventies. A reviewer at *Rolling Stone* called it "one of the most cataclysmic musical calamities ever released by a major recording artist." John Fendleman, the Unknown's lead guitarist, writer, co-founder, and self-appointed celebrity deity, never failed to remind Troy of that unmitigated failure whenever he could. *"What was the name of that record again?"* or *"Has Anyone Seen My Fledgling Career?"*

At first, Troy's slumming adventures, covert subterranean exploits into the mean streets of the city, consisted of mostly spontaneous explorations: biker bars, brothels, bathhouses . . . anything on the wrong side of the tracks. He insisted to Hilary that nothing of a sexual nature ever happened, and initially, the odyssey seemed innocent, an amusing if peculiar eccentricity. But the compulsion compounded into a full-blown obsession and had become a point of serious concern for Hilary and Bud, salacious or not. It was especially disturbing considering Troy had always been the band's backbone, the trouble-shooting, problem-solving, ego-mending voice of reason. The rock 'n' roll version of a medieval alchemist.

"What's the attraction?" Bud asked him. "What are you expecting to find? They're just like you and me, except more authentic. You want to see how the other half lives?"

Troy couldn't explain the cosmic energy that drew him to the

34

people of the street, to the adrenaline, danger, and desperation. But the last year with the band had been like running in waist-high water. The Unknowns were in the final week of an exhaustive world tour and despite their vow of sobriety, the band members had developed an unprecedented enmity for one another. This phenomenon was common at the end of tours, but never like this. Stony silence and fistfights had become commonplace. No amount of animosity in the band's history had ever escalated to this level. The indefatigable bickering and jousting had left Troy beyond disheartened to whatever comes after demoralized. He'd had enough. When Troy was feeling nostalgic, he'd recall the very beginning, when they had to live off their music and wits, sleeping in an old converted school bus. They thought they had it made back then. But now they weren't so much of a band as a business. Ten minutes after a show or a recording session, each person would scatter off in his own limo, with his own entourage.

Troy donned his flimsy disguise: sunglasses, Salvation Army clothes, long blond hair hidden up inside an old hat, half-pint of cheap bourbon. He tried to remember when this enterprise had started, this process of searching out the addicts, the hookers, and the hopeless, listening to their dreams, their heartbreaks, and where it had all gone wrong. He recalled that his virgin slumming expedition had been the very first night of the tour, eleven months ago, at the post-party hosted by the record label.

Outside, it had been an unseasonably cold night in Manhattan, and inside, a lavish ballroom of crushed velvet chairs and crystal chandeliers. The conversation with record execs had been the usual tap dance of flattery and accolades, then, after a few cocktails, the real conversations rose and converged. One young record mogul-in-training who wore a pin-striped suit and smoked a Cuban cigar had been particularly effusive with plastic praise for the Unknowns but later, as Troy eavesdropped in the background, he heard him say, "These big acts don't know how to bow out gracefully. They're like prizefighters who keep coming out of retirement only to get pummeled into raw hamburger. It's kinda pathetic."

His elder colleague agreed, "We love you, baby, you're superior, you have no equal, but your gross revenues are off twenty percent, and you haven't been on the charts since Nixon was in office. Your limelight has become more like a lame-light."

The young buck had chuckled and flicked the ash from his cigar on the floor. "The whole world's going disco. Rock 'n' roll is an endangered species."

"Don't get me wrong," his partner said. "I've got a nice condo in Waikiki from this act, but even I know when to shoot a crippled horse." They both laughed.

It would have been the perfect time for Troy to burst their little hubris-and-avarice bubble, but he didn't. He'd heard this talk before, whispers in shadows, unflattering concert reviews, smaller venues, but it was starting to make sense. For the first time, he could close his eyes and visualize the inevitable implosion of the Unknowns. Even the tour's first review confirmed it:

> The Unknowns opened an extensive tour at Madison Square Garden this evening to an audience that was far more enthusiastic than it had a right to be. The Unknowns still have the sizzle, but you'll have to shop elsewhere to find the steak. The old songs have the predictable zest and zing, but the new material is about as flavorless as yesterday's hash (and not the good kind, either!). While singer Troy Archer has always possessed more charisma than vocal dexterity, there were some truly excruciating moments for this opening night performance. More often than not, it was the acoustic equivalent of an old hound dog's pained wail after being whacked with a broom for peeing on the porch.

On a whim, Troy had managed to circumnavigate his way

out of the party, took a cab to the Bronx, walked through alleys, and started talking to a transient. That had been his first slumming excursion. A few days later, he confessed to Hilary that he felt rejuvenated.

"Why are you so intrigued with the ghetto? These ignominious creatures have nothing in common with you. If anything, they resent you."

Hilary loved to use fifty cent words like *ignominious*. Sometimes Troy would commit them to memory and look them up later in the dictionary. As for the street people, he didn't consider the less fortunate to be the other half. Humanity was a communal spirit, a circle. He was merely putting the puzzle together by attempting to understand the individual pieces. Somehow he had managed to retain his social conscience from the sixties. At the end of Woodstock, Jimi had summed up the entire antiwar movement with his rendition of "The Star-Spangled Banner." The sixties. Days Troy often longed for. But this was 1980, another Republican was running for office and threatening to *fire all the guns at once and explode into space*, and Troy had not responded to Hilary's inquisition except, like a defense attorney angling for an alibi to buy more time. Troy did admit to feeling a little mentally ill. Nothing too serious, about the equivalent of a nasty head cold. But unlike the past, instead of tripping on LSD, he was tripping on the truth. He was learning at age forty that he needed two keys in life: one for the doors he wanted to keep open, and one for the doors he wanted to stay shut.

Twilight was settling and he wanted to get an early start. He checked the answering machine, a new contraption called a Phone-Mate, another one of Bud's technological innovations.

"This is Nils. Remember me? Your fucking manager? Pick up if you're there. It really pisses me off when you don't return my phone calls. Nobody wants to play with you when you're like this. OK, listen. The place I told you about for tomorrow night is called the Blue Parrot. The act the label's trying to sign is called Central Air. Go down there, let the owner introduce you to them, and give them backstage passes for the Tucson show. Schmooze them. I gave Bud all the details. Also, I need to talk to you about this new cable TV thing they're calling MTV—Music/Television? It probably won't last a month, but we need to put some footage together 'cause I've got people all over my ass about it. So return my goddamn phone calls once in awhile, will ya? Hey, is the interview with *Playboy* finished yet? Don't ignore me, cowboy. Ciao."

Troy hit rewind. He didn't owe them shit.

As he was leaving, he found Hilary in the kitchen reading by candlelight. She was wearing a canary-yellow kimono with a black spider-web pattern on the back, no bra, diamond tennis bracelet, and her hair tied back into a ponytail. She was eating her favorite food—tiramisu, while reading her favorite novel—*Great Expectations*. Troy was reminded of the Greek goddess Persephone eating pomegranate seeds. According to Plato, Persephone was wise and touched that which was in motion. She'd been a fair maiden who picked flowers in the garden until she was kidnapped by Hades, raped, and forced to become the goddess of the underworld. Determined to escape, only the pomegranate seeds offered a respite, a temporary escape to her mother on the other side, and even then the visit was only long enough for the growing season to come and go. But the difference was that Hilary preferred tiramisu to pomegranates.

"Having the blue plate special?" Troy asked with a mollifying smile.

Hilary ignored him. She was well versed in the silent treatment.

"How many times have you read that book, anyway?" He kissed her on the cheek. "I'll be back soon."

Hilary shook her head. "What makes you so sure I'll still be here? Do you see a ring on my finger? You don't own me. You can't tell me what to do."

Troy didn't turn around. "Bud will fix us a late dinner." Like Hilary, Bud was a restaurant-quality chef. Unlike Hilary, he was also an avid hunter and ate only what he killed.

"I never thought I'd be stood up for a bunch of social malcontents panhandling on the streets and sleeping under bridges in cardboard boxes."

Troy turned to face her as he gently clicked open the door to the garage. He knew he was going, she knew he was going, and the only thing left was the shadowboxing and commensurate filibuster that would ensue. The human mouth was composed of dozens of muscles, sixteen in the human tongue alone, and when the silent treatment was over, he knew she'd be using every one of them.

"I find this incessant ennui to be highly insulting. You're losing it, Archer, you really are. So I'm just supposed to sit around all night like a spinster with my knitting needles?"

"Bud is here. Play some backgammon. Or cribbage."

"Fuck Bud. I see him more than I see you. You think you're so goddamn perspicacious."

Troy had no idea what that word meant, nor was he inclined to look it up.

"And parenthetically, are we ever gonna fuck again? Preferably before I become menopausal? I mean, if you can juggle it into your schedule. What has it been, a month? I can't even remember anymore. I know you're awfully busy with this *slumming* bullshit. Rubbing elbows with whores and hobos must be very time-consuming. Why can't you take me with you? I could be your loyal sidekick like Tonto or Keith Richards."

Troy delicately kissed her on the cheek, closed the garage door behind him, and her trail of vulgar invectives faded into the night. It was a relief to be on the other side of the wall of friction.

He fired up the old '64 Dodge, perfect cover for the evening's expedition. It was his first new car, financed a couple lifetimes ago by the band's early success in the Midwestern dance clubs of St. Louis, Kansas City, and Chicago. The paint job had weathered into a pale lime-green seaweed. The antenna was a wire coat hanger. Troy's rock star cars were far too conspicuous for where he was headed. Street life: pain, anger, resentment, despair. This was life or death. The real stuff. Rock 'n' roll had become nothing more than an illusion—a fog machine with synthesizers, and performing live had been reduced to fulfilling contractual obligations. It was all self-indulgent bullshit, Troy thought, and he no longer needed the adulation or to watch his inebriated band and crew tear down perfectly good hotel walls. Honest men built those hotels with their own hands. Honest men doing honest work. What he really needed was a double dose of reality. At one time, the Unknowns had helped light a fire in the belly of a rebellious nation—a country pissed off about Vietnam and Nixon and race and women's rights. These days, however, righteous indignation was in short supply. Maybe America was worn out.

Troy parked two blocks from the bus station, locked the doors, and strolled toward a nearby city park, where he found a pair of hardscrabble down-and-outers, prospective subjects. Troy sat among them with no trepidation, skipping formal introductions, and slowly removed the half-pint from his jacket pocket.

"Hey my brother, how 'bout a pull on that fire water?"

Troy passed the bottle to the pirate, who proceeded to belt down a healthy slug. He had a gaunt face with brooding eyes, and his head was covered by a red bandanna that was tied off in a triangle. A gold hoop dangled from his right earlobe. A modern day buccaneer, Troy thought. The pirate passed the bottle back.

"How's about a sip for old Rip? I call him *Rip* 'cause he looks dead. Rest in peace, you know what I mean? Rip Van Winkle." The pirate laughed. "He don't talk, so's I don't even know his name. But he been wit' me a few days and don't need much. You mind? Just a little somethin' to warm his insides up is all. A little booze for this bozo?"

Troy held the bottle up to the moonlight to see how much remained, a little method acting. He handed it to the raggedy derelict named Rip who took a sip and winced. Troy had learned to fine-tune his peripheral vision on these adventures, and from the corner of his eye he appraised Rip. His beard was tangled, his shoulder-length hair knotted and botched. He wore an Army surplus coat and kept scratching his neck and hair, then licking his fingertips. He appeared to have a severe dermatological condition and smelled like fresh feces.

"Who are you?" the pirate asked Troy.

"Franklin Roosevelt," Troy said. "Who are you?"

"Hey, I ain't tryin' to be nosy. I just wanted to thank you for the whiskey, that's all. Ain't you gonna drink none y'self?"

The bottle was for appearance only. Troy hadn't consumed drugs or alcohol since before the tour started. He discovered that he wasn't powerless over self-medicating, he was powerless over boredom. Banality was his constant companion. Troy didn't reply and avoided direct eye contact. The last thing he wanted was to be recognized.

The pirate continued, "Where ya from?"

"Albuquerque," Troy said reflexively, the site of the band's last gig.

"A guy shot me in the leg there one time," the pirate said. "That's a shithole town. Watered-down drinks, cops dressed like whores. The whole thing's really . . . " His voice trailed off. "A guy shot me in the leg one time."

Rip stood up and gingerly steadied himself.

"You gotta go again? This guy's gotta piss ever' five minutes."
Rip sauntered away toward a clump of sun-beaten palm trees.
"His bladder don't work so good and he can't talk, neither.
Ain't that a bitch?"

Troy nodded but focused on Rip, who didn't stop to urinate
but instead kept walking right out of the park. "Here," Troy
handed the bottle over. "Save some. I'll be right back." He
pushed up off the ground, dusted himself off, and surreptitiously
tailed his latest subject.

Rip slipped down an alley, and must have been ravenous because he was searching through metal garbage cans. Troy followed as clandestinely as possible. Finally, he decided to catch
up. "Psssst."

Rip turned around. His frightened eyes reflected the milky
moonlight; his handful of trash trembled.

Troy retreated a step. "It's OK, it's OK. Remember me from
the park? The one with the whiskey? I didn't mean to startle
you."

Rip stared at Troy's feet for a full minute.

Troy said, "Mind if I tag along?" He was thinking the old idi-
om was really true—*one man's trash is another man's treasure.*

Rip stood without moving.

"I don't mean to poach your territory," Troy said, not wanting
to distress his subject.

Rip stared at Troy's feet again for the longest time. He eventually went back to work and picked up a bent metal garbage can
with both hands, tilted it at an angle, shook it around a little as if
panning for gold, then set it down. He resumed his quest seemingly undeterred by Troy's presence. Troy could detect snarls of
hair hung over Rip's coat collar and the skin eating away from
his lower scalp. His forehead was wrinkled like mud that had
dried in the afternoon sun.

The stealth duo wordlessly made their way down several of

Tucson's alleys and back streets, shards of glass shimmering, and their increasingly comfortable silence interrupted by the random howl of a dog in the distance or a couple of cats fighting behind a garage. Rip was uncannily adept at avoiding backyard security lights and the occasional street lamp that invaded the privacy of darkness. He scratched his neck and sucked on his fingertips. Troy wondered if he had leprosy. They stopped at another overflowing garbage can. Troy removed the lid and set the can in front of Rip, who meticulously examined each item: last Sunday's newspaper, empty beer cans, orange peels, chewed gum, onion skins, peach pits, fourth grade math test, used Band-Aid.

They legged it a bit further, behind a neighborhood grocery store. Stenciled on the Dumpster were the words THYME MARKET. Among the sea of cardboard boxes and bruised fruit, Rip rescued a rotten cantaloupe. He settled himself atop a milk crate and squeezed the fleshy pulp into his mouth while Troy sat next to him. Rip positioned a wooden soda case on his lap and beat the fruit against it, tearing it open with his hands, but there was a problem. The acidic rind appeared to sting his fingers, and Rip groaned and dropped the fruit as if it were on fire. He immediately inserted his fingers back into his mouth, leaving a trace of dirt along his upper lip like a thin veil of lipstick. He reached out, pressed his hands against the cool metal of the store's back entryway and, to Troy's surprise, the door pushed open. Rip literally fell through the back door. As he reached up to balance himself, he tripped a switch and a flash of florescent light blinded him and knocked him to his knees. Troy tried to help him up but Rip was shaking. As Troy backed off, Rip got to his feet, sucked on his fingertips, and stepped all the way into the store.

Troy peered inside. He knew that to cross this threshold and trespass into this portal would be like stepping into Alice's rabbit hole. There would be no turning back. He would never be the same. He couldn't explain why, but in his bones he knew that whether it was destiny or just curiosity, going through this door would be jumping off a cliff into the sea without knowing the depth of the reef, simultaneously ominous and exhilarating. He could feel the adrenaline course through his nervous system. He took a deep breath, stepped gingerly inside, and closed the door behind him.

The market was quiet except for the low hum of a beer cooler. Troy thought he detected a smile from his new friend. It was easy to imagine local cops busting in, cuffing the two of them, stuffing their heads into the backseat of a squad car. He could feel the release of endorphins tickle his spinal cord. Troy further scrutinized Rip and wondered what a person who is literally starving would eat first after he'd stumbled into an unlocked grocery store? With an entire neighborhood market at his disposal, the possibilities were vast.

Rip stepped over to a plastic fifty-gallon garbage receptacle in the deli and began to fish through it for something to eat. He found a slice of pumpernickel bread and stuffed it into his mouth. Then he gnawed on an apple core while he slid the display case door open to fish out a pan filled with fresh ground beef. He placed the pan on the butcher block, stripped off its cellophane, and grabbed handfuls of the raw hamburger, kneading the meat with his fingers, squeezing and occasionally eating a mouthful. Troy sensed dermatological relief. Then Rip pushed the pan aside and moved toward some muffled sounds grumbling from another freezer in the front of the store. When he opened the top, cool air wafted toward his face and floated a frosty breeze against his tangled beard. He extracted a half-gallon of Neapolitan ice cream and sat down next to the plate glass window that was partially concealed from headlights and random pedestrians behind a newspaper rack. Rip tried to pry open the lid.

"Here," Troy said. "Let me help you." He removed the lid and handed the container to Rip whose fingertips danced in tight circles over the top of the ice cream like little skaters on a frozen pond. As the ice cream began to melt, he licked each delicious finger.

"Have you ever eaten ice cream before?" Troy whispered, squatting beside him.

Rip paused. He licked his fingers. It appeared he didn't quite know what he'd gotten his hands into. He licked his fingers some more.

Troy looked straight into Rip's faraway Donner-party eyes. "What's your name, my friend?"

Rip stopping licking but did not respond.

"Mi amigo, can you tell me your name? My name is Troy. What is your name?"

Silently, Rip continued his ice cream crusade.

Troy coaxed his accomplice back toward the deli, away from the front windows. They maintained a low posture, crouching like G.I.s behind enemy lines, and it occurred to Troy that Rip's entire life may have been spent behind enemy lines. Troy's heart thumped. He wanted to know about Rip's family, his past, who had pilfered his future. He checked the pockets of Rip's jacket for a wallet or ID.

"Would you like me to make you a sandwich?" Troy asked.

Rip returned Troy's gaze as if he understood.

"OK, let's see what we've got." Troy made a king-sized roast beef and cheddar sandwich on sourdough with extra mayo on both slices of bread. He delivered it on a paper plate with a carton of milk to wash it all down. As he watched Rip eat, he kept thinking that Rip was like a small child, and this was about as paternal as Troy was likely to ever get. He thought of his ex-wife, Gretchen, how she'd wanted a baby so bad, to make lunches for the kids and go to PTA meetings. She left him because in addition to being a philandering, hedonistic rock star piece of shit, he didn't have a paternal bone in his body. He was too selfish, and Gretchen had made this crystal clear on more than one occasion. In retrospect, Gretchen was the best thing that had ever happened to him, but he was too self-indulgent and self-aggrandizing to realize it. *Gretchen*. He liked saying the name.

"How's the sandwich?" Troy said, with fatherly concern. "Would you like some more milk?"

Rip yawned. His eyes seemed ready to surrender. There was a multi-colored puddle of melted ice cream all over him.

"Maybe we should get out of here," Troy suggested, hoping Rip could marshal what remained of his inner reserves so they could vacate before the cops crashed the party. Rip staggered to his feet and seemed to regain his composure, but instead of heading toward the back exit, he opened the glass door of the deli case, shoved aside a couple honey-baked hams, and climbed inside. He pulled his coat tightly around him, tilted his head away from the light, and curled up in the fetal position.

Rip's fetid smell permeated the deli case. Troy held his nose and tried to wheedle and persuade Rip out of his makeshift crucible.

"Seriously, we have to leave now," Troy said.

Rip didn't budge. He seemed to want to rest in peace.

"I want you to know I care about you," Troy said. "I want you to know that at least one person on this planet is concerned about your welfare. I don't know whether or not you can hear me, but I think you're brave as hell and if you were in Nam and need help, I know some people who know some people at the V.A. I could get you a bed. Were you in Nam?"

Rip's eyes were closed and his breathing was labored. In minutes he was snoring, accompanied by a plaintive rumbling in his chest. Troy had $267 in cash. He stashed it all into Rip's coat pocket and slipped out of Thyme Market the same way he had slipped in, inconspicuously, through the back door, the rabbit hole, the endless and confusing labyrinth of life.

3. Help Wanted

Jasper sat on the couch wearing nothing but a jock strap and white athletic socks, watching *Mighty Mouse* and eating Cheerios. Someone began pounding on the front door so violently that he sprang up like a jack-in-the-box and spilled the cereal all over the carpet. It was Saturday, his day off, so it couldn't be the boss. Shit, he thought, it's the old man! He found me! The phone was still unplugged. He accidentally kicked over an empty beer bottle that rolled across the floor as he searched for some gym shorts and cracked the blinds. "Who is it?"

"Me. Pam. Open up. Now!"

Jasper unlatched the deadbolt.

The owner's wife looked him up and down then abruptly turned her head. "Get dressed." She walked over to the phone. "Did you know this was off the hook? We've been trying to call."

"What's wrong, Pam?" Jasper had never seen her like this. "Have you been crying?"

She faced the door with her arms folded, tapping her foot. Jasper wasn't exactly fluent in body language, but Pam seemed to be cussing up a hurricane. She was wearing a pink and green jogging outfit that made a swishing sound when she walked. Her perfectly straight hair was frizzed out of control, and even her normally milky complexion was the color of Pepto-Bismol.

"Someone broke into the store, and the guy who did it is still there! Asleep! In my deli! Hurry up, get dressed. The cops'll be there any minute."

"Holy shit, how'd he get inside?"

She pointed at him, no longer shy about his state of undress. "No more questions. The car's running. You've got exactly ten seconds to get some clothes on, mister." She looked down at the mess of cereal on the carpet and winced. "NOW!"

As he dressed, he retraced his steps from the night before. Had he remembered to lock everything? He followed her outside, his attention drawn up to the ominous clouds that lingered overhead like a family of gun-metal zeppelins. He remembered the guy in the mailman outfit who'd predicted rain.

Neither of them spoke while they drove in the car. Jasper's stomach was turning like a bingo tumbler. A couple of university girls rode ten-speed bikes down the boulevard. A police cruiser was parked in front of Thyme Market, red lights reflecting sharply off the plate glass windows. The sign still read OPEN—WELCOME! The cops were just stepping out of the vehicle.

Pam unlocked the front door. "This way."

Jasper followed Pam and the officers inside. He attempted to avoid Tony's menacing death-stare.

"Your sign says OPEN,'" the shorter cop pointed out.

The owner switched it to: CLOSED.

"Where is he?" the tall cop asked.

Tony led them to the deli in the rear of the store, and Pam motioned toward the display case. Inside was a scrunched-up body.

"Holy shit," Jasper said. "It's King Rat."

The tall cop opened the deli case and recoiled at the rancid

48

smell. He reached inside with his nightstick and tapped the man's shoe. "Hello sir," the cop called out. "Would you mind stepping outside of the deli case for me, please?"

"Is he dead or asleep?" the second officer asked.

"Oh, he's alive all right," Tony said, still glaring maniacally at Jasper.

The body twitched. The tall cop holstered his nightstick. "King who?"

"He's a transient who eats out of Dumpsters," Tony said.

The cops assisted King Rat from his refrigerated cocoon. He was shivering, eyes red and frightened, hair a ghastly mess. He trembled and licked his fingertips, avoiding direct eye contact.

"Everything is contaminated," Pam said.

Jasper felt culpability bulldozing a path decidedly away from King Rat and toward himself. "So how am I involved with this?"

"The minute I pulled in," Tony said, "I knew something was wrong. The back door was wide open. No chain, no latch—nothing. I go to call nine-one-one when I hear this shriek and my wife sees this . . . thing, hunkered down inside the deli. The only explanation is that the back door must've been unlocked. The front door's padlocked and no windows are broken, so it had to be through the back. There's no sign of forced entry."

As the police officers escorted King Rat away from Thyme Market, Jasper taxed his memory. He recalled smoking a joint and calling Lani, he recalled being distracted all day by Pop's happy birthday wake-up call, but he couldn't recall locking the back door. He lowered his head as he heard the tall cop inform King Rat of his constitutional right to remain silent.

"Can I see back door?" the other cop asked.

"What will you charge him with?"

"Trespassing, for starters. Probably criminal mischief. We'll take him downtown, clean him up, process him, and the judge will want a psychological exam on Monday. Chances are he'll be back out on the street by the end of the week."

When the cops had departed with King Rat secured in the back of the squad car, Pam started to cry as she began to inventory the ruins. Tony stood in front of Jasper. "Did you leave that back door unlocked?" he whispered. "And don't say you didn't."

"I don't remember locking it," Jasper's voice lowered, "and I don't remember not locking it."

"Well, the front door was padlocked and no windows are broken, so he must've come in the back. You must've forgotten to lock the goddamn door." Tony pointed his finger and his eyes bulged like a bullfrog's. "I thought I could trust you. I thought you could handle a little responsibility. And to think I was gonna promote you. Jesus H. Christ. Give me your keys."

Jasper inhaled and exhaled. "Does this mean I'm fired?"

"Hell no, you're not fired. You're not getting off that easy. First, you're going to help Pam clean up so we can open. Then you're going to work the eight-to-five shift so I can get the place back to normal and hire a new clerk. *Then* you're fired."

"That's not fair. I'll quit."

"Like hell you will." Tony took a step in his direction. "Don't fuck with me, kid."

Jasper disliked threats but not as much as he disliked pain, and Tony was nearly hyperventilating.

"I treated you pretty well," Tony said. "Gave you a chance when you bottomed-out in school, gave you a free lunch every day. I even paid you four-fifty an hour when I know for a fact that the guy over at Twelfth Street doesn't pay his people more than four bucks. I tried to tell you this store is all I got. Me and Pam ain't rich, We each spend seventy hours a week in this place. Do you realize how my insurance premiums are going to sky-rocket? I could kick your ass right into the middle of next week. Store manager. *Ha!* I must've been out of my mind."

"I'm sorry, Tony. I was so freaked out yesterday by my old

man's phone call. Remember? I told you? I was so freaked out, Tony. I'm sorry. I'm really sorry. You've been like a big brother to me, I know I messed up, but please give me one more chance." Tony's voice dropped an octave. "You should've thought of that last night." His eyes were cold and small, like ball bearings. He didn't look at Jasper when he said, "I need someone I can depend on, and you're not it. Pam will have your final paycheck ready at the end of the day. You can skip lunch and leave a half hour early if you want." He hung the HELP WANTED sign in the front window and retreated upstairs to his office on the second floor. Pam, now wearing rubber gloves, was delicately extracting meats and cheeses from the deli case as if they were from Three Mile Island.

Jasper noted the HELP WANTED sign—a perfect summation of his own mental state. He thought of giving his mother a call but, of course, she was dead. Still. He sometimes forgot.

Tony turned on the stereo system, elevator music, in this case a symphony orchestra playing the Beatles. This was no life for a serious poet, Jasper lamented. He tried to block out the vortex of violins, the melancholy old man, school, his mother, unemployment. Pam finished clearing out the deli case. Jasper could tell she didn't like this music, either.

The market opened an hour late, and Jasper sensed it was destined to be a bad-to-worse kind of Saturday when the first customer trotted in wearing neon-pink micro-shorts, expensive New Balance running shoes, and a big handlebar-mustached grin.

"Good morning. Would you happen to sell the lotion used for maintaining erections?"

"What?"

"Erection lotion. You know, hard-on juice. I'm entering a wet boxer-shorts contest at that new gay bar called Starz. Ever heard of it?"

"Try the Twelfth Street Meat Market."

The guy jogged away still grinning, undaunted. The next customer was a regular, the bombastic Iris the Virus. Jasper was in no mood to hear about her latest entrapment by Tucson's vice squad. Iris was a working girl in the old-fashioned sense and didn't care who knew.

Jasper rang up a box of maxi-pads and a half-gallon of Chablis."Is that all?"

"Well, there is one other thing," Iris said. "Can I warm my hands on the heat of your cock?" Her smile showed a new missing tooth.

"Iris," Jasper said, "is that necessary? It's not even ten o'clock."

"How bouts you and me drink a little wine when you get off work? I bet you got some sweet lips on you. Can I call you Sweet Lips?"

It had been a long time since Iris had unnerved Jasper, but today she'd made a resounding comeback. In honor of providing quality customer service at all costs, even on his final day of employment, Jasper resisted the temptation to ask why in the hell he'd want to fuck a whore on the rag.

"Ooh, you're quiet today, ain't ya? I bet you got a hot date tonight, huh? I think you're a little heartbreaker, that's what I think. Anyone ever told you that you look like that guy on Three's Company?"

"Twelve eighty-five." Jasper held out his hand and Iris paid, winking and whistling away. She wasn't subtle and she understood the way money binds the planet. Pay the piper, hit the road, get in and get out.

By the time the next customer, androgynous Man-Woman, arrived at the counter with her lemon yogurt, Jasper was in even less of a mood for witty repartee. The more he thought about his meager existence, the more he seriously considered suicide as an alternative lifestyle. Would anyone notice? Other than Robert McPherson?

"How are you today, Mr. Trueblood?"

"Never better. Will that be all?" Jasper envisioned Man-Woman gobbling down her lemon yogurt, a glob falling on her beard.

"You don't seem very talkative today."

He looked in her eyes. "Sorry, Charlene."

"Does this have anything to do with the police being here this morning?"

"I accidentally left the back door unlocked. Somebody came in last night and decided to go camping in the deli. This is my last day at Thyme Market. Tony's firing me." He bagged her ten lemon yogurts.

She shook her head and mumbled something intended to be inspirational, something about Jesus closing doors and opening windows, but Jasper wasn't paying attention.

Saturday slogged along, punctuated by Muzak, and Jasper spent the rest of the afternoon being rude to customers, something he had always been tempted to do anyway. It was a job made simple by the unending procession of complaints about the heat. Jasper's suggestion was to heed Harry Truman's advice and get out of the kitchen. Later, he tried to think of a metaphor he could use in a poem that would describe his current mood. The first thing he thought of was a rat in a sewer—King Rat in a deli. It was all just grist for the mill, he tried to convince the poet inside him.

An old Mexican woman bought champagne mustard, three fifty-nine for six ounces, and pulled a wad of food stamps from the darkest recesses of her brassiere. It wouldn't be long before Jasper, too, would qualify for food stamps. He might be a heartbeat away from sleeping in neighborhood deli cases all over the greater Southwest.

A young divorcee sashayed up to the counter to buy cigarettes. She was fashion-model-gorgeous, one of the most attractive women Jasper had ever seen, and she lived around the cor-

53

ner. Jasper had read that fashion models often complained of loneliness because their looks intimidated men and made women envious. She didn't come in often, so when afforded the opportunity, he would gape at her. She had chameleon eyes and she wasn't afraid to show her curves. Jasper knew he was in bad shape when he suggested she read the Surgeon General's warning on the side of the pack.

"Those things'll kill ya," he said.

"Who in the fuck asked you?"

Jasper smiled. He deserved that. She disappeared around the corner in a cloud of smoke. Have a nice day, he thought. As the dreary Saturday afternoon crawled to its inevitable conclusion, images flashed in Jasper's mind like frames of an old newsreel: King Rat in the deli, Jasper's mother vomiting in a bucket, his father talking back to the evangelists on TV. He made a mental note of the day and time. He wanted to remember the exact moment he decided to hate every living creature on the face of the earth.

The mailman with the pith helmet purchased a nice Bordeaux and some specially aged cheeses just before the store closed. "How's it goin'?" he asked.

"So far, so what," Jasper replied.

"Look," he motioned toward the window and the steady rain. "The gulches are going to flood. Remember I predicted this? The leaves never lie."

Jasper shrugged and closed the front door behind him.

Tony locked it.

So this was it. He had hoped Tony would soften over the course of the day and reconsider, but apparently no official do-overs would be forthcoming.

"How many applications did you give out today?"

"Several," Jasper lied. He'd given out none.

"Leave through the back door. I'll mail your last paycheck on

Monday. Pam didn't bring her checkbook today."

Jasper felt like he was about to be keel-hauled. The phone rang.

"Just a minute." Tony put his hand over the receiver. "Hey, do you know a Robert McPherson? It sounds like long distance."

Shit, Jasper thought, this is perfect. "That's my father. Tell him I left."

"What?" Tony shouted. "Speak up."

"No," Jasper said. "I don't know a Robert McPherson."

"Wrong number," Tony said and hung up the phone.

"Boss, I apologize for everything. It was all my fault and I'm really sorry. I know this store means everything to you and Pam."

"This isn't personal, it's business. I'll mail your check on Monday."

* * *

When Tony failed to respond further, Jasper trudged down the breakfast aisle for the last time, oblivious to the symmetry of the cereal boxes and the purr of the freezer, through the back door that he would never have the opportunity to leave unlocked again. He walked in the rain and dripped down the street dodging puddles of gasoline rainbows, trying to reconcile the distance between his two lives—Junior and Jasper. Then he wondered if he had any beer left in the refrigerator.

4. The Earth Shall Inherit the Meek

Jasper trudged up the twelve wooden steps that led to his loft apartment and unlocked the door. He removed his wet shoes and shook his head so that a halo of raindrops sprayed the room. With no money saved, he couldn't afford to be unemployed for long. He began to consider what a cheaper residence might look like. The loft came furnished and even though it wasn't much, it had become a respectable sanctuary.

The kitchen was modest: an oak dining table where Jasper wrote poetry, two straight-back chairs, a few small appliances and a sliding glass patio door that led to an old redwood sundeck, perfect for observing the Tucson skyline. Lani had been up there twice, but that was a long time ago. Whatever happened to Lani? Against his better instincts he had fallen hard for her, despite the voice in the back of his head warning against it. Lani liked the sundeck, especially at night when the constellations and celestial wonders created a romantic sphere where people might say things they would later forget.

While he popped a frozen pizza into the oven, he found a poem-in-progress under his dictionary, one he'd written a couple days earlier. He read it, started to crumple it into a ball then stopped, smoothed out the page, and put it in a peach crate he'd lifted from Thyme Market. The word POETRY was scrawled in black magic marker on one side, and it was a foot deep in near-poems and parts of near-poems, mostly on yellow legal pads. He did not own a typewriter but even if he did, he lacked the courage to type anything up, never mind submitting them for publication. That was too permanent. Still, he felt good about a few pieces in the box. When he wasn't sure about the quality, he kept it just in case.

The loft was owned by a Mr. O.E. Parker, to whom Jasper mailed a money order once a month. He'd only seen his land-lord twice in the duration of his residence, the day he answered the ad in the student newspaper and once in an off-campus pub. Mr. O.E. Parker had been sitting all cozy next to a frosty mug and a buxom coed who, Jasper guessed from her excessive gig-gling, was not Mrs. O.E. Parker. Jasper bought two beers and had a cocktail waitress deliver them. When Mr. Parker looked Jasper's way, his face became ashen. Jasper nodded and waved. Since that night, Jasper was never too concerned if the rent was a few days late.

* * *

After draping his wet clothes over the shower curtain rod, he switched on the small green radio he'd bought at a thrift store for six bucks. He also turned on the TV—without sound—the only way to watch the evening news. The video unscrambled and a tanned anchorman with helmet hair mouthed the day's tragedies as rock 'n' roll blared from the radio. Jasper ran in place, pumping his knees at a frenzied pace, exercising the car-diovascular, exorcising the day's demons. He tried to ignore the extra pounds vibrating at his waist as he lip-synched the lyrics to the song and assaulted an imaginary guitar in an impromp-tu rampage. His heart was dancing by the tune's end and for a minute, he forgot where he was. He walked over to the window, peeked out the blinds, then pulled them tightly closed.

Resting on the couch, he gazed blankly at the TV until he smelled dinner. Then he sat naked at the kitchen table, eating pizza and reading a list of ominous-sounding chemicals that were printed on the back of the box. He hit the shower, humming with the radio, lathering himself in a southerly direction with a bar of blue soap, and remembering the immortal words and revisionist history of Robert McPherson: *at least I never hit her.*

He rubbed some of the fog away from the mirror, shaved, nicked his chin, applied the tissue to the dot of blood, stung his face with musk, brushed his teeth, and returned to the bedroom to dress: gray corduroys, blue-and-white-striped western shirt with pearl button snaps, cowboy boots, wallet. He sipped the last of his last beer. It being Saturday night, his former dormitory buddies would surely want to kick up some dust in one of the local watering holes, but Jasper decided to lone-dog it. Tonight he was uninterested in companionship or anyone else's problems. He preferred to wallow in private. By this time on a Saturday night, Lani would be sitting in a posh restaurant across from some smug smile in a tailor-made suit. To hell with her. Jasper was determined to celebrate his twenty-first birthday, albeit alone and a day late. *A day late and a dollar short*, as Robert McPherson always said.

"Tomorrow night," the voice on the radio announced, "live in concert at the Tucson Performing Arts Facility, Desert West Productions presents the incomparable musical majesty of a rock legend, *the Unknowns*! Don't miss Tucson's premiere rock event of the year. Special guest, Freezing Rain. Remaining tickets are still available at the box office. Don't delay, get yours TO-DAY!"

For weeks Jasper had waited to purchase a ticket to the Unknowns show, hoping one of his old dormies would wind up without a date and sell him a good seat. With the advent of his newfound unemployment, he could hardly even afford to park, and he didn't have a car. The Unknowns, a super group from the days of flower power and free love, had always been one of Jasper's favorites. He remembered hearing them for the first time back in fifth grade, the same year nuns showed anti-drug filmstrips wherein hippies smoked pot and subsequently played Russian roulette or dropped acid and stepped out of a nineteenth-story window. The Unknowns had pumped out some good tunes in their day, but were definitely past their prime. It was likely to be their final tour.

He killed his beer. Several months before he'd vowed to switch to hard liquor so as to reduce the size of his belly. These days, he was lucky to be buying food. If he could lose some weight, maybe there would be a bright side to getting fired. Jasper knew he had to get down to fighting weight to compete for Lani. Poetry wasn't enough. He needed to be perfect, whatever that was. Faulkner once said he felt a "defiant inferiority" to the fairer sex. As soon as he read it, Jasper understood the sentiment. He combed his hair and hit the road. Solo. On foot.

The street lamps on University Boulevard cast a yellow luminosity into the night and onto the wet pavement. The rain had come and gone, rinsing the air clean. Jasper hiked through the dark campus amongst the joggers and palm trees, past a ridiculously abstract metal sculpture, huge and beginning to rust. Every college campus onto which Jasper had ever set foot included one of these strange steel pretzels. In addition to being highly regarded as an academic institution, the university was replete with diverse extracurricular activities. In his brief academic exposure, Jasper had been introduced to the Marxism Club, the Gay & Lesbian Student Coalition, and Iranian students burning Uncle Sam in effigy outside the student union. Growing up in the Midwest, he'd seen the brewery workers go on strike, but nothing like this.

Inside the classroom, the focus was directed toward learning more and more about less and less. Professors in outdated suits mumbled while scribbling on the chalkboard. Mental masturbation on a grandiose scale. A student in Jasper's lit class once asked the instructor how long the assigned term paper should be. "Approximately the length of a woman's skirt. Long enough to cover the good parts but short enough to be interesting," was the answer. It seemed so much easier to be stupid: no brains, no headaches. And someday he would have to answer for his soon-to-be delinquent student loan.

He walked down the mall, the largest stretch of grass for miles in this desert, and sat on a cement bench in front of a girls' dormitory. Nine floors and seventy-two bedroom windows filled by silhouetted coeds in various stages of undress. Tonight, none of them mattered.

Jasper stared at the full moon which looked close enough to touch. The light made his eyes water and his tendency was to turn away, but he concentrated fiercely and the glowing moon seemed to double, then triple, in size. He experienced a strange calm. His body felt buoyant, almost as if defying the laws of gravity. Rather than resist the mysterious sensation he allowed it to envelop him, to release him from himself in a kind of homespun astral projection. He sat there, blinded by the moon, while his mind and spirit crisscrossed the universe until he was distracted by coeds being escorted from their dorms by their Saturday evening suitors. Jasper left campus, flashing back to the image of King Rat in the deli. Where would he fit into Sister Constancia's fourth grade catechism lecture: *The Meek Shall Inherit the Earth?*

Jasper wasn't sure what to think of the God thing anymore. In private moments, he speculated as to whether God was a delusion, Marx's opiate of the masses, someone's idea of a practical joke. If not, did God have good seats for World War I, World

War II, or occasionally sneak a peek through the keyhole of life at all the children who starved in Africa? The entire planet was replete with suffering and pain, and Jasper had had enough of God's working in mysterious ways. When it came to theology, Jasper's ex-roommate from the dorm, Elmo, had it all figured out. Elmo Maroney, a.k.a. Elbow Macaroni, was a doctoral candidate in philosophy from Duluth, Minnesota.

"If you don't believe in God," Jasper had asked, "how do you explain the creation of the universe? I know about the big bang theory, I'm talking about before it all blew. What was that initial mass of matter? Where did that come from?"

"God," Elmo explained, "*was* the mass of matter. The big bang occurred at the instant of God's demise."

Maybe Elmo had something. Maybe the moment the Almighty foresaw the impending mess that loomed when human beings emerged on the evolutionary landscape, He Himself self-destructed. For Jasper's money, there was too much tragedy in the world to warrant blind faith in a deity who was supposed to be all-knowing, all-loving, and all the other bullshit that the nuns and priests professed. He no longer trusted the idea of God, an admission that would have impaled his mother's heart. When he was seven years old, she once said that nothing in the world would make her happier than if he decided to become a priest. For the next two years, Jasper devoted himself to this sacred task. He went to Mass and received Holy Communion every day. He was the first altar boy in his class and confessed his sins promptly whenever he thought he had committed any. In fact, sometimes he fabricated sins and then had to confess the fabrications. And he prayed for ten consecutive hours on the special day of the year when one could say a rosary and parole a poor soul from Purgatory straight up to Heaven with no questions asked. Jasper fully apprised his mother of each religious achievement with great enthusiasm and vowed one day to become the first American pope.

"I believe you can do anything you set your mind to, Junior," she would say matter-of-factly, then hug him around the neck.

Of course, when Margaret Cantrell's breasts developed in the fifth grade, Jasper's aspirations toward a career in divinity began to wane. These days, theologically speaking, Jasper was leaning more toward Elmo's theory. Jasper wasn't sure if life could have any real meaning without a God, without a heaven to aspire toward, but he intended to find out.

Walking around directionless during this spiritual musing, he finally headed toward an enormous edifice that epitomized contemporary religious convictions in suburban America. Stone steps and a slanted gangplank for wheelchairs led to an awe-inspiring cathedral, overwhelming in its size and design. White columns anchored high arches that were sculpted in ornate detail. Rose windows shaped in semicircles lined the clerestories flanking the brick basilica. It was the desert's gothic tribute to Rococo architecture. Ornamental obelisks, spikes, leaves, kinks, and interlaced garlands were carved under two sky-high spires. It reminded Jasper of the encyclopedia photo he'd seen of the Notre Dame de Paris with its strange beasts leaning over the parapets, some half-human, some right out of nightmares. These, the people had said, were the demons of Paris shut up in the Cathedral where they stood gazing over the rooftops of a city in which they could no longer do mischief. He never knew churches could go bankrupt, but this one had and after years of sitting dormant, it was transformed into Dooley's, Tucson's most ostentatious discotheque. The moneychangers had converted this house of God into a lucrative den of strobe lights, disco balls, and watered-down drinks. The gargoyles were back and running amok. Jasper hated the place with every cell of his mortal soul. He walked inside.

When the bouncer checked his driver's license, he smiled and Jasper smiled back. Finally legal. He stepped into the club. Several couples were gyrating on the dance floor to swirling techno music, girls sporting big hair and sequined cocktail dresses, male companions wearing white shoes, white belts, and unbuttoned silk shirts. A disc jockey in a glass-encased booth was spinning records, filling the room with 112 pulsating beats per minute.

Jasper climbed the spiral staircase to the mezzanine level, bought a beer, and watched the glitterati engage. The regulars, narcissistic aristocrats at balcony tables, were sizing up the captivity on the coliseum floor. Periodically, a vapid sorority girl would strut by in a haze of hairspray and perfume, a Lani but without the wit and charm. If he were more intoxicated, he'd strike up some insipid conversation with one of them because Dooley's was, above all else, an exercise in jejune chit-chat. He observed the muscular bartender selling mixed drinks from a computerized machine that measured, mixed, and poured with zero margin of error. There was no romance to be found in the cocktails at Dooley's.

Saturday night continued to strut through the double-door entrance. Bouncers in bow ties checked for dress code compliance and proper identification, while the fashionably attired customers in gold chains and platform shoes mingled and danced. Stained glass windows depicted a variety of Biblical scenes. Jasper, impervious to the evening's artifice and glee, directed his blank stare toward the floor.

His mood had swerved from self-pity to complete numbness, an improvement really, and as he sipped his beer, he rotated on the bar stool just in time to find none other than the disco queen herself, Lady Lani. She was headed for him at three o'clock with dead aim, predictably embracing the arm of a guy almost prettier than she was. Jasper's eyes met hers at ten paces.

"Hey, what's the word, bluebird?"

"Lani."

She was wearing an aqua-colored chiffon number with white cloth buttons fastened just below the collarbone, ivory-white earrings, and a matching necklace. Her jet-black hair was piled high on her head with a French curl spiraling down along each cheek. Behind her right ear was a white hibiscus, a Pacific Islander trademark that indicated its wearer was searching for a mate. Had the flower been behind her left ear—closer to the heart, it would have signified being spoken for. And as always, Lani's eyes were impossibly blue, almost translucent. Blue eyes were a rarity for an island girl. In fact, Lani claimed to be the only native girl on Guam who had them, inherited from her American-born grandmother. But perhaps Lani's most distinguishing feature was her hands, her smooth, supple, delicate, luxurious, surgeon-like hands, which gesticulated when she spoke.

"Jasper, this is my friend, Maximilian."

Jasper shook his hand waiting for the limp-fish return handshake, but the guy practically broke Jasper's knuckles.

Lani went on to provide a truncated biography of her escort's personal history, which Jasper completely ignored, and he would have missed his name, too, had it been anything other than *Maximilian*. The guy probably got his name out of a phone book, Jasper thought, and smiled a fake smile. His real name was probably *Junior*.

"You been writing me some poems?" Lani shouted over the din of the music.

Jasper didn't respond and an awkward silence lingered in the air like a plume of cigarette smoke.

"Maxie, why don't you go find us a table? I'll be over in a sec." As he left, Lani looked through Jasper with those glacier blues. "What's wrong with you?"

"Nothing's wrong with me. What's wrong with you?"

"Come on, don't give me that. What's the problem?"

"Why must you insist there's a problem?" Jasper sipped his

drink as indifferently as he could muster.

"Because," she said, pointing her finger at his chest, "whenever you're pissed off, you pout like a petulant child and it's irritating as hell."

"So, enough about me. Let's talk about you."

"Stop joking around for once. I'm being serious."

"What do you want me to say? I called you last night. Hell, I call you every night. You're never home, I never see you. You always have to study or be somewhere. If you don't want to see me anymore, just tell me. I can take it." Jasper swallowed hard. He hadn't meant to go that far.

"First of all, school is kicking my ass," she said. The Donna Summer decibel level was deafening, so Lani sat Jasper back down on his barstool and half-whispered, half-shouted in his ear. As she leaned over he could smell her shampoo and feel the curvature of her breasts against his shoulder. "Anatomy and Physiology is killing me. Plus, I hate math and we have all these things happening at the sorority house. So give a girl a chance, will ya? Don't make this a big deal."

"You're not avoiding me?"

"No, I'm not avoiding you. You're just too damn sensitive. You're a poet, that's all."

"I feel like we're playing hide-and-seek and I'm always the one seeking. I know I can't wine and dine you like these rich frat rats, and all that money is intimidating to a poor Catholic boy like me. Plus, just look at this place. I mean, seriously." He set his beer on the bar. Glitter and glam were splashed everywhere like stars smeared across the Milky Way. "There's enough pretense in this place to fill the Grand Canyon. The drinks are mixed by a machine for crissakes!"

Lani smiled. "There's a little man in there mixing those drinks." She indicated the man's size by a space between her thumb and forefinger.

Jasper suppressed the laugh.

"If Dooley's is so terrible, what are you doing here?"

"I decided to celebrate my twenty-first birthday. By myself."

Suddenly Lani's mood seemed to shift. "Today?"

"Yesterday," Jasper said. "Plus, my old man tracked me down and I got fired from my job. Other than that, life has been relatively uneventful."

"I'm sorry, baby," Lani said. She hugged him close, caressed his face in her hands, and French kissed him. The song stopped and she whispered, "First of all, happy birthday. Second of all, you know I like you. But I told you up front that after three years with Marcel, I wanted to date around. Remember that?"

Jasper exhaled and nodded reluctantly.

"Three years is a long time, haole boy. That guy really broke my heart. So like I said, give a girl a chance. If you want to know the truth, you're all over my radar. So don't screw it up. Capiche?" She kissed his cheek.

"I'm not asking you to move to a pig farm in Nebraska and have my children. Just dinner would be nice."

"Look, I gotta go," Lani said, "but next week I'll pick you up in the convertible and we'll take a bottle of wine up to Gate's Pass. I promise." She kissed his cheek again and then just behind his ear, a sweet lingering kiss.

He could feel the warmth of her breath and smell the hibiscus.

"And as for the rich frat boys?" She pointed at his chest with her perfect finger. "You got poetry in that heart. No amount of money can compete with that." She touched his nose and smiled. "I wouldn't trade you for all the frat boys on Greek Row." And before she walked away, Jasper glanced one last time into her eyes, her mesmerizing, humbling blue eyes, which somehow made it impossible to hate her. Still, he realized he couldn't sit and watch her coo over Mr. Universe all night.

Jasper made his way past the dancing strobe lights and exited

Dooley's through the double doors. Lani was right, what was he doing here? Softly humming, he strolled down the sidewalk not wishing, not wanting, not wondering. Going out of his way to avoid Thyme Market, he headed down Fourth Avenue, a thoroughfare that originated in the swimming pool mansions of the Catalina foothills and meandered all the way through the valley of the desert, downtown. Good street sense was knowing to avoid it after dark. But tonight Jasper was fearless, his personal safety secured by the psychotic look in his eye. He stared down the faces of passersby as he read billboards, signs in store windows, and flyers plastered on telephone poles, all of which he'd seen a thousand times before without noticing. A tattered poster caught his eye, a strapping young executive wearing an expensive suit and dashing smile with lots of sparkling white teeth. It said: THIS MAN IS IN NUCLEAR RESEARCH. THE FUTURE BELONGS TO DYNAMIC INDIVIDUALS WHO ENJOY EXCITING CAREERS. FOR HIS CAR, OF COURSE, HE CHOOSES MARBLE WAX.

5. Inside the Blue Parrot

Jasper was unable to turn off his brain and the numbness eventually converted into nausea as he wandered down Fourth Avenue. His day-late solo birthday bash was about to detour toward the blue neon lights blinking outside a raucous punk bar called the Blue Parrot.

"Well, well, look what the cat dragged in. If it ain't Thyme Market's own Jasper Trueblood. Five bucks cover." A thin woman with stringy brown hair and wire-rimmed glasses stood smiling at the door, collecting cash and stamping hands.

"Hi Julie. Five bucks cover? Really? Are you giving away free appliances or something?"

"No. Wet T-shirt finals."

Jasper gave her a five. He had twenty-three dollars left to his name and almost no food at home.

She looked at his license. "Your birthday?'

"Yesterday."

"Happy birthday, Jasper. Here's your change." She cupped her hand and returned the five with a wink. "Good to see you again. You're gonna love this band. They kick ass."

"Thanks, Julie." Jasper knew her from the market and a couple of local poetry readings. She seemed too bright to slave away in a dystopia like the Blue Parrot. He wriggled carefully past the bouncers into the clamor. The word was that Doc, the pernicious proprietor, had installed an electronic weapons scanner due to the high percentage of patrons who were packing more than just wallets. Allegedly, Tucson's law enforcement community didn't fancy the Blue Parrot's long history of parking lot fistfights, blaring car stereos, and open drug transactions. But allegedly, what the cops resented even more was that the Blue Parrot had made Doc a millionaire many times over, yet the city had to pay the tab for all the fights, vandalism, and public disturbances. That's why they leaned on him so vehemently.

In stark contrast to Dooley's, the Blue Parrot was raw, devoid of pretense or affectation. When Jasper's mother had told him not to talk to strangers, this collection of people were what she'd had in mind. Each customer seemed to be the product of a genetic accident or an experiment in animal husbandry. Designer labels were not likely to be found on the hips of these jeans. Even the waitresses had funky hairdos and freaky tattoos.

A couple dozen tables were occupied by a menagerie of drug-addled brains, select representatives of the criminal underground, and a bevy of weekend nymphomaniacs. More of the same undulated on the dance floor in one large public grope. The body heat generated from this fertility ritual made the air sticky and makeup run. Girls from the Blue Parrot weren't the coquettish type who required flowers or romantic dinners before you could get to first base. In-the-park homers had been hit without ever leaving the coat room.

Jasper ordered a glass of draft. A biker sitting next to him was yelling to a woman at the other end of the bar; she was wearing a bubblegum-colored halter top and had a copious amount of hair. The sound system drowned out any kind of intelligible conversation. In that respect, the Blue Parrot was just like Dooley's.

In addition to wooden beams, the décor included a mural of a runaway freight train that had jumped its tracks and was soaring high above rooftops, trees, and telephone wires, climbing through wispy clouds and into the sky toward the stars. On other walls, neon beer signs winked and posters advertising past and future events were plastered everywhere. The bar's overall color scheme could be read as prolonged illness. Jasper felt right at home.

As he sipped his beer and quietly observed the mob throbbing at full throttle, a rugged punk rocker with a safety pin impaled in his left nostril was attempting to coax a girl into dancing. She seemed hesitant but he was drunk and undeterred. He towed her by the arm past the pool tables and cigarette machine toward the dance floor. Jasper tried to keep in mind that Blue Parrot girls weren't the type to play tennis because they liked the little white outfits. They expected a man to take the initiative, and the night was overflowing with possibilities for any guy unwilling to take no for an answer.

The dense aroma of beer, smoke, and perspiration was infiltrated by a dust cloud of thick perfume. A woman poured into a pair of black leather pants strutted past and ordered a Tom Collins. When the drink arrived, she sipped it, then plucked the maraschino cherry seductively from its stem and chewed it while waiting for her change. A leather-clad biker with chains dangling from his jacket stepped up to the bar, his face polished red from too much sun. The girl swallowed the cherry and began to slide her lips against his, behind his neck, in his ear. Jasper decided to move.

He managed to catch an open bar stool close to the stage where he watched a bartender working his trade, flipping bottles over his shoulder, expertly mixing a multitude of drinks and lining them up on the waitress trays. There were no computerized booze machines at the Blue Parrot. Suddenly, a wall of speakers interrupted his concentration. Jasper pivoted on his barstool as the band took the stage.

Most of the musical groups at the Parrot should've spent a few more months practicing in the drummer's garage, but it soon became clear that this ensemble, Central Air, was an exception. The guitars blended melodically and the keyboardist seemed to be playing piano, organ, and synthesizer simultaneously. The drummer remained in the background, thumping out an up-beat tempo with a guy in a gray fedora playing stand-up bass. As sharp as they sounded, there could be no doubt that the main attraction was the singer, Hollace Pacer. She was a black wom-an of medium build with a short brown Afro, tie-dyed lavender T-shirt, cutoff jeans under which she wore nylons with seams running up the back, and black stiletto heels. She was sensuous and captivating and could sing like a church choir. The veins in Hollace's neck throbbed as her resonant soprano rose above the wailing guitar. Her ability to range from a whisper to a scream within a single song was exhilarating. Jasper got lost in it drift-ing with eyes closed, oblivious to the rest of the world.

A massive tattooed woman sporting wild porcupine hair tapped Jasper on the shoulder, shattering his trance, and nudged him toward the dance floor. He shook his head. She grabbed his arm and he yanked free. She flipped him off and told him what he could do to himself, an act that wasn't even physically pos-sible.

Hollace belted out the final chorus, chest expanded, and the song faded out to enthusiastic whistling and applause. She wiped her brow with a white towel and bowed. This was Doc's cue. In his role as master of ceremonies, he entered stage-left wearing a fire engine red military jacket with gold-tasseled epaulettes, a red top hat, and goatee. He looked like a ring announcer fur-loughed from the Ringling Brothers.

"The amazing Hollace Pacer and Central Air. And yes, they'll be back for a final set but first ladies and gentlemen, the main event you've all been waiting for. The Wet T-shirt Contest Finals!"

There was a smattering of applause. Pre-recorded stripper music played in the background, a scratchy rendition of "Big Spender."

"And while we're setting up, let me take this opportunity to welcome all our special undercover friends from the Narcotics Division and the DEA. Please give them a round of applause. It's great to have you with us." Doc tipped his hat, clicked the heels of his black boots, and saluted.

There were a few half-hearted jeers.

As he droned on about upcoming acts, two bouncers carried out a plastic blue wading pool with little red fish stenciled on the side. Stage hands covered the amps with plastic and removed the guitars and other vulnerable sound equipment. Two girls sashayed onstage to boisterous clapping and wolf whistles. They were wearing yellow panties and white T-shirts with the Blue Parrot logo on the belly, a giant blue parrot sipping sarsaparilla through an oversized straw.

"In this corner," Doc said in his ring announcer voice, "at a combined weight of two hundred and fifteen pounds . . . "

The girls stepped cautiously inside the plastic pool and a bouncer muscled his way onstage carrying two large pitchers of water.

"What's your name?" Doc asked the contestant closest to him. "Lindsay."

Doc repeated it into the mike. Her opponent was named Carla. Both were curvy but Carla held a discernible edge. Lindsay would have to do something spectacular to compensate, and her smile exuded a halcyon confidence that she would do just that; when it was all over, Carla wouldn't know what hit her.

Doc signaled and the music began. The girls wiggled around

a bit and then their eyes froze as the bouncer poured water on their respective chests. They began to dance salaciously in a display of vulgarity everyone seemed to enjoy.

Lindsay's nipples were hard enough to poke holes through her shirt. Water splashed her panties, accentuating her black triangle under the stage lights. Carla had a slightly darker complexion with stringy bleached-blonde hair and though her face wasn't quite as appealing as Lindsay's, her body was. Her tan lines displayed a fondness for diminutive swimwear.

"Nice boobs, Carla. Let's see 'em," an anonymous voice shouted. Jasper didn't consider himself a prude but felt his stomach roiling. He wasn't titillated. The whole spectacle felt—obscene. Carla unabashedly tantalized the audience by shimmying her T-shirt up and over her head. Lindsay had done a one hundred and eighty degree turn to show the crowd her shifting hips, but when she heard the cacophony of cheers, she retaliated by pulling her T-shirt off completely, then tugged it between her legs like a feather boa, rolling her hips, licking her lips, and massaging her breasts. Lindsay was counterpunching with purpose late into the round.

The record stopped and Doc rang a cowbell. "OK, ladies, OK." There was boisterous applause and catcalls. Carla looked wistful as Doc stepped center-stage. Lindsay grinned, apparently pleased with her performance.

"The winner comes back for the final round and a shot at an all-expenses-paid weekend at spectacular Caesar's Palace in Las Vegas. Number one!" Doc held his outstretched palm over Lindsay. The crowd howled its support. He stepped around the pool and gauged Carla's ovation. Lindsay had a distinct advantage. Doc repeated the voting process but the ballots were in. Democracy had spoken. The way Doc put it, Lindsay was victorious by half a tit.

"Lindsay, we'll see you later in the final round."

"Is that shit unreal?" A man with long hair and a thick beard diverted Jasper's attention from the stage.

"What's that?"

"These babes may be amateurs, but you don't see this kind of action in legitimate strip clubs. And these chicks ain't doin' it for the dough, neither."

"Why are they doin' it?"

The man shrugged his shoulders. "Beats me. But it ain't for the dough."

"Have you ever seen this band before?"

"Yup."

"That girl can sing," Jasper said.

"Hollace rocks. I talked to the drummer last night between sets. Record companies are in a bidding war to sign them. They're about to cut their first record."

"Really?" Jasper said. "How come they're stuck out here in the middle of the desert?"

"Same as everybody else, I suppose. Fighting the water shortage by drinking their liquor straight." He laughed and pushed his hair back, but his smile dissolved when he turned his attention toward the stage. "Oh good mother of God."

The next contestant was of average physical attributes, legs a little too long for her torso, but not bad. However, the girl following her had frizzy red hair sprayed in indeterminate directions, and her panties bulged at the waist. She was a good fifty pounds overweight and had a face full of acne. Jasper looked closer. It was same woman who had asked him to dance. She was working the wire without a net.

"Wow." Jasper didn't know what else to say.

"Yeah," the hairy man added with a smile.

"I thought you had to win at least one week to be in the finals."

"She did. There was hardly anyone here that night but a few bikers. She went up against one of their bitches and lost. Then the biker chick slipped in the pool and started screamin' she was gonna sue, so Doc disqualified her and declared this big momma the winner. Then the bikers and bouncers beat the shit out of each other."

Jasper considered women's breasts magical, and what was transpiring on stage was a travesty to mammary glands everywhere. He ordered another beer.

The large woman twisted in lurid contortions, grinning slyly. The gal next to her appeared to be uncomfortable and self-conscious, understandable considering she was soaked to the bone and parading around in her underwear. This was the stuff of nightmares. Jasper thought he'd use it in a poem.

Doc stopped the music. The shy contestant received mild though sustained applause and a few shouts. Then Doc placed his hand over the larger woman. The first three excruciatingly-long seconds there was nothing but stone-cold silence, no clapping whatsoever, not so much as the accidental tinkling of a glass. In no time her face ran the full gamut of emotion, a metamorphosis from hopeful and high on hard liquor to embarrassment and finally abject shame. The deafening absence of sound was soon broken by booing, howling, retching, and jeers. Jasper felt so sorry for her that he began to clap but it was too late. His feeble applause was drowned out by an onslaught of catcalls and derisive laughter. The large woman's head hung dejectedly. Mercifully there would be no recount.

The last semifinalists swaggered front-and-center. On the left was a hot-looking Latina whom Jasper had seen a couple times in Thyme Market. Unlike the other girls, she was not wearing the standard-issue yellow panties, but, rather, a white G-string. Then, when Jasper saw the girl who was next to her, he became weak-kneed. He stared closer. Lani. Doc announced her name but Jasper couldn't hear it. He stood up on a rung of his bar stool and peered over the crowd. The only thing he could think was, please God, don't let that be her.

He wormed through the crowd toward the ring apron where he was prepared to yank her offstage by the ankle bracelet, but as he got closer and the girl was doused and dancing, he realized her hair was too short, too brown, and she had no ankle bracelet. Plus, those weren't Lani's hands. He got within a few feet when she turned his way and they exchanged glances. He exhaled. She had brown eyes. She definitely wasn't Lani. But she was so gorgeous. The guy at the bar was right; this woman didn't need a vacation in Las Vegas. She was up there for reasons unrelated to monetary gain.

The Lani look-alike was stunning but as Doc had explained in the introductions, Tracy had won seven of the twelve weeks of competition. She was certain to have a few tricks up her sleeve despite the fact she wasn't wearing sleeves. Sure enough she immediately pulled her G-string up tight and bent over at ninety-degree angle to afford the front row a view of her peach-shaped derriere. Jasper had to laugh when one guy got too close, grabbed handfuls of air, and the bouncer motioned for him to move back or else.

Tracy was ultimately too lewd and won a resounding finish, which culminated in sustained applause. She went on to reign victorious over the other panty-clad gladiators in the final round by making suggestive motions with her fingers and being the first girl to completely disrobe. The runner-up won a modest cash prize.

"It's been a business doing pleasure with you," Doc said.

Jasper searched the crowd, determined to meet the Lani look-alike, but by now she was probably back in Doc's office being seduced by long lines of sparkling cocaine. Jasper went to take a piss.

The john was standing-room-only and smelled like a wet dog. Someone was whizzing in the sink and moaning in relief. Jasper eventually stepped up to a urinal and began to obliterate to-bacco from a dead cigarette with a steady yellow stream as he read the delirious prophecies and snippets of wit on the walls. Among the rather cubist array of anatomical drawings were po-ems of questionable meter and rhyme, ethnic and racial slurs, profane limericks, and phone numbers with going prices for group rates. Some of the sentiments were original, some cliché, some amusing. These lavatory philosophers weren't eloquent enough to write their congressmen or send letters to the editor, but they could certainly brighten up your commode.

Jasper had just flushed when he felt a commotion stirring behind him. The guy squirting in the first urinal had a billow-ing red Afro, roadmap eyes, and was singing to himself off-key when the sudden swell of bodies cramming through the door-way surged forward and pushed into his back, slamming his head into the cinderblock wall and his torso against the porce-lain. The crotch of his pants was splashed with his own urine.

"You fucking motherfucker," he said. He turned and thrust his hands into the shoulders of the unfortunate man behind him, the penultimate domino. The blow separated the man from his dark glasses and derby hat. A long blond ponytail fell free. The livid redhead glared down at his wet trousers, seemingly more incensed by the stain than his skull which had just lost a head-on collision with the wall. As his fists clenched and muscles tight-ened, the blond patron who'd been pushed retreated a step. Peo-ple stopped in mid-motion as heads peered from the threshold. Curious eyes appeared like periscopes from the stalls.

Red was soon hyperventilating, obviously drunk, probably drugged, and clearly intent on hurting someone. Jasper was right next to them forming a human triangle.

"That was an accident." The blond man didn't seem particu-larly frightened but rather appropriately apprehensive. He was a head taller and held a definite reach advantage. More faces crowded the doorway. "I didn't do it on purpose," he said.

Red reexamined his blotchy wet crotch. "You made me piss all over myself. I'm gonna kick your fucking ass, bitch."

The blond guy eyeballed him. "I apologize. Is that what you want me to say? I'm sorry, all right?"

"No, asshole. It ain't all right," said the irate redhead, aware of the gathering audience. "It ain't all right at all. I want you to suck the piss stain out of my pants."

Jasper thought he recognized the blond man from somewhere.

"Eat shit," said the blond man, barely moving his lips.

Red reached into his cowboy boot, activated a catch-release, and with an audibly metallic *click* a long silver blade shot out of a black casing. The switchblade's tip glinted in the phosphorescence of the overhead light. Spectators scrambled out of the way.

"Let's just see who's gonna eat shit."

Anyone who couldn't escape the restroom altogether took what little cover was available as the redhead crouched into an attack position and the blond man countered in a defensive posture. Just then, as they were staring each other down, Jasper, devoid of any emotion, of any malice or premeditation, telescoped his line of sight on the weapon and with one fell swoop kicked the redhead's hand to send the blade spinning straight up. It ricocheted off the ceiling, off the wall, and boomeranged right off Jasper's shoulder. Jasper then threw a roundhouse right that landed squarely on the redhead's cheekbone and knocked him flat on the floor. Red's lump of a body didn't flinch. Jasper hadn't punched anybody since he was Junior McPherson in seventh grade. His hand hurt, but other than that, it felt pretty good.

"Is he alive?" a voice finally asked from the first stall.

The blond ponytailed man shot Jasper a cursory glance as he turned Red over, his face as pink as raw hamburger. Blood trickled from his nostrils. The blond man checked Red's wrist for a pulse. It occurred to Jasper the guy might actually be dead. The color in his eyes had rolled back in his head.

"He's alive but he's gonna have one hell of a headache." The blond man rose to his feet and gave Jasper a nod of appreciation. "Thanks." He retrieved his hat and dark glasses, put them on, and picked up the blade. "This thing catch you on the shoulder?" He deposited the switchblade into a trash receptacle.

Jasper, in his sudden burst of testosterone, had forgotten to check. "It just tore my shirt a little," he said. He inspected it further and noticed blood.

"You sure?"

Jasper nodded.

The spectators turned their attention toward Jasper.

"Hey, any of us could have been castrated!" Jasper exclaimed. "Did you see the size of that blade?"

While everyone laughed and started clapping, Jasper noticed the blond man sizing him up.

"Look." Someone pointed to the unconscious Red who was sending a new stream of urine inside his pants.

"I guess he wasn't done," someone said.

Another chimed in, "You can shake and you can dance but the last drop stays in your pants."

Jasper stepped over Red feeling neither guilt nor satisfaction nor much of anything else. Normally he would have been stupefied by this display of aggression, but not this time. He felt numb. He passed through the cheers and pats on the back. The blond man, under his hat and behind his glasses, watched him walk away from it all, past Doc who was leading the cavalry, two beefy bouncers, toward the scene of the crime.

Jasper returned to the comparably sedate hysteria in the bar. Hollace was back onstage. The dance floor percolated. He stood in a tight space by the waitress station when, before long, he caught the blond man spying on him from a couple of tables away. Jasper knew he'd seen the face before As Hollace slipped into a ballad that was as slow as you could get away with in a place like the Parrot, the man approached.

"Excuse me."

Jasper acted surprised. "Yeah?"

"Can I ask you a question?"

"Sure."

"Why did you do it? I mean, why did you jump into the fray like that?"

Jasper paused. "I don't know."

The man nodded and smiled.

"You look familiar," Jasper said. "Ever been in Thyme Market? A few blocks from here? I work there."

The man peered over his sunglasses and squinted into Jasper's eyes. "I don't think so. Whatever you're drinking is on me."

Jasper didn't feel much like conversing but if the guy thought Jasper was a hero, the least he could do was drink the man's liquor. "Rum and Coke."

The bartender walked by three other people waiting for refills and directly up to Jasper's new friend as if he were a foreign dignitary.

"A double rum and Coke and a grapefruit juice on the rocks." The barkeep was back in a jiffy. The man handed him a twenty. "Keep the change." He slid the drink over in Jasper's direction. "Hey look," he said, pointing at Jasper's shoulder. "You're bleeding."

Jasper shrugged.

"Maybe you need a couple stitches?'

"I'm fine. Just a flesh wound."

The ballad was over and guitars were thrashing with Hollace deftly hitting the high notes. The man spoke directly in Jasper's ear. "Can we go somewhere so we can hear each other talk?"

"If you're trying to pick me up, no offense, but I'm into girls."

"No," he laughed. "I want to show you my appreciation, not my genitals."

Jasper laughed. "You got any smoke?"

6. The Two-Beer Tour

As they approached Troy's car, an alley cat hopped off the hood and darted off into the shadows. Troy hoped the kid wouldn't place his face, reasonably sure of his anonymity, though the kid had seen him without the disguise. Troy turned the ignition and revved the engine. Bud kept the old Dodge in tip-top condition and even though it looked like hell, it had a souped-up engine and ran like a race car. He thought again of his ex-wife, Gretchen, who'd cracked it up pretty good back when it was still new. He wasn't sure why he'd been thinking so much about Gretchen. Dreaming about her. The more distant he became from Hilary, the more he realized how much he missed Gretchen, and the more he regretted his lack of fidelity. "All these girls on the road? I don't go near 'em," Troy had once assured her. Gretchen had insisted she wouldn't marry him without a solemn vow of monogamy. "It's like they don't even exist," Troy would say. And for a while they didn't.

"What's your name?"

"Jasper. Hey, there's the fag bookstore." He pointed to a small adobe building.

"Oh." Troy smiled at the kid's homophobia. He believed every human being's sexual composition was part homo, part hetero, and that individuals differed only by degree. They stopped at an intersection. Troy called out to an old man who was stumbling along the sidewalk, "What's the word, old-timer?"

The wino staggered to the driver's side window. "*Life* is the word," he slurred. "And a hamburger with onions. You got any spare change for a war veteran like m'self?"

"Which war?" Troy asked.

"W. W. Two. United States Marines, Fifth Regiment. Guadalcanal. You wanna see my war wounds?"

"No thanks," Troy said and handed him a ten, then another. "I just want to thank you for your service. Let's get those fucking hostages out of Iran."

The man squinted at the two bills. "Hey!" he said with a flash smile and diamond-sized glint in his eye. "I know who you are. John F. Kennedy!"

Troy grinned as the old soldier stashed the bills in his hip pocket and hobbled away with renewed pep.

"You rich or something?" Jasper asked.

"It's all relative," Troy said, wishing he'd been more subtle. "Hey, I heard a joke today. Why do men have nipples?"

"I don't know," Jasper said. "Why?"

"So old geezers know how high to pull up their pants."

The kid laughed but didn't say anything else, so Troy drove without talking into the foothills, hoping his enigmatic passenger wasn't struggling to find himself. Troy had been endeavoring to lose himself for quite some time. But it was apparent this kid had fallen into an emotional black hole, as evidenced by an aura of doom surrounding him. Jasper hadn't questioned Troy's age, occupation, or even asked his name. The street lamps cast a soft amber glow that angled through the windshield and framed the kid's face. Troy theorized that most people were, spiritually, either living or dying. His new friend had bad color.

"How's your shoulder?"

Jasper was staring at the moon, then tugged at the jagged, bloodstained fabric of his shirt. "It's fine. It barely nicked me."

"We'll go out to my place for a nightcap and get it dressed. Looks superficial, but you can never be too sure."

"And you're not gay, right?"

Troy smiled. "Right. So what're you lookin' at?"

"The moon," Jasper said. "When I was a little kid I used to think the moon was following me around. Whenever my family would drive somewhere at night, I'd look out the window and watch it. And it seemed like it was following only me, no one else. I would whine if I couldn't see it because clouds were in the way. I'm not sure why it took so long to figure out the moon follows everyone, but for the longest time, I remember thinking it was only me."

They were driving past the edge of town, gliding up a long foothill road when Troy caught a white Buick sedan out of his peripheral vision headed straight for them. The vehicle had run a stop sign and was aimed toward the passenger side doing at least sixty.

Jasper screamed, "Look out!" He tucked and ducked under the dashboard.

Troy slammed on the horn and punched the brakes, swerving and fishtailing to the right, missing the honking Buick's left rear bumper by a fraction as it swished by at top speed. Troy's Dodge narrowly avoided skipping down into an arroyo. The kid emerged wide-eyed from his death crouch.

"Jesus!" Jasper said. "That guy almost killed us."

"Have you noticed that people don't know how to drive anymore?"

"No shit!" Jasper pressed his hand on his heart. "I thought we were history. I thought we were about to become past tense. That guy's headlights were right there."

Troy maneuvered the car off the gravel shoulder and wheeled

back onto the road, leaving a wake of dust.

"Well, that didn't take long."

"What?" Troy asked.

"If I saved you at the Blue Parrot, I'd say now we're even."

Troy smiled.

"Where in the hell do you live, anyway?"

"Not much farther. What's your name again?"

"Jasper Trueblood. I'm sure I've seen you somewhere before."

"Doubtful. I live in Tucson, but I'm on the road most of the time."

"You said you had some loco weed?"

Troy glanced at the rearview mirror. "Oh, yeah. Check the ashtray. My friend Bud drives this car around the ranch a lot. He smokes this killer Cambodian shit that'll knock your dick in the dirt. You can actually see chunks of blond hash in the buds."

There were several large roaches in the ashtray.

"Don't mind if I do," Jasper said, then fired one up. It smelled pungent, like church incense. Jasper offered the joint to Troy, but he declined. Smoking meant coughing, which meant laryngitis, postponements, cancellations, litigation. And these days, it put him straight to sleep.

The car labored along over the roller coaster roads through the serene desert night. Jasper used the car lighter to keep the joint lit and inhaled deeply, trying to hold it in, but the smoke expanded in his lungs and escaped through his nose. He coughed hard, red-faced and glassy-eyed. He studied the moon again.

"Do you have a personal relationship with the moon?" Troy asked.

Jasper's eyes remained fixed skyward. "Sorta. It kinda transports me sometimes, you know? Like a little escape. I remember in high school, two guys from NASA brought a moon rock exhibit. The stone was about the size of my fist. I stared at it for a while, and I was so bummed out. There was nothing special about it. It looked like an ordinary rock, like a million rocks I had seen a million times. I don't know what I was expecting. Maybe for it to glow? I was very disappointed. What did you say your name was?"

"Troy. Did you get a kick off that pot?"

"Hell yes. That shit is totally decent. I feel a lot better. I can still see those headlights comin' straight at me."

Troy was pleased to have revealed his name without trace of recognition. "We're almost there."

They curled around a few more bends and curves, past the contorted vegetation and finally there it was like a vision in the night, Troy's mansion, nestled at the base of the Santa Catalinas and shining in the moonlight. The silhouetted mountains stood behind it on the horizon, imposing.

"That's it," Troy said. "That's my ranch."

Even from a distance, it was evident the estate was a full city block long.

"Holy shit, Batman," Jasper said. "That's the biggest house I've ever seen in my whole life." Then, with a hint of suspicion he asked, "You really live here?"

"Well, I own it, but like I said I'm on the road a lot so I don't actually spend much time here. Not as much as I'd like anyway."

Troy neared the wrought iron gate and fished a remote control from under the seat, activating floodlights. The gate, anchored in a stone pillar, slowly swung open.

"Wow," Jasper said. As they entered, he turned around and watched the gate close and the lights fade to black. "This is bigger than my whole neighborhood."

They idled up the stone drive bordered by sand, enormous rocks, and numerous varieties of cacti. They rolled to a stop. Troy switched off the ignition.

"You live alone?"

"I live with my girlfriend, Hilary. My best friend Bud runs the place, I just pay the bills."

"Because you're on the road."

"That's right." Troy opened his car door but did not get out. "Will you be in town tomorrow night? At the Unknowns concert?"

Troy grinned like a child found under a cardboard box in a game of hide-and-go-seek. He removed his hat and extended his hand. "Troy Archer."

Jasper studied Troy's face. He wiped his palm on his shirt and shook Troy's hand. "Un-fucking-believable. I'm sitting in a car with Troy Archer. *The* Troy Archer. Man, you guys are like my favorite band of all time! I read something in the paper about all the celebrities who own property in Tucson, and I remember they mentioned you and Paul McCartney. I knew I recognized you from somewhere. Wow, this is unreal. And the hat and glasses, it's a disguise, right?"

Troy shrugged. "I guess you could say that. Going incognito is just my way of deflecting unwanted attention. "

"I was looking at your car radio when it hit me. Remember the picture of you on the cover of that one album where you're underwater, listening to that old radio—"

"*Sound Waves.* That radio was one of the first Victrolas ever made."

"Yeah, that's it. The *Sound Waves* album. So what were you doing in the Blue Parrot?"

"My record label's trying to sign the act. Central something. . . "

"Central Air."

"Yeah, that's it. I was supposed to introduce myself but I never got around to it."

"Why didn't you tell me who you were?" Jasper said.

"You didn't ask. Let's go inside. Bud'll patch up your arm."

"Holy hell, I'm sitting here with Troy Archer. OK, here's an admittedly dumb question but I mean, when am I ever gonna get a chance like this again, right?"

"Shoot."

"All the magazines say this is your last tour. Are you guys really breaking up?"

Troy laughed. He was expecting something serious. "They've been saying that since our first tour. Forty years from now we'll probably be doing an octogenarian tour in wheelchairs and adult diapers. In this industry, don't believe anything you read. I think the Unknowns are going to be around for a while. At least, I know we'll be around tomorrow night. I'll get you some tickets."

"Wow, that'd be so cool, Troy. Can I call you *Troy*? Man, I gotta tell ya, a rock 'n' roll hero was about the last thing I was expecting tonight. Lately my life has been careening out of control like that car back there."

Troy didn't want to press him for more information just yet, but it was somewhat disheartening that this animated exchange was prompted by Troy's celebrity. Heroes rarely measure up to their advance billing. Back in that restroom, Jasper's attention had been reflexive and genuine. Now it was circumspect.

As they moseyed up the winding sidewalk, Jasper was thinking that to whomever had built the place, rocks were serious business. It was dynamically constructed with carved, cut, and stacked stones in shades of white, off-white, and tan. The roof's turrets and gables sliced at elongated angles from the promontory, and it had more windows than Jasper had ever seen. As they neared the portico lined in mosaic tiles of blue, white, and copper, automatic security lights flicked on which illuminated the front door and leaded glass side panels latticed in floral designs. Curiously, embedded into the frame was what appeared to be a pair of binoculars. Troy peered into them. A small green light clicked on.

"What's that?"

"It's called an Eye-dentifier, spelled e-y-e. You look into it and a computer records the blood vessel pattern in your retina. Or maybe it's the iris. I'm not really sure, it's one of Bud's gimmicks. Anyway, they're like fingerprints. No two people have the same pattern. If your pattern computes in the security code, the door unlocks. Go ahead, try it."

Jasper tentatively peeked in. The light clicked red. "You really need this thing? Do groupies beat a path to your door or something?"

"These days, the guys in the crew get all the girls. It's just another gadget. Bud's hobby." The door opened. "Aha, speaking of whom. Jasper, this is Bud. Bud, this is our new friend, Jasper Trueblood. We need to fix his arm."

Bud shook Jasper's hand a bit warily and looked at the cut.

"It's nothing," Jasper said. "Nice to meet you." He stepped inside and stood gawking. The squat, semicircular doorway exploded into a foyer the size of an opera house. Jasper stared at the proportions of the high ceiling, but the center of the sunken room quickly commanded his attention. A glass shaft the size of a freight elevator reached majestically up to a skylight in the ceiling.

"It's a terrarium," Bud said as if anticipating a familiar question.

Multicolored sand, rocks, and cacti of various sizes were positioned on three glass shelves. The foyer's exposed wooden beams accentuated the skylight and solar panels. When the front door closed, intricate crystals of a chandelier danced and pinged. Plush white carpeting and soft leather furniture surrounded the terrarium, its three-foot marble base streaked with pink and gray veins. Jasper peered up toward the moon.

"Reflectors push sunlight down for the plants," said Bud, "and moonlight for the night-blooming cereus. Those are the tall slender ones, top shelf. The white flowers open at night and hibernate during the day."

"It's like a desert under glass. All you need are a few rattle-snakes."

Bud and Troy looked at each other and smiled.

"Perhaps you should give Jasper the two-beer tour while I call Nils."

"OK," Bud said. "Troy, may I see you in the dining room for a moment?"

"Sure. Jasper, have a seat. The bar's over there. Make yourself a rum and Coke or whatever you'd like."

Bud followed Troy into the dining room while Jasper dream-ily inspected the terrarium out of earshot. "Who is he?"

"I'm not really sure," Troy said. "Some drunk with a switch-blade came at me in the restroom of that fucking dive bar Nils sent me to. The kid kicked the knife out of the guy's hand and clocked him. I figured that was worth a cocktail or two."

Bud peered gravely into Troy's eyes. "This is dangerous. If you're going to start bringing your slumming buddies out here to the property, that's a serious breach of security."

"First of all, I wasn't slumming, Bud. I was doing a favor for the record label, a professional courtesy. And second of all, the last time I checked, my name's still on the deed to this place. I'll bring anybody I damn well please."

"You own it but I'm living in it, and if someone decides to rob the place and not leave any witnesses, it's my obituary in the morning paper."

"Listen, I didn't meet this kid on the street. He broke up a knife fight, all right? I was only in the club because Nils said the label wanted me to schmooze the act. That's it. Like I told you this morning, my slumming days ended at that grocery store last night."

"Good."

"Where's Hil?"

"Asleep, I guess. How the fuck would I know? She never says

two words to me."

"Trust me, Bud," Troy said. "This kid is no security risk."

As Bud led Jasper on a tour, Troy headed up the spiral staircase, steadying himself on the brass banister. Each stair was anchored to create the illusion of being suspended in mid-air. The master bedroom door was slightly ajar and he tiptoed inside. The drapes were drawn, and a familiar lump occupied the middle of the canopied bed, breathing heavily, cocooned in a comforter like a badly-rolled cigar. Her hair was festooned all over the pillow and smelled like fresh strawberries. The air-conditioning was on full blast. Hilary once said the only dreams she remembered were the dreams Troy was in. At the time, he thought it was one of the most romantic things he'd ever heard, but that was back in the Dark Ages. He kissed her gently on the cheek. She repositioned herself and turned away. She could have been sleeping or playing coy. Troy wasn't sure.

He returned downstairs to the music library and switched on an old reel-to-reel featuring rhythm-and-blues numbers he used as pain relievers, songs that could have been written specifically about his jigsaw life. They were the kind of tracks John Fendleman used to write for the Unknowns before he became so utterly specious, obsessed with overdubbing and applying endless layers of orchestration to create the sophistry that the record label referred to as "complexity with broad appeal and commercial viability."

Troy wondered if the music was killing him or keeping him alive.

He called Nils.

* * *

As Jasper followed Bud down a wide corridor that was more like a runway than hallway, he soon became numb to all the finely-crafted antiques and stained-glass windows. The opulence reminded him of a museum, and he could hear his mother's voice warning not to touch anything. Jasper had trouble assimilating too much beauty, whether it was a mansion or a college coed. While Bud pointed out various nooks and crannies, Jasper sized him up. He was an aging James Dean, but with lots more facial hair, wearing old jeans and occasionally gesturing toward one artifact or another. His biceps were like coiled cables twisted together. A threadbare Mexican wedding shirt hung loosely from his shoulders, and his tennis shoes squeaked as he walked along the polished marble floors. His blasé inflection suggested he needed to impress no one, and Jasper speculated that Bud didn't appreciate unexpected guests.

They arrived at the main dining room which included tables with white tablecloths, a dance floor, chandeliers, and a disco ball. They moved onward and the ceiling dropped from thirty feet to twelve. They poked their heads into bedrooms, a fireplace in each, and in one of the bathrooms, Jasper removed his shirt. Bud disinfected the cut then bandaged it with gauze and tape.

"Thanks," Jasper said.

Bud didn't respond.

Farther along and around a corner, they entered a combination greenhouse-spa that afforded a panoramic view of the property out back. Footlights reflected in the swimming pool and well beyond stood tall shadowy forms which Bud said were sheds, a guest house, and stables for their twenty-head of horse. The dark mountains, fat and sassy, were almost close enough to touch.

Bud hit a switch that activated four small overhead spotlights. In one corner, a white cockatoo, perched in a wicker cage, squawked and turned its head inquisitively, reminding Jasper of the onlookers at the Blue Parrot during the wet T-shirt contest. Under the cage was an ornate Jacuzzi fashioned in a byzantine décor, steps on either side descending into the steamy pool. Woozy from booze, weed, sadness, and exhaustion, Jasper was tired of the glamorous two-beer-tour, but Bud had saved the finest foci for the grand finale. They entered what Bud referred to as the drawing room. Built into a wall flanked by books on either side was an immense glass case crawling with live rattlesnakes. Wrapped behind rocks, coiled around branches, and nestled snugly in the sand were at least a dozen of them slithering together. They didn't seem to appreciate the disturbance and showed their annoyance by clattering their rattles like castanets.

"I don't like taking wild animals out of their natural habitat and plunging them into captivity, but they're just so damn cute. Actually they were lucky. I was going to shoot them."

"You shoot rattlesnakes?"

"Sure. You take a four-wheeler into the desert after dark and inch along ever so slowly with your headlights on bright. The warmth arouses 'em and the light freezes 'em. Then you blow off their little heads, eat the meat, and treat the skin to make a hat band for your Stetson."

"Pretty amazing." Jasper inspected a massive globe on a gold stand and gave it a spin. It stopped at Bolivia. Another wall was lined with books from floor-to-eye level and above them, portrait after portrait of sad-faced clowns. The colors were subdued, leaving no room for an interpretation of mirth. Mounted on the opposite wall was a bighorn sheep head, who appeared not much happier than the clowns, and surrounding the sheep and clowns was a collection of clocks: a gold-faced grandfather, a finely carved Buddha figurine with a timepiece in the belly, a scaled-down replica of Big Ben, a small flock of cuckoos. And each ran counterclockwise.

"How come they all run backward?"

Bud shrugged. "I don't know. My ex-wife said I couldn't do it, so I guess it's just my infantile way of proving her wrong. It looks confusing but everything's just reversed. Each of them tells perfect time."

Farther down, against the rear window-wall, a splendid cheetah skin was spread out, colors in stark contrast to the white carpet below. The cheetah's eyes stared out in frozen terror, the world's fastest land animal unable to escape his fate. Jasper thought that if he were a wild jungle animal, the last place he'd want to end up was on the floor of some rich rock star.

Bud directed Jasper's attention to the fireplace, which was not really a fireplace at all. There was a cluster of red sandstone rocks and extended white polished stones supporting small plants and family portraits. The hearth was actually a pool of water, cool and green. Bud activated a dial and a ceiling-to-floor waterfall came to life. "The design was conceived by Frank Lloyd Wright. Ever hear of him?"

"Yeah," Jasper said. "Famous architect." He didn't mention that he'd also read that one of Wright's house managers, someone not unlike Bud, had set one of Wright's creations on fire and then killed seven people with an axe as they tried to escape.

Bud readjusted the dial and the artificial rain came to an abrupt halt. He pointed at the bighorn sheep. "See that red button behind old Lazarus there? Press it."

Jasper complied. There was a buzz and then slowly, a black panel as tall as Jasper and a good twenty feet wide began to pull sideways and disappear into the opposite wall to reveal a breathtaking spectacle.

"Holy shit. What do we have here?"

The aquarium was gargantuan and teeming with life. Red rock sparkled up to knee level from which crystal white coral sprouted like little snow-covered trees. In a clearing, a gray Chinese pagoda stood as tall as the tank, and slender fish slid hurriedly through intricately carved openings as if rushing through a train station.

"Eleven hundred and ninety-two gallons of synthetic salt water and fish from all over the world. My miniature ocean."

"A whole separate world," Jasper said, staring and envying the fish and their uncomplicated lives. "How come all that water doesn't break the glass?"

"Gravity pulls the water down, making it more-or-less dead weight. But everything else is tricky. Time-consuming as hell."

"Feeding?"

"Feeding, cleaning. Bad water causes most of the problems. You have to consider heat, lights, filters, air pumps, a dozen other things."

"What's this down here?" In a section at the far end of the tank cordoned off by a pane of glass were several sea horses clinging to watery plants with tiny prehensile tails.

"I'm trying to breed sea horses, with only minimal success. The four large ones are Man 'O War, Citation, Whirlaway, and Secretariat. I haven't named the others yet."

Some were bright red, others bright purple. Their tiny faces were a combination of horse and crocodile. One had a pouch at the stomach. "Is she pregnant?"

"Yes. But that's not a she. It's a he."

Jasper looked at Bud. "Get outta here."

"No, really. In this species, the male gives birth."

Jasper's eyes got big. "Cut it out."

"Seriously," Bud insisted. "And see the long eel-like fish up there? Those are pipefish, like a stretched-out sea horse. The male gives birth in that species, too. With a sea horse, you're supposed to remove the females from the tank when the male starts the birthing process because he tends to go into violent contortions and may try to kill the female."

"Hell yes," Jasper said. "I would, too."

"Reminds me of this buddy I had over in Nam, Billy Callison. Came home and got his wife pregnant and all through the preg-

nancy he attended classes, coached her on the breathing tech-
niques, everything. But when the big day came, at the moment
of truth, the pain was too much and she started screaming at
him to never touch her again." Bud chuckled. "The doctor made
Billy leave the delivery room."

They both laughed.

The sea horses looked studious, milling about a porcelain
shipwreck as if assessing the vessel's damage. Jasper loved them.
"Why sea horses?"

"I don't know. Never had any children. Maybe secretly I want
to be a daddy sea horse."

Jasper was drawn to the other end of the tank. "What kinds
of fish do you have?" He'd completely forgotten about Troy.

"Kinds you don't usually see together."

The fish cruised by patrolling territorial boundaries, fins and
tails waving delicately like lingerie blowing on a clothesline,
their shadows following on the rocks below. "Most of the fish
I've had are too aggressive. Some are entirely peaceful except
with their own kind. See that mandarin over there? Pretty non-
violent except with other mandarins. Other species will fight
anybody." Bud pointed, "See that yellow one over there with the
black spot by his tail?"

"Yeah."

"Other fish think that spot is his eye so when they attack, he's
able to get away."

"No shit. I could use one of those."

"And see the small school in the corner?"

"They're swimming straight up and down!" Jasper exclaimed.
"Look at their little fins!"

"Shrimpfish. Their body structure has been modified in the
evolutionary process to make them harder to find in cracks."

Jasper pointed up toward the surface. "Bud, look."

Bud squinted toward the top. "One of the shrimps." The long, thin fish rocked demurely with the waves. "That's the second dead one this week. They're not adapting to the water. If you're going to stay alive in this world, you've got to adapt to the water." He lit a cigarette and offered Jasper one.

"No thanks. Pretty spectacular place." Bud was affable enough, but he seemed like he was suppressing a significant burden. "You and Troy own this place together?"

Bud pursed his lips like one of the sea horses. "Troy and I have been best friends since grammar school. He owns it, I'm paid to appreciate it and make sure it appreciates." He exhaled again and smoke filtered through his mouth and nose.

"You run it all by yourself?"

"I have hired hands to work the horses and a full-time cleaning lady, Betty. She's off to see her son in Denver this weekend. She's not especially fond of Troy's entourage. My ex used to live here too but she split."

"Sorry."

Bud shrugged. "It happens."

"How'd you get that scar on your neck?" Jasper asked.

Bud laughed. "You're forward. I like that. It happened in Nam. Shrapnel. Mekong Delta. Ninth Infantry Division. My ex used to have to wake me up with a broomstick from the opposite side of the bedroom because of the nightmares. I'm not sure why but in dreams, it takes forever to kill the other guy."

"Thank you for serving our country." Jasper remembered Troy's words to the old wino on the street.

"Thanks. I appreciate that. When you're over there, all you can think about is going home and when you get home, all you can think about is going back."

"How come?"

"'Cause all the people you left behind are the people who kept you alive."

Jasper nodded. "Shall we see what Troy's up to?"

"Can I give you a little advice first?" Bud crushed out his cigarette. "Don't kill him with questions. He's got a lot on his mind."

"Kill him with questions? I don't even know why I'm here. This wasn't my idea."

"Troy said something about a knife fight."

"Some drunk in a bar with a bad attitude, that's all. Happens every day. A simple 'thanks' would've sufficed. Why would someone like Troy Archer give a shit about me?"

"Troy has a tendency to collect people. I collect clowns and clocks, some people collect coins or baseball cards. Troy collects people."

"Yeah, well I imagine he's got some real collector's items, fashion models and movie stars, the beautiful people and all that shit. But why me?"

Bud smiled. "The beautiful people aren't exactly the type Troy's been collecting lately. They're more the type he's been avoiding. Sycophants, parasites, and leeches otherwise known as promoters, agents, and entertainment lawyers. They don't know whether to shit or wind their fucking watch. The talent's the shark. The entourage is the suckerfish mooching a free ride on the shark's back and eating the bacteria. The hangers-on love to eat bacteria. They're so low on the evolutionary food chain that they'd have to work their way up to become bottom-feeders."

Jasper noticed a flash of anger in Bud's eyes. "It's the buzzard syndrome," Jasper offered. "They're vultures who can't kill anything on their own and get frustrated when nothing's dying."

Bud smiled. "Most of Troy's associates are about as authentic as a spray-on tan. All I know is Troy must like you," he said. "He doesn't ordinarily bring people out here. He's extremely guarded about his privacy and if it's all the same to you, I'd just as soon keep it that way."

"Yeah, that's cool. I completely understand. Hell, I don't even know where we are. The last two days have been so surreal."

"Yeah? How so?"

"Yesterday was my birthday."

"Congratulations."

"You don't understand. The surreal part is I haven't had any contact with my father since I moved out here last year from the Midwest. I even changed my name. Yesterday was my twenty-first birthday, and somehow he managed to find my phone number and call me. Then he called me at work, too. That was right about the time I got fired from my job."

"Fired for what?"

"I work at Thyme Market. I forgot to padlock the back door. Some vagrant snuck in late at night, and you'll never guess where he decided to bunk down for the night. Inside the deli case! And my boss? No shit, I thought he was actually going to beat me."

"What's the name of the store?"

"Thyme Market, down by the university."

"Thyme Market? On the corner of Third Street and Third Avenue?"

"Yeah."

Bud broke out laughing so hard he started coughing and had to sit down. "Thyme Market? Are you serious?"

Jasper nodded.

"You work at Thyme Market, on the corner of Third and Third, and you got fired because someone vandalized the store?"

"Well, not exactly. I got fired because I forgot to lock the back door. Can you believe the guy was sleeping in the deli case? How fucked up is that? I'd seen him loitering around the store a lot. The boss hates him, says he scares customers away. Of all the transients, he's definitely the craziest. I call him King Rat. The cops came in and hauled his ass away. My boss was so pissed. You should've seen him. I thought he was gonna spontaneously combust."

Bud studied Jasper as if all this might be a practical joke. "You're serious?"

"Serious as the bubonic plague."

Bud scratched his head, played with his sideburns a little, and for the first time smiled. "That's the most incredible story I've heard in a long damn time. Sorry to hear about your Pops, too. I can sure recall having some real power struggles with my old man, God rest his demented, whiskey-drenched soul. Come on, Troy should be off the phone by now. Let's go see what the legendary rock star is up to. You know," Bud said, "you may have done something stupid, but you didn't do anything malicious. You made a mistake. People make mistakes."

Jasper raised his eyebrows a little. "That may be true," he said, "but it doesn't make me any less unemployed."

7. Your Karma Hit My Dogma

C ool house."

"Thanks," Troy said. "I owe it all to Bud. It's really more his pad than mine." Troy sat at the far end of the spacious dining room table, spinning a gyroscope on a string.

"What's that?" Jasper said.

"A gyroscope." Troy's face was boxed in by shadows and flickering candlelight. Instrumental music was barely audible in the background, and a silver serving dish filled with venison stew steamed away on the table. Next to it was a crystal decanter of Puerto Rican rum.

"How's the arm?" Troy asked.

"Great. Bud patched me right up."

"Try some venison stew," Troy said. "It's Bud's specialty."

"Hilary said she refused to eat anything that used to look like Bambi." Bud snickered. "Hey Troy, can I see you in the other room for a second?"

By the end of the two-beer tour, Jasper thought he should have been inspired and invigorated by all this opulence and any other time he probably would have, but he couldn't help comparing Troy's astronomically successful life to his own, which was no comparison at all. His poetry was mediocre and this was as close to real fame as he was likely to ever get. His preoccupation with prestige and winning literary awards was nothing more than a pipe dream. And what did Bud mean about Troy collecting people? The numbness and nausea returned and under the circumstances, food of any sort should've made him want to retch, but it smelled pretty good. He took a bite. It was nice and spicy and as Jasper ate, he tried not to think about the muses or the mischievous gods or Bambi strapped to the hood of a pickup truck. He was hungry. Deer meat sure beat frozen pizza.

* * *

"Still think he's a security risk?"

Bud laughed. "No. In fact, quite the opposite. As it turns out, *you're* the security risk. You're gonna love this, I shit you not. I can't wait to see your face."

"What're you talking about?"

Bud poured himself some coffee. "It seems that until yesterday, your friend out there was gainfully employed by a local neighborhood market."

"And?"

"Well," Bud smiled, "the store in question is a quaint establishment called Thyme Market. Ever heard of it?"

Troy noted the amusement in Bud's tone. "No. Why? Should I?"

"The kid got fired 'cause he forgot to lock the back door of the store, and in the middle of the night someone snuck in. Does any of this sound familiar?"

Troy squinted at Bud, and then it hit him. He flashed back to Rip, to the deli, to the Dumpster in the alley stenciled THYME MARKET. "I don't believe you."

"Isn't karma a beautiful thing? What do you suppose the odds are of something like this? A million to one? A billion to one?"

Troy shook his head. "Don't ask me how, but the second I stepped into that store I knew some weird shit was gonna happen."

"All this is even more ironic if you consider he allegedly stepped into the middle of a knife fight for you. Oh, the cosmic paradox of it all!" Bud said, the back of his hand dramatically placed against his forehead. "Nobody expects their karma to hit their dogma!"

Troy's head shifted back and forth like a pendulum. "Are you sure?"

"Ask him about someone they found sleeping in the store named King Rat. And if I were you, I wouldn't mention this to Hilary."

Troy grabbed him resolutely by the arm. "You know how I am when I make up my mind about something. When I say this slumming bullshit is over, it's over."

Bud tapped Troy on the shoulder. "Don't worry, I won't tell her."

"Tell her anything you want," Troy said. "I'm saying this for your benefit, not hers. Because you're my best friend and because of all the shit we've been through together. And I guess I'm saying it for my benefit, too. This insanity has finally gone too far. As for the kid, I'm sorry I had to fuck up his life in the process, but don't forget I specialize in damage control. Can you find him a job?"

Stirring his coffee as he left, Bud said, in the most condescending voice possible, "Whatever you say. After all, *your name's still on the deed* to this place."

Troy heard him in the other room say to Jasper, "I'm glad you liked the aquarium."

* * *

"Stew?" Jasper said as Troy sat down. "This stuff is incredible."

"No thanks. I had some earlier." Troy sipped some coffee.

"I've never had deer meat before. It's very good. I like the little carrots and potatoes and onions, too. Jasper ladled a modest second helping onto the cream-colored china plate and ate fastidiously, as if good table manners might lend him an air of sophistication. Between bites he asked, "Do you drink? I noticed at the bar you ordered grapefruit juice."

"Nope. Quit booze years ago." Troy slapped his stomach a few times, "Gotta stay in shape or the road'll kill ya. My body's a temple."

"My body's more like a gas station restroom," Jasper said, still chewing.

"I used to drink a lot. Did a lot of dope, too," Troy said, wondering if he had the guts to confess his role in the subterfuge that had cost the kid his job. "It all got old. To the point that being sober was more intoxicating than being intoxicated. I've tried it all: transcendental meditation, Zen Buddhism, biofeedback, yoga, racquetball. All of it works temporarily, but music's the only substance with any staying power. For me, the eighties will be alcohol-and-drug-free. It's time to give my body a chance to catch up. Hell, I'm still three drinks ahead of the rest of the world." Troy was afraid that if he just blurted out his admission about the store, the kid might panic. He wanted to explain what life had become, how the illusion of celebrity had degenerated his soul. Still, blurting it out was what he wanted to do more than anything. Just get it over with.

"If I lived in a house like this, I'd never leave." Jasper's eyes drifted toward the light from candle sconces that reflected off the mirrored blinds. He remembered Bud's admonition: *don't kill him with questions.* "Bud seems pretty cool."

"Yeah, we've been best friends forever. Life's been hard for him. First there was Nam and more recently his divorce. But he's very resilient. Brilliant, too. He wants to grow cocktail trees."

"What's that?"

"One of his professor friends at the U. is a master arborist who specializes in grafting. Bud knows a lot of geniuses. Anyway, they're going to use the orange trees out back and graft limbs onto them from other trees: lemons, plums, apples. In a few years, the damn thing could look like a slot machine. Who knows what fruit might pop up?"

"Can you can mess with Mother Nature like that?"

"I don't think so, but if anyone can, it's Bud. He came back from Nam completely blind, a psychological condition caused by battlefield trauma. The doctors called it 'conversion disorder,' but James prefers the pre-Freudian term 'hysterical blindness.' The war attacked his psyche, and his psyche attacked his physiology."

"Wow. How'd he get his sight back?"

Troy shook his head. "Long story."

Bud's voice transmitted over the intercom, his newest technological innovation, and startled both Troy and Jasper up off their chairs. "Go ahead, tell him."

"Jesus, Bud. You about gave us a fucking heart attack. If you're going to eavesdrop, why don't you come in and join us?"

"Just tell the story. I want to hear it."

Troy rolled his eyes at Jasper. "I don't even know where to start."

"Start where Charlie blows Joey Duco's fucking head clean off while we're on perimeter. Tell him about how Joey took two decapitated steps before his corpse collapsed. And how later that night—" his voice cracked.

Jasper looked at Troy; Troy looked at Jasper.

"And how later that night I went back to the village and slaughtered every ox, chicken, goat, and human being I could catch in the cross hairs of my night scope. And don't forget to tell him about the next morning when I couldn't remember a goddamn thing, and I was stone cold blind."

"Geez," Jasper said. "How did you get your sight back?"

"You tell him the rest, Troy."

The sudden absence of Bud's voice left a void in the room.

"Bud was shipped stateside and declared legally blind. For a year, specialists tried to diagnose it: ophthalmologists, neurologists, even a faith healer. No one could figure it out. Then he started working with some psychiatrists in Phoenix, a dream management team they called it. They monitored his sleep because of the nightmares and with acupuncture, hypnosis, and extensive psychotherapy, they were able to break through and restore his sight. Quite a comeback."

Jasper's problems paled in comparison to Vietnam and hysterical blindness. "So how come you asked me to come out here?"

"I figured I owed you one, from the bar. It's been a long time since anyone stepped up for me like, you know, a fellow human being. I usually get special treatment."

"Well, your house is spectacular and you're the first famous person I've ever met, but you don't owe me anything."

Troy smiled. "There's something else. The guy with the knife. You nailed him pretty good and showed practically no emotion. That intrigued me."

"I might've shown more emotion had I known who you were."

"That would've ruined everything."

Jasper liked Troy. He had the presence of a dignitary, yet he was still a pretty regular guy for a rock star.

"Are you from Tucson?" Troy asked.

"No, southern Illinois. I've been out here about a year."

"Where in southern Illinois?"

"Belleville. Home of Jimmy Connors. The tennis player."

"Really!" Troy said. "I'm from Alton. Home of Miles Davis. The trumpet player."

"No kidding," Jasper said. "I knew the Unknowns were from

the Midwest, but I didn't realize you were from Alton. I grew up in Wood River until I was five. Wood River's right next door to Alton. You could piss on Wood River from Alton."

Troy laughed. "Southern Illinois is a good place to be from. As good as any other, I guess."

"I guess," Jasper said. Normally he would've asked Troy something stupid like, how does it feel to have everything you ever wanted? But it seemed Troy Archer did not have everything he ever wanted, that being famous just provided a different amalgamation of problems. "If you could be anything else in the world, what would you be?" Jasper mixed himself another drink.

Troy volleyed it in his head for a bit. "Our drummer Larry Toon once told me that if it weren't for percussion, he would've been on the FBI's Most Wanted List. As for myself, if I could pull the tablecloth out from under all this, I'd probably be something painfully conventional. Kiss the wife, drive the kids to school, nine to five, no more waking up wondering what day it is or what city I'm in. Probably sell insurance or clean gutters. Something simple."

"Sounds dull," Jasper said.

"Exactly. As dull as humanly possible. My girlfriend's father is a retired physicist," Troy said. "In his day he was quite distinguished in the scientific community, a real pioneer. She worshipped him but mostly from afar. He was always busy lecturing at Cornell or smashing atoms in some laboratory. In grade school, Hilary had trouble pronouncing *physicist*, so she used to tell her classmates that her daddy sold shoes. That's the kind of job I'd have. Selling shoes."

Jasper smiled.

"What's your ideal profession?"

"A rich poet."

Troy smiled. "Isn't that a contradiction in terms?"

"Probably," Jasper said.

"End rhyme or free verse?"

"Free verse."

"That's great." Troy said. "I love poetry. We did some innovative things with free verse lyrics on a few of the earlier records, back in the psychedelic days. Some of Fendleman's best work came out of that era."

"I'm not very good yet. I haven't even tried to publish anything."

"You will," Troy said. "When you're ready."

There was a pensive expression on Jasper's face. "Is it fun being famous?"

Troy smiled. "Performing is like a drug. Thousands of people screaming and singing your song?" He shook his head. "Nothing can top that. But the music industry is not what it appears. Years and years ago, Fendleman and I were driving around one day when we heard our first single on the radio. Now *that* was cool. Another time I was at a college football game, Missouri against Illinois, and at halftime the marching band broke into a rendition of 'Lost and Found' from our first record. Lots of brass and high-stepping, twirling batons, and John Phillip Sousa. Fendleman wrote that song at four in the morning after doing a hit of mescaline and drinking a bottle of vodka. Anyway, that's when I knew we had arrived. But there've been precious few moments of that caliber. Music is a commodity to be bought and sold just like blue chip stocks. You don't see free concerts in the park anymore and you never will. No one can afford the insurance. Tour buses and hotels may sound exciting, but try livin' in 'em for a year at a time."

"My real name," Jasper confessed, "is Junior McPherson."

"No shit. How come you changed it?"

"I was trying to reinvent myself."

"Did it work?"

"No. Can I use your bathroom?"

Troy pointed down the hall. "Past the stairs, first door on your left."

As Jasper walked away, Bud's voice resounded from the intercom.

"Troy, phone call."

"Who is it?"

"Your percussionist."

Troy glanced at the clock. "I'm sorry about earlier. I didn't mean to—"

"It's OK. Did you tell the kid you were in the store?"

"No," Troy said. "But I will."

* * *

Heading toward the john, Jasper saw a shadow descending the spiral staircase, a scintillating blonde whose hair bounced as if spring-loaded. It must have been the aforementioned Hilary. Her face had the bone structure plastic surgeons promise, and there were traces of mascara near her eyes. She was still half-asleep and wore an apricot-colored peek-a-boo negligee with white lace trim that hugged her breasts. She was very tan, and her dark nipples hid behind the sheer lingerie. As he marveled at her legs, they stopped in mid-stride.

"Hey grasshopper," she said. "Who are you?"

She didn't seem the least bit inhibited. Her age was difficult to gauge, somewhere between twenty and thirty. "Uh, hi," Jasper said. "I apologize for staring. I was just on my way to the bathroom. I'm Jasper."

She studied him for a moment, then playfully slapped his cheek with her hand. "Who said staring was against the law?" She winked and walked away.

As she passed him, Jasper admired her back side as well. She returned with a glass of wine.

"Good night, grasshopper," she whispered.

"Good night," Jasper said and watched her climb the staircase.

* * *

"Was that Bud?" drummer Larry Toon asked Troy indignantly.

"Yes," Troy said.

"The fucker acted like he didn't even know me. What's his problem?"

"I don't know, Larry, it's late I guess. What's up?"

"I'm sick of taxis and limos, Troy. I can't stand being driven around anymore. Driving helps me think, you know that. I need a car. I need to drive and think."

"You sound inebriated."

"Not at all, just a glass of sherry with dinner. I tried to rent a car but there's all that gobbledygook about a valid driver's license."

"Where are you right now?"

"Downtown. In a pay phone. There's a cabbie outside with his meter running. I offered him six grand in cash for his taxi but he wouldn't take it. So what d'ya say? Can you lend me some wheels? No intoxicants, you have my word. Can you help me out?"

"Promise to keep it between the curbs?"

"I swear to it, and what a darling man you are. I knew I could count on you. It won't end up like that one time. Remind me, how do I get to your palatial estate?"

Troy inhaled deeply and in doing so, relented against all sense of reason and logic. He gave Toon the address. "Tell the cabbie it's at the end of Secret River Trail."

Toon's checkered driving record was infamous in eight states and on three continents. Over the years he'd logged dozens of moving violations and although he had behaved admirably on the current tour, he wrecked Troy's convertible BMW just two summers ago. The agonizingly slow death of the Unknowns

110

was wearing on everyone, especially Larry Toon. Something in his voice sounded like surrender.

"I'll see you shortly. Oh, I found out some nasty shit about the evil Dr. Fendleman tonight."

"I don't want to hear it."

"He hired a law firm and filed an injunction. Not only is he going to quit the band like a spoiled little bitch, he's also going to prevent us from replacing him. Well, see you soon. Kiss, kiss!"

Troy liked the softer side of Toon, the vulnerable, lost-little-boy side. Toon usually concealed it but had confided earlier in the tour that he felt no purpose in life without the band. He wanted to belong to someone, to some guiding principle. "I'm afraid," he had said, "I have grossly underestimated the value of a tether. Technically speaking, I have no one."

The only thing worse than Toon's driving were his battles with Fendleman. Earlier in the tour, the two engaged in a fist-fight onstage in Atlanta. Troy had been having his own skirmishes lately with Aubrey, the bass player, who wanted to sign a new manager to replace Nils. Ultimately, Aubrey and Troy would compromise in order to concentrate on the bigger issue, preventing Fen and Toon's mutually assured destruction. There had been a time when the emotional edge had worked to the band's advantage, but now it was just bilateral vitriol with no redeeming qualities.

Troy had been facing the intercom, and as he turned around he was surprised by Jasper, who had slipped his mind . "You're back."

"Sorry, I couldn't help overhearing."

"Larry has a tendency to exaggerate. He lives for high drama."

"I think I just met your girlfriend. She left the kitchen with a glass of wine."

Troy finished his coffee. "Wine helps her sleep."

"She's a fox."

"The other night," Troy said, "she told me she liked me better when she didn't know me so well." He laughed.

Jasper thought that men and women must incite riots in each other at every socioeconomic level because regardless of fame or fortune, no one in the world seemed very happy.

"Bud told me you got fired today. Tell me about King Rat."

Jasper related the entire saga. "Can you believe the guy was actually sleeping in the deli?"

Troy looked down at his bare feet, not knowing where to start.

"I'll find another job," Jasper said. "The real problem is that my old man tracked me down. I disappeared a year ago and he finally found me. It was my twenty-first birthday, and we had this ugly scene on the phone. I haven't been able to think straight since. Then he calls me at Thyme Market just as I'm being fired, so I decide to drown my sorrows and the first place I go, guess who I find? None other than my quasi-girlfriend Lani on the arm of some rich fraternity brat. Then I go to the Blue Parrot and jack a guy's jaw in the restroom," Jasper raised his arms up in the air, "and voila, here I am!"

"About your job," Troy swallowed hard and smiled, "you're not gonna believe this, but I have a confession. I was there. I was there, with King Rat. His street name is Rip."

Jasper laughed. "Yeah, right."

"I'm serious. I know it sounds like the most improbable coincidence, it is to me too, but I've been in some sort of spiritual vacuum lately, and I've been mingling with people who are quite out of the ordinary. People like Rip, er, King Rat." Troy went on to explain his night at Thyme Market in specific, incontrovertible detail, describing the store in a way only a genuine accomplice could.

Jasper's smile dissolved. He was half-flabbergasted, half-crestfallen. He stood up and backed away from the table. "You really were there." Suddenly he felt set up, a pawn in the game of some rich rock star with nothing better to do. He was no better than Troy's cheetah-skin rug.

Troy rushed around to Jasper's side. "Sit down. I'm sorry. It was a stupid mistake that won't happen again. I'm so fucking sorry. Please. I really am a good rock star, I'm just a bad wizard. I'll make it up to you, Jasper, I swear."

"How did you know I'd be in the Blue Parrot?"

"I had absolutely no idea whatsoever that you were going to be in that bar. I swear on my mother's grave the whole thing was just an extraordinary coincidence. I didn't know you'd be in the Blue Parrot, I didn't know you worked at Thyme Market, I didn't know anything about you. At all. Ever. Until tonight. I never intended for any of this to happen. I don't know how else I can say it. *I'm really sorry.* But in the big scheme of things, it'll all work out for the best. Bud will find you a new job. A better job. A *much* better job. Bud knows everybody who's anybody in this town. You'll make double whatever they were paying you before."

Jasper was suspicious the charade might still be in progress.

"Look, I'm not sure why you and I have been linked by fate, but we have. You and me. Don't worry, I'll make things right. Tell me a little more about your quasi-girlfriend."

Jasper sat back down and finished his drink. "Well, OK," he said. "Lani. What can I say about Lani Sablan from the island of Guam? She makes me feel invincible and impotent. She's a phenomenal girl, she's just not phenomenal often enough. I'm in love with her, but she's still in the gee-it's-great-we-both-like-Chinese-food stage. You know what I mean?"

"Yeah."

"And she's swarmed by these filthy rich frat rats driving nice cars and wearing gold chains. I wish I didn't care about her so much, but I do. I love her."

"Love—" Troy sighed. "The other night I saw something on TV," Troy said. "A drought in Africa, right? A herd of wildebeests migrate to this river, their only source of water. They're dying of thirst, and they know they'll never survive if they don't drink. But there's a problem. The water is brimming with hungry crocodiles. The dilemma of the wildebeest is the dilemma of love. If you don't take a chance, you die a slow, miserable, parched death. If you do take a chance, you could be chewed up and spit out on the rocks to dry in the sun."

"That's me all right." Jasper managed a smile.

"If you're so sure she's interested in money, maybe she's not your type. You're a poet, right? Poets don't fucking care about money. They're too pissed off and passionate to be seduced by money. Hell, it's all fool's gold anyway. You're so young. Fall in love twenty times. If she's not into you, move on. There are plenty of delightful women out there who are lonely as hell. I meet them every day."

"I was hoping it would be different with Lani, but it's like watchin' a movie I've already seen and pretending the ending will be different. It never is. Same movie, same ending."

"It won't always be that way," Troy said trying to reassure the kid despite the fact it had always been that way for himself. "You'll bounce back. You'll see."

"Have you ever thought about suicide?"

"No," Troy said. "Doesn't seem like there's much future in it. You?"

"No," Jasper said, "Well, maybe a little. I was just thinking that this would be a time some folks might start to wrestle with it, you know? I wouldn't want to end up like King Rat."

Troy pointed his finger right between Jasper's eyes. "Let me tell you something that not many people know," he said in his business voice. For the first time all night he struggled to maintain his composure, shuddering to think his antics had contributed to this. "When I was a junior in high school, my old man shot my mother and then shot himself. For a long time I wanted to do myself in. I loved her. I loved him, as crazy as that may sound. But it made me a stronger person. You gotta play out your hand, man. Wouldn't you want to know if you were destined to be the next Robert Frost?"

Jasper noticed the tiny specks of gold in his brown eyes.

"Hell yes you would. I know guys who swore they'd be happy if they just had one hit on the charts or a gold record, but it doesn't work that way. Happiness comes from right here." Troy tapped his heart with his thumb. "Forget about being a rich poet, just be a poet. The rest will come. Forget about reinventing yourself, just invent yourself. Find out who you are and then be that person. Like Bud always says, *embrace that which defines you.*"

"Don't worry, man, I'm not going to do myself in."

"Good. As for this girl, what's her name again?"

"Lani. Short for Leilani."

"Lani. No matter how it works out, someday you'll laugh about it."

"The thing is," Jasper sighed, "I've made peace with the fact that I'm completely at Lani's mercy. Women aren't actually my main problem. Neither is Thyme Market. You and King Rat probably did me a favor as far as that goes."

"So what is your main problem?"

Jasper exhaled with a flourish. He buried his face in his hands and rubbed his eyes.

8. Love May Cause Cancer

M y main problem is my old man," said Jasper.

"Tell me about it."

"Well, basically, I hate the motherfucker. Can't seem to get past it."

"What about the rest of the family? Brothers and sisters?"

"No. Just me."

"And your mother?"

Jasper felt like he might start to cry for the first time he could remember. He had not cried at her funeral, had not cried since her funeral, and his heart had become so indolent, he had been emotionally anesthetized for so long, it had become the status quo. "She died a year and a half ago. Cancer. Me and Pops had been arch-enemies for years but after she died, we kinda called a truce. He did his thing, I did mine. The people at his job convinced him to check himself into a psyche ward over in St. Louis. Five weeks later they released him, and he was so despondent and drugged up he hardly left his room. He was worse when he came back than when he went in. When he wasn't sleeping, he was reading the Bible or watching Christian TV. We didn't make direct eye contact. It was like an episode of *The Twilight Zone*. I was living with two ghosts, his and hers. When I finished junior college and the loan went through, I was in Tucson before I knew what hit me."

Troy sipped more coffee. "You and your mother were very close?"

"Yeah. She was everything to me. She saved me from him. Without her around, he woulda killed me or I woulda killed myself. For sure."

"What happened when you got to Tucson?"

"I got this bright idea to legally change my name from *Junior McPherson* to *Jasper Trueblood*. I liked the name Jasper right from the start. It has a j in the beginning and an r at the end, just like my real name, so I figured it'd be easy to remember. But I really struggled with the last name. I sat up with the phone book for four hours one night until I found *Trueblood*. My first act of defiance. I liked Tucson. Being a stranger in a strange land. The anonymity was cool. But after eleven months, the old man sniffed me out."

"How did he find you?"

"He hired a private investigator. When he said my real name on the phone, *Junior*, I nearly shit my pants. It was like a dream. I was paralyzed by the sound of his voice, and then it kept echoing in my head like we were standing inside the Grand Canyon. I'm not even sure what I said to him. And you wanna know the weird thing?"

Troy was silent.

"The weird thing is I *knew* he was gonna call. Don't ask me how, but I absolutely knew he was gonna call. I knew it in my blood. I knew it in my bones. He said he wanted to come out here and see me. I told him no way. Then he called me at the store. It's just a matter of time before he ends up on my doorstep. I told myself he was dead for so long that I actually started to believe it. But he's not dead. Jasper Trueblood may not have figured that out yet, but Junior McPherson has."

"Why all the resentment? Sounds like the typical father and son carpet bombing."

"Yeah. I mean, he had his good moments but couldn't control his temper. The littlest things would set him off. The *TV Guide* is missing? Oh my God, here comes World War three. Dinner isn't on the table at the prescribed time? Duck and cover. Even after my mother was diagnosed with cancer, he still treated her like an indentured servant. I can't stop thinking about that." He stared into his cocktail glass, the cut crystal corners glinting in the candlelight. "I've been having nightmares about him, nightmares about her, nightmares about both of them together . . . It's exhausting."

"Wow, Jasper Trueblood, you've got a lot of poems to write. You should be at home writing one right now," Troy said. He recognized this state of perdition. "Believe it or not, I think I know what you're going through. I haven't told many people about my parents."

"Your dad killed your mom?"

Troy nodded. "Uh huh and then himself." Troy's scalp tingled when he thought about that day twenty-five years ago. "Junior year in high school. He came home early from work, got drunk, and wanted to have sex. But apparently she resisted. According to the homicide detective, there'd been gin and torn clothes all over the living room. When I came home from school, cops were crawling all over the neighborhood. I thought it must have been a burglary because the neighbors had been robbed the week before." Troy smiled a fragile smile. "I was in therapy for a while, but what saved me was meeting Fendleman and forming the band. Music was my therapy. Fen and I devoted every waking hour to the Unknowns. Hell, when we started, we didn't even know how to read music."

"Did you idolize her? Your mother?" Jasper asked.

"Yeah," Troy said. "But I idolized him, too. That's been the hard part. I can remember the two of them holding hands in public, and making out on the couch. They used to dance in the living room all the time and whenever he dipped her, she smiled. They were in love. Many years after that terrible day, I found out from an uncle that my old man had been molested by a next-door neighbor when he was five. The neighbor was fifteen or sixteen, I think. As soon as I heard that, everything fell into place. That's why he was so prone to anger. Why he drank so much. I used to find solace that he put the revolver in his mouth and finished the job. Morbid, but I respected that."

"I can relate."

"Not so fast. The funny thing is," Troy said, "despite what he did, I still wish he were alive. He might even be out of prison by now. You may find that hard to believe considering his crime. You're right, I did idolize her. But I miss him. We might've been able to help one another. I might've been able to forgive him."

Jasper imagined Troy coming home from school to flashing lights, blood on the carpet, chalk lines marking the boundaries of what had once been his parents.

"Years later, I got into some serious psychotherapy and dealt with all this. Sometimes you have to go backward to go forward."

"Counterclockwise," Jasper said. "Like Bud's clocks?"

Troy smiled. "Yeah. If you let it, this family shit will follow you around like a shadow. If it gains momentum, it can swallow you whole."

"Our situations aren't so different," Jasper said. "My mother was only forty-eight. Never smoked a cigarette. No family history of cancer. Used to walk every day and played shortstop on our parish's women's softball team. She took care of herself and was big on nutrition. And she was a devout Catholic, so God was supposed to be on her side. The week after she died, I cornered one of those so-called specialists at the hospital and asked him how someone like my mother could get cancer. He said it was stress. He said there was a lot more about stress they didn't know than everything they did. My old man caused all her stress. It's not the same as your situation, but—"

Troy sipped his coffee.

"What really pisses me off is that even after her terminal diagnosis, he never gave her flowers. Never took her out to dinner. Or vacation. I mean, take her to fucking Paris or something, you know? She still cooked his meals and even shined his goddamn shoes. Can you imagine? Even worse, when he was in the Navy, he had her first name tattooed on his forearm. D-O-R-I-S. Pretty romantic, right? Later, he had it bleached out. Now there's just a big white spot on his arm where her name used to be. This is *after* the diagnosis. How fucked up is that? Maybe he was ashamed of her hair falling out, I don't know. He singlehandedly manufactured every ounce of stress in that woman's life."

Troy slowly inhaled and exhaled through his nose. "What was he like as you were growing up?"

"Hair-trigger temper, regularly kicked in doors, punched holes in walls, threw furniture . . . One morning at breakfast he called her a bitch, flipped the table over, then gave her the finger. I'll never forget his stubby finger with the chewed-off fingernail. And right before church on a Sunday morning, he slapped her in the face. It was the only time she wouldn't let me talk to her. She locked herself in the bedroom and I was shocked that she didn't go to Mass. She never missed Mass. Never. In our world, that was a mortal sin! And according to our religion, if she would have died with a mortal sin on her soul without going to confession, she would have gone straight to hell. My father could have made my mother go to hell! That's what I used to believe, and I hated him for it. I hated him as much as you can possibly hate another human being."

"How old were you?"

"I don't know. Ten, maybe eleven. And then on the phone he had the nerve to tell me he never hit her. Apparently the distinction was whether or not it was a closed fist."

"Did she ever consider getting a divorce?"

"Nah," Jasper said. "She was too Catholic. She'd rather be a martyr. I think almost every day about her memorial service. At the cemetery, the wind chill factor was something like five degrees below zero, and I was the only one there without a winter coat. I was wearing a suit jacket, truly freezing. I wanted to remember that feeling for the rest of my life. I never wanted to forget how cold it was that day in that cemetery. People kept asking me where my coat was. At one point, I started punching this massive fucking oak tree over and over as hard as I could until one of my uncles pulled me away. I must've hit that tree at least ten times and my hand shoulda been broken in ten places, but the next day there wasn't a mark." Jasper looked at his hand and flexed his fingers.

"Marriage is a bitch," Troy said. "I was married once, and I thought it'd last forever. I really did. Gretchen was the best thing that ever happened to me. I was too much of an asshole to realize it."

"In first grade," Jasper went on, "Sister Mary Frances told my parents I had an unusually high I.Q. She said I was gifted, whatever that means. But I never earned good enough grades to please my old man. He said I was too busy being the class clown. To him, the exalted Robert McPherson, the only excuse for someone with a genius IQ to get low grades was laziness. He started calling me a no-good bastard. Age six."

"Did your father have a formal education?"

"He dropped out of high school and lied about his age to join the Navy. Him and me?" Jasper laughed, "We're like night and day. Polar opposites. When I was in the Cub Scouts, he tried to teach me how to tie a slipknot. That sailor knew his knots. I got

121

so frustrated I ended up quitting."

"I know the type," Troy said. "Ask 'em what time it is and they tell you how to build a clock."

"We must've developed the opposite hemispheres of our brains," Jasper said. "His idea of fun was to spend an entire weekend taking the engine out of our station wagon, laying it all out piece by piece in the driveway, and then putting it back together. Completely left brain. I'm completely right brain. I like to read poetry, go to concerts, watch movies. As for my left brain? A couple weeks ago at work, I couldn't figure out how to load a pricing gun to save my soul."

"Did your father want you to be a sailor?"

"Of course. He thought I was a big pussy for not enlisting. He said that as fat and spoiled as I was, the service was the only way to make a man out of me. In the second grade, he whipped me with a leather belt in the bathtub because I was taking a bath like a woman instead of a shower like a man. I had welts all over my legs for a week."

"Did your mother save you?"

"She tried," Jasper said. "She did her best." He sighed. "It's hard to resurrect all this. I feel like such a whiny asshole when I think of what you've been through with your parents, what Bud's gone through—my little problems seem small by comparison."

"We're all fighting our own battles," Troy said.

"I thought I was getting over all this until he called. I can't afford a shrink so I write poems as therapy. I used to write about this stuff sometimes but I spend a lot less time writing poetry than I do fantasizing about winning awards for writing poetry. My whole life is going nowhere fast." Jasper took a drink. "Can I ask you a question?"

Troy nodded.

"What were you doing in Thyme Market with King Rat?"

Troy tapped his finger on the table. "My life has become . . . rudderless. I was doing some misguided research. I have so much and they have so little, yet they're more or less content and I'm more or less miserable. I want to know why. I *need* to know why. I tried to get him to leave that deli case but he refused."

Jasper drank his drink.

"You know what you should do? You should tell your father exactly what you've told me. All of it. Get it off your chest. Once you go back and face it, you can go forward and rise above it. Jasper Trueblood and Junior McPherson should get together and double-team his ass."

Jasper laughed.

"It seems a little disingenuous," Troy said, "to remember everything positive about her and everything negative about him."

"I don't know," Jasper said, his voice now raw. "Like I told you, she was everything to me. She taught me how to laugh. She taught me how to stay down on a ground ball even if I got hit in the face. To read. She was the one who explained where babies come from. What a horrifying little chat that was. To realize that my very own mother had engaged in this disgusting perversion known as sexual intercourse and with the old man no less! And then it dawned on me that every married couple in St. Martin's parish was doing it! The O'Connors down the street were highly respected members of the community, and they had nine kids! Holy hell! I remember staring at them in church one Sunday and thinking to myself, these people are sick. They've actually fucked nine times!"

Troy laughed.

"Just before I moved out here, I found a picture of my mother in her twenties. Doris was one fine-looking lady: high heels, V-neck sweater, fox fur wrapped around her shoulders. I never thought of her as being sexy until I saw that photograph. Up until then, she was just my mom. I never really thought of her as a woman."

Troy said, "Tell me one positive thing about your father."

"Well, one time I had been misbehaving all day. I remember my mother saying, 'Wait till your father comes home, mister. He's gonna tan your hide.' And when the old man walked in the front door, my mother gave him the full report. So he marched me downstairs just below the kitchen where she was making dinner. He leaned over and whispered, 'It's been a long day and I'm really tired, so just play along.' Then he removed his shoes and slapped them together. I took his cue and yelped like a wounded animal. He did it again and so did I and in no time, we were all doubled over on the couch, laughing as quietly as we could. At one point, he handed me the shoes and I slapped them together myself. After five or six resounding thunderclaps and accompanying screams, we walked upstairs and there was my mother in the kitchen, wearing her apron with the hearts, holding a spoon and a mixing bowl. My face was so red that she must've thought he really lit into me because all through dinner she kept asking if I wanted more yams. That was about the coolest thing I can remember the old man doing."

"That's actually very revealing," Troy said. "Your father's traditional role of breadwinner and disciplinarian demanded a lot. How would you like to knock yourself out at work all day just to come home and find it's time to whip Junior's ass?"

Jasper nodded. "Yeah. I guess."

"I think you should confront him. Then you can get on with your writing and your life. It's an obstacle that will only get bigger. I know, I've got one myself."

"You mean with your parents?"

"No, with my ex-wife. Just before Gretchen and I split up, her period was late. Gretchen was *never* late. Suffice it to say, it was not an amicable separation and when she said she never wanted to see me again, I took her at her word. I didn't want a kid. I was too busy being a pretentious rock star. Hell, I'd cheated on her three weeks after the wedding. She had explicitly said not to marry her if I couldn't be faithful, but I did anyway. Big mistake. I really hurt her. And for years I was so wrapped up in my own shit that I didn't care." A tear formed in Troy's eye. "I find myself thinking about her all the time." Troy opened up his wallet and pulled out an ancient photo. "That's her."

Jasper could barely distinguish the faded features of her face.

"I can't stop thinking about her. Maybe Gretchen had been pregnant. I have no proof, but I've regretted never having had enough guts to find her and support our child, if there is one. It's always bugged me, but lately it's taking on a life of its own, no pun intended. Maybe after the tour, I'll look her up and find out once and for all. Hearing your story inspires me to take the initiative. To go backward in order to go forward. Maybe enough time's passed that she wouldn't guillotine me or impale my head with a pitchfork. You should confront your old man, too. It could be our mutual quest. Maybe that's what this is all about. To force each other to do what we least want to do?"

"Maybe." Jasper yawned and checked his watch. "I think I need to crash."

They shook hands over the table.

"OK," Troy said. "Bud'll give you a ride home. And I want you to know I meant every word I said earlier. Bud will help you get a new job, a better job. And as for your old man, if you decide to face him, I'll even fly you back to Belleville, home of Jimmy Connors and Junior McPherson, It's up to you." Troy buzzed the intercom. "Bud?"

"Yes."

Troy knew he'd been listening. "Would you mind giving Jasper a lift home?" He gathered up the dishes as Bud made his entrance.

"Thanks for the stew," Jasper said. "Bambi never tasted so good."

"You're welcome," Bud replied. "Let me give you a hand with that," he said to Troy.

They converged at the kitchen sink.

"Well," Troy said, "So how did I do?"

"Leave Gretchen alone. You've done enough damage in that arena."

"Fuck off, Bud. You barely even knew her."

Bud dropped his load of cups and dishes into the sink with a resounding crash.

They returned to Jasper who was slumped back with his eyes shut.

Troy jostled his chair. "Go home Jasper Trueblood. Get some sleep. You need to rest up for tonight."

"Tonight?"

"I'm sending a limousine for you and a guest. There'll be two backstage passes waiting at the press gate for the show tonight. Your name will be on a list."

"Wow, thanks." Jasper didn't know what else to say. He'd never been in a limo or had his name on a list.

Troy gave Jasper a brotherly hug. They headed toward the foyer and Bud opened the front door. There, peering into the Eye-dentifier, stood Larry Toon.

"Greetings, Earthlings." He wore a starched white shirt, blue pinstriped vest, jeans, Italian loafers, and too much cologne.

Troy made hasty introductions and noted that Toon appeared reasonably sober and lucid.

"Hey, ladies, don't let me break up your little tea party," Toon said.

"You're not," Troy replied. "Jasper's gotta go home and rest up for tonight. Right Jasper?"

"Damn straight." Jasper yawned again.

"Be good to yourself," Toon said.

Bud led Jasper outside toward the garage and they sped off in a red Jeep. A coyote dashed across the road, and Jasper snored as Bud drove into the desert, into the dawn creeping over the horizon.

* * *

The car closest to the open garage door was a white Cadillac. Toon climbed inside. "Who's the kid?"

Troy hadn't the energy nor desire to define Jasper Trueblood. "Just a fan. I met him at a bar and we got to talking,"

"And you decided to show off your luxurious digs, ply the lad with premium liquor, and solve all his problems, right Troy my boy?"

"Fuck you, Larry."

Toon reached outside the Caddy and playfully punched Troy on the hip. "I was just kidding. You're a good man, Archer. A kind soul, indeed. Now, if you don't mind, I'm going to go drive off into the sunset or the sunrise as the case may be, and I'll see you later at the hotel. Keys please?"

"What's this shit about Fendleman?"

Toon fired up the engine and the Caddy purred. "My girlfriend's girlfriend in New York was at a restaurant and overheard some guys from Atlantic Records talkin' about Fen and his new attorney. The skinny is that five minutes after the tour is over, he's going to cut us off at the knees."

"Meaning what?"

"He's fixin' to split and make it illegal for us to replace him. He's gonna arrange things so that when he goes solo, we can't cut records or play gigs unless we change our name. He's gonna make some grandstand play for all the rights, the royalties, our name, our logo, everything. If we had a mascot, he'd sue for that, too. It's a musical version of a scorched-earth policy."

"He can't just take everything because he has a new lawyer. Read the contracts."

"According to my girlfriend's girlfriend, Fen's lead counsel is someone named Trevor Randall Alexander III. He's supposedly known in legal circles as 'Lord Loophole.' He's very expensive and very good. If I had to bet, I'd say the official expiration date for the Unknowns is the day this tour is over."

Troy shrugged. For the first time, the end didn't seem so calamitous. "So be it. Maybe it's time."

"You're giving up, too, Troy my boy? You? Our beacon in the night? The lighthouse of our darkened shores?"

"I wanna ask you something. Larry," Troy said, "and I want you to tell me the truth. If you could be anything else in the world besides a musician, besides a drummer, what would you be?"

"God."

"No, seriously. What would you be?"

"Man, Troy, you sure are in a mood tonight. Have you been taking your vitamins? You don't look so hot."

"What would you be?"

After some deliberation, Toon said, "An astronaut, I guess. As long as I got to walk on the moon, I'd want to be an astronaut."

"That's good," Troy said. "I like that." He handed Toon the keys. "And by the way, if you wreck this car, I'm gonna cut off your dick and feed it to Bud's rattlesnakes."

"You say the sweetest things." Toon honked the horn with a thumbs-up and wheeled away.

Back inside the house, Troy turned on the radio and made himself a piece of toast. While he was eating, an Unknowns song came on, the title cut off their second album. He'd still been with Gretchen back then. He hummed the melody. Their child, if there was one, would be almost ten by now. He softly mouthed the lyrics and looked blankly out the window where a captive audience of giant saguaros held their applause, arms frozen in mid-clap.

Retiring to the bedroom, Troy disrobed and slipped in between the sheets next to Hilary and her fragrant hair. He rested his ear on her chest and listened to the rhythm of her heart. She cuddled closer and hooked her warm ankle around his. Maybe, Troy thought, there was hope after all.

PART III: SUNDAY

9. Acts of Contrition
at the El Cerrito Hotel

Sunday afternoon sunshine spilled through the bedroom window. It was nearly two, the day of the Tucson show, and Hilary was predictably missing in action. Always an early riser, by this time of day she could be almost anywhere. Troy rarely crawled out of bed before the sun reached its zenith. Like it or not, rock 'n' roll was the graveyard shift, and it played havoc on the circadian rhythms. He stretched his legs and hit the jogging track, an Astroturf path that Bud had installed that circled most of the ranch's circumference. There was a treadmill in the greenhouse, but running in place was too much like real life.

On the day of a show, Troy limited himself to a couple miles at a casual pace, maybe less today as the sun was menacing and beads of perspiration trickled into his ears and rolled down his cheeks. Usually the best part about running was stopping, but today Troy enjoyed the purple mountain majesty of the desert in her best dress when he happened upon Bud's newest addition to the ranch staring at him from the stable.

The thoroughbred was seventeen hands, chestnut with white markings on his nose, and Bud had raved about his potential on the racetrack. Troy didn't know much about horses, but this looked like a good one. The stallion avoided the blistering sun of the corral by hiding in the shade, snapping at flies with his tail. A ranch hand tipped his hat, and Troy waved back as he jogged at a casual pace down the path which curved away from the stables and toward the pool. He would have loved to spend more time in the serenity of the ranch when the tour was over, but Hilary hated it and warned she couldn't be away from her East Coast connections much longer.

Troy recalled the previous evening: Jasper Trueblood, gabbing like a school girl about Gretchen, how Bud had warned him not to cross that threshold. He accelerated until his chest started to burn. He pumped his knees around the winding path and then briskly turned to run backwards, watching his shadow follow behind. He walked a lap to cool down, then picked a leaf off a jojoba plant. Bud said the jojoba was magic. His friend, a tribal elder named Hototo whose name in Hopi meant "warrior spirit who sings" had explained its medicinal properties, how it didn't need water and could grow out of a rock. The more desperate the climate, the more the jojoba thrived. Troy crushed the leaf and rubbed it into his hands for good luck. A bald eagle swooped in cursive loops high overhead. Hototo had also said that eagles carried prayers to the Creator. Upon Bud's return from Vietnam, Hototo had performed a spiritual ceremony with fire and drums to heal Bud's soul.

Time to punch the clock.

Troy switched on a cassette player and showered, playing conductor to Berlioz's "Symphonie Fantastique" and singing out a series of vocal exercises. He had just started to lather up when he realized he'd accidentally picked up Hilary's perfumed beauty soap. With armpits destined to smell like lavender for the rest of the day, he shaved his face and nicked his chin. He licked his finger and dabbed it on the dot of blood.

"Nils called," Bud said when Troy walked into the kitchen. He handed Troy a glass of grapefruit juice. "The sound check is at five. Also, Aubrey called. He says he needs to see you pronto."

"About what?"

"I don't know, but he's awfully neurotic for a bass player," Bud said. "And the guy from *Playboy* said he'd catch up with you at the hotel. Says he only needs a couple more hours."

"Where's Hil?"

"Your guess is as good as mine. And I called your driver. He'll take Jasper Trueblood to the concert tonight, so I'll give you a ride to the sound check."

"That's OK, just drop me off at the hotel."

"Chance said he misses the days when everyone rode in the same limo and arriving at the show was a spectacle."

Troy pondered for a moment. "Yeah. Thanks, Bud," Troy said. "After the show maybe we'll come out here for a cocktail."

Bud nodded. "I like Jasper Trueblood. He says what's on his mind."

"You know, after the tour I was thinking Hil and I might return to the ranch for some r&r. Decompress. Think you can you put up with us for a few weeks?"

"I'm glad you asked," Bud said. "I've been thinking about looking for my own place."

"Bud, Bud, Bud. Listen, I mouthed off last night and said some shit you know I didn't mean. I consider this place as much yours as mine. When I bought the property, it was nothing more than a broken down old ranch house with a couple of dilapidated stables. It looked like a reject off the set of *Gunsmoke*. You transformed it into what it is today. I'm gonna add your name to the deed. Fifty-fifty. And don't bother arguing. My mind's made up."

Bud squinted at Troy eye-to-eye. "What about Hilary?"

"Hilary owns a half million shares of Yummy Yogurt. What does she need my money for?"

Bud smiled. "Really?"

"Really."

They shook hands and briefly embraced. "Thanks, brother. That means a lot to me. I don't know what to say."

* * *

They drove into town with the air conditioner on high, discussing ranch business: ranch hands, escalating property taxes, and Betty the maid. Then they were quiet and enjoyed the ride.

"You really think it's a bad idea to look up Gretchen?"

Bud checked his rear-view mirror. "Yes."

"I hadn't seriously considered it until my conversation with the kid last night. Suddenly I got this prescient feeling that she no longer wants to kill me." Troy made a mental note that *prescient* was one of Hilary's favorite words.

Bud checked his rear-view again, the blind spot over his left shoulder, and pulled over into the passing lane. "I never knew you thought there might be a kid. When did that happen?"

"At the end. She was late. She was never late before."

"Sounds like you've already decided to find her, so just make sure she doesn't get hurt again."

Troy laughed. "That's what I like about you, Bud. I give you half the fucking farm and you still cut me absolutely no slack whatsoever." Troy stared out the window. Bud rolled to a stop at the front entrance of the El Cerrito.

"You sure you don't want me to leave you a couple tickets at will-call?"

"No, thanks. I've got work to do."

"OK, we'll see you after the show. Can you find a job for Jasper?"

"If I can't find him a job, I'll hire him myself. I got all kinds

133

of chores for him to do. Those stones behind the stables? I need someone with a strong back to clear them out."

"That's great," Troy said. "Be sure to overpay him."

"I will. Break a leg." Bud U-turned away into the sporadic Sunday traffic.

* * *

The El Cerrito Hotel had once been a proud Spanish-colonial resort on the edge of town. When westerns were filmed down the road in Old Tucson, the cast and crew would often stay there. The brochure boasted of being a vacation getaway for Truman and Eisenhower, as well as countless other dignitaries and VIPs, but over the years it had deteriorated right along with the South Tucson neighborhood in which it was located. Four stars dwindled to—on a good day—a star and a half. Nils thought it was quaint, and the band was in no position to be particular. After all the years of maliciously redecorating hotel interiors, high-end luxury hotel chains had blackballed the Unknowns. The Hilton and Sheraton were no longer amused by smashed-up TVs, holes ripped in walls, or motorcycles revved up in the lobby at four a.m. Anarchy had become a hard sell by the spring of 1980.

The El Cerrito's exterior was constructed of weathered white adobe: two stories, sixty rooms with high ceilings, three luxury suites. It included a bar, restaurant, and pool, which in Troy's opinion was all anyone could rightfully ask of a hotel. He approached the front door and peered around a privacy fence, its wooden planks interwoven like a basket. Green awnings were supported by a checkerboard trellis with several squares missing. A marquis in front read: VACANCY.

An elderly Mexican couple tended the registration desk, the gentleman tall and lanky, his wife short and squat. Together they looked like the number ten.

"Buenas tardes, Senor. May I help you?" the gentleman said.

"Yes. I'm Troy Archer of the Unknowns. I believe my girl-friend Hilary Hightower has already checked in?"

The woman regarded Troy briefly, then returned to reading her magazine.

"Si, Senor Archer," said the man. "My name is Carlos, and may I say it is such an honor to have your band staying with us. Miss Hightower has checked into room twelve, which is adjacent to your luxury suites. Here's a key. There is a fully stocked bar and buffet in the hospitality suite, just down the hall in Conference Room B. Enjoy your stay, Senor, and if there is anything I can do for you, anything at all, please don't hesitate to ask."

"Gracias," Troy said. Room twelve was empty except for Hilary's overnight bag, so Troy made his way to the pool and found her reading, her glistening body absorbing the sun. She read voraciously, more than anyone Troy had ever known. She was sprawled out on a chaise longue with a sprinkling of other baking tourists; between the chairs were large clay pots of barrel cactus and prickly pear. The courtyard was enclosed by the basket fence on one side and the hotel bar on another. Hilary was wearing her Bimini bikini, a-silver two-piece purchased on one of their trips to the tropics. Like Ponce de Leon before them, they had searched assiduously but unsuccessfully for the elusive Fountain of Youth. She was lying face down with her top unfastened, her neck and back the color of an old penny. Her hair was pulled over to the side, and she adjusted her sunglasses as she read. She was always working through a new novel. Always.

Troy pulled a lawn chair close and sat next to her. Without any salutation or even direct eye contact, she reached for a smoke. He lit it, a diffident gesture of cigarette etiquette.

"Buenas tardes, Seniorita."

"Oh, it's you," Hilary said. Her jewelry, a turquoise bracelet in a silver setting with matching earrings, glinted on a table nearby. Hilary never wore jewelry when she tanned.

"New?" Troy asked.

She nodded petulantly, fastened her top, and returned to reading. Her body language was peppered with dirty words.

"So how's it going?"

She lifted her sunglasses. "I'm bored. So what else is new?"

Now that the seismic activity had officially registered on the Richter scale, Troy knew it wouldn't be long before another tremor struck. "Is anyone else here?"

Hilary flicked out her thumb like a hitchhiker toward the pool and went back to her book.

John Fendleman floated on an inflatable raft. He was co-founder of the band and wore dark glasses, a black cowboy hat, and white swim trunks. Everything he wore was either black or white, that was Fen's fashion statement. He politely asked two pre-teenagers who were sitting on deck chairs to turn down their portable radio. One of them lowered the volume and Fen thanked him. When Fen turned around, the kid flipped him off and his friend laughed.

"I'm suffocating," Hilary said.

"It's hot. This is the desert."

Hilary raised her sunglasses again. "I wasn't referring to the heat. *You're* suffocating me. Smothering me with neglect." She sat upright, squirted a thin, translucent line of tanning oil on her thighs and calves, and rubbed in the lotion with a circular motion. The faint dots of freckles on her legs sparkled in the brilliant sun.

"I'm sorry," was all Troy could manage to reply. He stripped down to his trunks and walked toward the pool.

Hilary hurled her sunglasses to the cement. "That's right, run away," she said loud enough so that several people took notice. "Just like you always do."

Troy dove headfirst into the deep end of the pool. He opened his eyes underwater and imagined a living room with no furniture. He thought of the times Hilary had run to him and hugged his neck whenever he walked into a room, the kinetic energy of new romance. The chlorine began to sting his eyes, so he rose to the surface and clung close to the edge of the pool. Although he wanted to patch things up with her, it occurred to Troy that after awhile women just seemed to get tired of him. Gretchen had, others had, too. He did a submarine dive across the pool, knifing his way underwater and swamping Fendleman's raft.

Fen stood up in the shallow water dripping and irritated. "Goddamn it Troy, I was trying to get some rest."

The kids with the radio laughed.

Fen placed his floating cowboy hat back on his head and hopped up on the raft. "Where is everybody?" He glanced at his wristwatch. "We should be leaving for the sound check."

"It's not until five. Get your beauty sleep." Troy wanted to interrogate Fen about his alleged mutiny from the band, but he climbed out of the pool when he noticed Hilary: taciturn, crestfallen, tear-streaked cheeks. He shuffled over and waited for the war to recommence.

Coaxed out of her blank stare, Hilary lit another cigarette. "I can't do this anymore. You're too obstreperous for me. You're too self-absorbed and self-centered to genuinely love another human being."

"Let's keep our voices down," Troy said, assuming *obstreperous* meant something akin to self-absorbed and self-centered. "Can't we discuss this in the room?"

"What's to discuss?" Hilary started to cry. Sun worshippers again leaned in and took notice. "I feel like the whole world's been designed for right-handed people and I'm left-handed. I'm thirty-one years old. What am I doing? What contribution am I making to society?" She started crying harder. "I don't have a f-f-future. I'm just a f-f-fucking groupie with no identity."

Troy sat down and put his arm around her. "I was thinking

this morning about the early days of our relationship. Remember how wild in love we were, Hil?" Troy asked. "Remember that loft apartment we had in Chelsea, and that trip to Bombay? What happened to those days?"

"I don't know. I'm so far removed from them that it feels like they happened to someone else."

Troy backed away. "I should warn you that what you're about to say can and will be used against you."

"I'm not joking, Troy. I feel like a corpse inside."

"You know, you've really changed," Troy said. It was an observation more than an accusation. "You don't need me the way you used to."

Hilary laughed. "Maybe you're right. I've been doing a lot of thinking, what with you off wandering the slums and doing whatever it is that you do. The part of me who needs a man is the part I admire least. That includes you, my father, and all the boyfriends in-between. I've never been just me. I don't even know who *me* is."

"Hil—"

"The problem isn't even men. I like men. And I don't trust women, you know that. I've never had a female friend in my life. Men are powerful. They lead interesting lives. They open doors for you and pay for dinner. Plus, they can save you from other men. The problem is not men. The problem is me. I've always measured myself by the man I was with instead of just measuring me for me. Even in high school when I was valedictorian, I always had to show cleavage and wear short skirts to get any attention."

"Why am I suddenly lumped into a category with half the world's population?" Troy asked.

"Look, I'm not in love with you anymore. I don't know if you were ever really in love with me but if you were, it's over now. We'd be better off cutting our losses than prolonging the inevitable. It was great while it lasted, we had a nice run, but now I want out. I've been walking into a machine shop and the farther I get in, the louder it gets. I need peace and quiet. I can't hear myself think. I have a literature degree from Cornell, that ought to be worth something. Maybe I could go to grad school. Maybe I could teach. I know for sure I can't do this anymore."

"I don't get it, Hil." Troy scratched his cheek and smoothed out his ponytail. "Why have you given up on us? The tour's over in a week, and then we'll reconnect like we always do. We'll go on a fabulous trip, just the two of us, and realign the cells in our bodies and get back in tune with each other's soul, like we always do. What's the big deal?"

Hilary shoved her book into her purse. "Remember at the beginning of the tour when you told that reporter your life would be nothing without the Unknowns? It didn't really click then but now it does. In fact, it rather eloquently articulates exactly how extraneous and superfluous I am. We've become nothing more than traveling companions. We don't even have sex anymore. You're no longer a part of me, and I'm no longer a part of you. We've become inconsequential. But you have one big advantage. You have the band. And what do I have? I have nothing but me. And for the first time in my life, that's enough. *Me* is enough." She laughed. "I'm taking an extended sabbatical from men. I'm going to focus exclusively on me. I'm going to stop trying to change everybody else and start changing myself. I'm finally going to start doing my own thing as soon as I figure out what the fuck that is."

"What if your thing totally wrecks my thing?"

"Your thing is the band, Troy, you said so yourself. And whether it impacts your life even a little doesn't matter. I don't want that much responsibility for another person if it's not reciprocal," Hilary said. "It's exactly that attitude convincing me to move on. I want to discover myself. I feel like a massive block of marble just begging to be sculpted."

Troy could see that it had all unraveled like a poorly kept secret.

"We're clouds, Troy. You and me? We're like clouds."

Troy looked quizzically. "We're *clouds*? What does that mean, Hilary?" It wasn't until that very moment Troy realized they were speaking in dead languages. "If you ask me, this whole relationship has been one big fucking sham."

"That's not true, Troy Archer, and you know it." The tears fell again. "You're just trying to be deliberately hurtful," she said with a sniffle. "We were special. We had synergy. But we're like clouds that have drifted away from each other. I can't live like this anymore. My whole life is vicarious and insignificant. I'm going to find out who I am and build a person around it. I've never lived alone in my whole life? Not once. I've never even been to a restaurant by myself."

"Hil, come on," Troy implored. "The tour's almost over. We'll work it out. You'll see. We just need some time to reconnect, that's all."

"In three years we've never once discussed the subject of marriage. Not even casually. Not even by accident. You've never asked if I wanted a baby."

"You always get so offended when someone inadvertently refers to you as my wife. I just assumed you didn't want to get married."

"I'm offended because *you* don't refer to me as your wife." Hilary started to weep once more. Now almost everyone was staring at them. In a small act of contrition, Troy moved over and let her sob on his shoulder.

"Do you want a baby, Hilary?" he asked. ·

"No," she said, sniffling again. "Not necessarily. But I want you to ask me about it. I want you to be invested in me emotionally."

"I'm sorry, Hil. About everything."

"Don't be. No one can ever take away what we had. You know I could never forget you. But I have to do this. I have to do it for me."

As she said the words that were reducing him to a memory, Troy stopped consoling her and collected what little remained of his dignity. "So this is really it? You've thought this all through?"

She dried her eyes with a beach towel. "This is it."

Troy recognized the stubborn resignation in her voice. He rubbed his chin. "Is this about those two chicks in Detroit?"

"I told you I was over that. As far as I'm concerned, you can get blowjobs by all the rock 'n' roll reclamation projects you want. I'm done."

"Don't forget, Hilary Hightower, how you fucked that guy after that funeral last year. I never hardly said shit about that. And with a pallbearer, for godsakes."

"Troy, it's over," she said almost nonchalantly.

"I never knew you wanted a baby. You had that abortion before we met, so I just assumed you weren't interested in having kids."

"No," Hilary said. "Not with *him*. I was eighteen years old, and he was a goddamn heroin junkie who told me he was dying of cancer. I wanted to escape my mother so badly I believed him. Why would I want to be a parent with him? You should have asked if I wanted a baby with you, Troy." Then she whispered, between sobs, "You should have asked."

Troy took one of her cigarettes and lit it. He hadn't smoked a cigarette in six years.

"Are you going to be OK?" she said.

"Yeah," he said, though in truth, a dull pain gathered momentum in his chest. He reached out but she turned away, and then suddenly from the edge of the courtyard came a resounding, thunderous, monstrous crash. It sounded like a ballistic missile had struck the El Cerrito Hotel. Hilary jumped and screamed as did a cadre of other sunbathers.

Troy turned just in time to see a large section of the wooden fence splintered into smithereens and blasting through it, a large, white, and very familiar-looking automobile. The runaway vehicle carried a portion of the fence on its grill as it rampaged through the open courtyard. Beach towels unfurled in the air, and lawn chairs overturned as bodies careened off one another, dodging and darting to flee its path. A flower pot was crushed, a gas barbeque decapitated. Fendleman and other swimmers leapt out of the water like spawning salmon. Hilary cowered behind her lawn chair. And despite all the chaos, Troy didn't flinch. He recognized the car and had no doubt as to the identity of the driver.

The sun worshipers shrieked in panic as the automobile plunged squarely into its rectangular target—the swimming pool—with an enormous splash. Water slowly enveloped the vehicle and finally swallowed it whole as it sank in a bubbly rush to the bottom.

Hotel guests cautiously approached the water, peering as if the car might hop out the same way it hopped in. Larry Toon navigated his way through the window on the driver's side and swam to the surface. The hushed crowd backed away as Toon pulled himself up onto the cement and stood dripping before them. He shook his head like a wet dog after a dip in the lake.

"Can anyone tell me how to get to Phoenix?" Toon laughed maniacally.

The kids with the radio broke out laughing and applauded. "Hey mister," one said, "who taught you how to drive?"

Toon took a gracious bow and blew kisses. The youngsters clapped furiously while the rest of the pool's patrons maintained a healthy distance.

"A ten from the American judges." Toon struck a pose.

Hilary came out of hiding. She was not fond of Larry Toon under the best of circumstances. "You could've killed somebody, you crazy piece of shit." Her eyes were crazed, feral. "You could have fucking killed someone."

"I've always liked that swimsuit on you, Hilary."

"It's not a joke, The world is not your personal playground."

Toon said with a grin, "I've never told you this before, but secretly I think you wanna sleep with me."

"Ha!" Hilary laughed. "I'd rather sleep with crawling bugs." She pointed at him, then Troy. "I'm sick to death of all you garrulous, over-the-hill rock stars."

Toon sat on the diving board and pulled off his custom-made loafers, sloshing water back into the pool. "Hey Hil, why don't you hop in? Let's see if witches float." He cackled out a new peal of laughter.

"You bastard," Fendleman screamed, red-faced. *"I was in that pool!"*

Toon smiled. "Then my timing was perfect you Benedict Arnold motherfucker."

Fendleman stood glowering at him, not backing down. "I don't care if you commit suicide, I really don't. Drummers are a dime a dozen. But I don't intend to go down with you. You're a menace, and I'm tired of this sophomoric bullshit. I thought you'd changed. You're destined to wind up in a prison yard or a graveyard, and I won't be a party to it. Hilary's right, it's not funny anymore. No one's laughing."

Toon stepped off the diving board and took a couple strides in Fendleman's direction. "Don't tread on me, bitch." He wiped the chlorinated water from his eyes. "The life you save may be your own."

Fen didn't budge. "You're more irresponsible now than ever. When are you ever going to grow the fuck up?"

"Don't let him fool you, folks," Toon said. "It's just a little lov-

143

er's spat. We're homos."

There were a few restrained laughs. Fendleman continued his tirade. Troy remembered the fistfight in Atlanta had started like this. Toon ever the provocateur, Fen unwilling to acquiesce.

"The reason we're in these piece-of-shit dives in the first place is because you've destroyed every respectable hotel in the country."

"Yep," Toon said. "Some of the best. See, the way I figure it, what with you planning our demise with your secret little acts of treason, who knows when I'll get another chance to drive a Cadillac into a swimming pool?"

"Wait a minute. Where did you get that car?" Fendleman said.

Toon glanced at Troy.

"I should've known," Fendleman said shaking his head. "I shoulda fucking known."

The spotlight settled on Troy, who felt as though he'd just breached national security. But Fen was right. This was exactly why Troy hadn't invited the band to the ranch. Troy remained silent. He saw Hilary shake her head, pick up her purse, walk away.

"I blame you for this, Troy. He's hopelessly infantile," Fendleman pointed at Toon. "We all accept that. But you're the one who keeps putting the gun in his hand."

Fen followed Hilary through the flotsam and jetsam of the courtyard. As they approached the entrance to the bar, the Mexican couple who managed the property rushed past them and found the fence smashed to pieces. When they saw the car in the pool, the rotund woman sat down in a lawn chair, crossed herself, and began to recite Hail Mary's in high-speed Spanish. Her husband gestured with his hands, cursed, and threatened to call the authorities.

Troy stepped up. "Carlos. Mi amigo."

"Senor Archer?"

Troy took him off to the side as Toon slithered away. "This was all my fault, Carlos. My car has touchy brakes. But there's no need to call the police. I'll pay for everything, you have my word on it. Call a tow truck, hire someone to build a new fence, and there will be plenty left over for you and your wife, I promise. I'll take care of everything. Believe me."

Troy smoothed things out to the tune of three thousand dollars in cash, and Carlos' spirits seemed to elevate each time another C-note landed in his palm. The fence would be repaired, the Caddy fished out of the drink and towed back to the ranch, and the pool and courtyard closed to guests for the rest of the day. Hotel employees were marched in to clean up. But no amount of damage control was going to fix Hilary Hightower.

10. Sound Interlocks the Universe

By the time Troy finished negotiating with Carlos, the door to room twelve was wide open and inside was nary a hint of Hilary, not so much as a hairbrush, toothbrush, or bathing suit draped and dripping over the shower rod. Troy sat on the faded chenille bedspread and hoisted his feet onto a coffee table that was too large for the room. Miniature roses were carved into the table's borders. The wallpaper was a chalky yellow, and there was a hint of Hilary's favorite perfume in the air, Head Over Heels. Troy picked up Gideon's Bible, read a passage at random, and returned it to the nightstand. He imagined his affection for Hilary collapsing into an affliction not unlike the unrequited love a coyote with built-in telemetry has for the full moon. He pounded his fist on the bed and bounced his head against the headboard.

His options were limitless now. He could get drunk, go on a crime spree, get a tattoo, or engage in a sex-a-thon with a litany of rock 'n' roll tootsies. It was universally understood that a jilted lover was capable of just about anything in this world, the evening news reported it every day. And as he vowed to ignore her if she ever came crawling back, there was a knock at the door and he rushed to answer it.

It was Bobby Lee, the interviewer from *Playboy*. He rubber-necked over Troy's shoulder from the hall and glanced inside. "Is this a bad time?"

Troy laughed, "Couldn't be worse. I just broke up with Hilary."

"Oh shit, really? I'm sorry, Troy. You want to shoot for later?"

"No, let's do it. What the hell, we've all got deadlines, right? Besides, didn't you tell me there were documented cases of people who actually bought your magazine to read the interviews?"

"I lied about that," Bobby Lee said. He popped open his silver suitcase and set up the recording equipment. "Another couple hours and a few photos oughta do it."

"Clothes stay on, right?"

Bobby Lee smiled. "Unless you do *Playgirl*."

Troy wanted desperately to disappear, to find Hilary and fix everything, but the commotion of his life pushed on undeterred like Sherman's March to the Sea, and even though three years was the longest relationship he'd ever had, even longer than Gretchen, Hilary was probably better off without him.

After some paper shuffling, Bobby Lee was ready. Troy explained that normally he would have room service send over cold drinks, but under the circumstances, he was not on the best of terms with the hotel management. Bobby Lee said he understood.

Troy had come to know the ubiquitous Bobby Lee pretty well in the last month: forty-five, slightly hunched, cerebral, prematurely bald, journalism degree from somewhere, and a contemporary music scholar who had written freelance for *Rolling Stone*, *Cream*, and an assortment of other rock 'n' roll rags. Today he wore pleated charcoal pants, a white linen shirt with the sleeves rolled up, and sandals. His alert eyes and well-groomed mustache formed a smile that Troy had grown to trust. Bobby Lee believed that if Beethoven, Bach, or Mozart were alive today, they'd be playing rock music. He also believed that in-depth interviews with cultural icons ought to entail more than coquettish schoolgirl inquiries about sex and drugs. He researched his subjects exhaustively and always found a few surprises to toss into the mix. Troy had learned things about himself in this process that probably weren't interesting to a reader, he thought, but were personally revealing, to say the least. Like that he still had feelings for his ex-wife. Previous interview sessions had covered Troy's traumatic childhood, Vietnam, Woodstock, Watergate, punk rock, disco, and the Iranian hostages. Bobby Lee flipped a switch. Tape began to filter onto a reel-to-reel. In his current emotional state, Troy thought he was likely to say something he'd later regret.

Bobby Lee consulted his notes one last time then picked it up from where they had last left off. "There was a story we heard about you meeting Jimi Hendrix. Can you tell us about that?"

"Yeah," Troy said. "I met Jimi at a hotel in New York, in an elevator, just the two of us. We recognized one another, introduced ourselves, made a little small talk. It was cool, too, because he was wearing all the psychedelic garb just like one of his posters. I remember his hands were enormous. Each of his fingers was the size of a praying mantis. Amazing. Anyway, I mentioned that I really dug his work, and he said something that I'll never forget."

"What was that?"

"Sound interlocks the universe," Troy said.

"*Sound interlocks the universe?*" Bobby Lee smiled. "What does that mean?"

"Beats the hell out of me," Troy said, "but I thought it was pretty heavy. A couple days later I got a telegram with four letters on it: J-I-M-I. He was playing Madison Square Garden, so I made arrangements to get backstage."

"What happened?"

"After the show, I gave his road manager the telegram. He led me back to the dressing room and there he was, sitting all alone with his guitar in his lap. Just Jimi and the guitar. I remember, too, there was a plant on the table next to him. A fern. He must've just fixed because he was all fucked up. I put my arm around him, and he sorta leaned against me. Then he dropped his guitar, and I'm convinced he would've collapsed on the floor if I hadn't been there to catch him. His people hurried in and hustled me out the door. That was it. That's the last time I ever saw him. Sound interlocks the universe. His death had a monumental impact on the Unknowns. Think about it. Less than two years after Woodstock, Jimi Hendrix, Janis Joplin, and Jim Morrison were all dead. Giants, each and every one. Fucking giants. And what did they have in common?"

"Dope?"

"Unlimited amounts of dope and alcohol. There was no such thing as moderation. Hell, that's what fucked up the Black Panthers. They couldn't handle all the cocaine. So when we decided we were going to do a world tour last year, it was with the proviso that we'd stay clean, all four of us. No drugs, no alcohol."

"And have you?"

"I have," Troy said. "I'm not sure about the others."

There was a knock at the door, and Troy leapt back into the present. *Hilary!* Bobby Lee switched off the recorder.

Troy threw the door open. "Aubrey."

Aubrey poked his head in. "Sorry to interrupt. Did Bud give you my message?"

Troy checked his watch. "Shit. I was supposed to come see you. Sorry, Aubrey. Can it wait? We're just wrapping this *Playboy* piece."

"No," Aubrey said firmly. "It can't wait. This is urgent."

Bobby Lee jumped in. "It's OK, really. I understand. I'll talk to Nils and make arrangements to catch you later. And Troy, I'm really sorry to hear about Hilary."

Aubrey sat on the bed and tapped his foot. He had a shaved head, salt-and-pepper beard, and the prototypical body for a bass player: six-foot-four, two hundred and sixty pounds.

"What's wrong?" Troy asked. "What's so urgent?"

"What did he mean about Hilary?"

"We broke up."

Aubrey stood up then sat back down. "Shit. Then this is probably not the best time to tell you."

"Tell me what?"

"We've got real problems, Troy."

Troy laughed. "What else is new?"

"Fen's preparing to disband the band. He's hired a new lawyer."

"I already know all this," Troy said. "Toon told me."

Aubrey exhaled deeply. His shoulders were slumped over, and his hands covered his face. He stood up and paced across the coffee-colored carpet. "Fen will not do another record with Larry, or another tour. And you really fucked up today, my friend."

"Me? What did I do?"

Aubrey lit a cigarette and paced the floor. Ribbons of smoke swirled in his wake. "You fanned the flames by giving him a car. Bad move. Fen thinks Larry tried to kill him today."

"Oh Jesus Christ, Larry didn't try to kill anybody. How is he supposed to know Fen was in the fucking pool? He was just blowing off steam. Toon's depressed about Fen being such a diva all the time. You know how Larry is. Actually, I think he's behaved rather admirably until just recently. As for Fen, he's been threatening to break us up ever since I can remember. We've heard this shit before."

"Not with lawyers. This is how the Beatles died. We used to say that could never happen to us, and now look at us." Aubrey french-inhaled a stream of bluish smoke and blew a chain of smoke rings in the air, one inside another. "Whether Toon was trying to kill him or not doesn't matter. Fen is pissed. He says this was the final straw."

"Bullshit, Aubrey. There are plenty of straws." Troy stood up, took Aubrey by the shoulders, and sat him down on the bed. The incessant pacing was nerve-wracking. "Let me ask you something. Did you ever think about what you might do after the Unknowns? I mean, this gig can't go on forever, right? Have you ever considered that? We're like boxers, we have a short shelf life. So what are you going to do when it all ends?"

Aubrey resumed pacing and smoking. "Listen, I have a plan to save the band. Drastic times call for drastic measures."

Troy had hoped to be taking a nap with Hilary before the sound check.

"I propose we get a new drummer."

Troy stared at him and slowly shook his head. "I can't believe what I'm hearing. That's so ridiculous I don't even know how to respond. A couple days ago, I told *Playboy* that you and Toon were the best rhythm section in the music industry. We've been together for what, fifteen years? And you're gonna dump him just like that?" Troy snapped his fingers.

"I know it sounds radical, but I think Fen could be persuaded to stay if we did. It's a concession I don't want to make, but—"

"If you get rid of Toon," Troy said solemnly, "then I'm out, too."

Aubrey pointed a shaky finger. "You're bluffing."

"I'm as serious as fucking bone cancer, Aubrey. I'm gettin' too old for this shit. We'll talk before we go on stage tonight, just the four of us, just like we always do. We'll lay all our cards out on the table and find out what's what. If Fen has a lawyer, we'll get to the bottom of it. But there's something you gotta remember. One day, *this will end.* And what I'm beginning to discover is that it may not be so terrible. I've been with Hilary every single day for the last three years, and it took me this long to realize I'll miss her more than I'll miss the band."

Aubrey kept walking around the room as if he were cold and trying to generate body heat. "I'm not ready to let go. Let's fight this thing together, Troy. Maybe we can get Fen and Toon to come to some sort of a compromise. The tour's over in a week. After that, we agree to take some time off and let cooler heads prevail. Let the shit shake out of the trees, you know? Why rush to any hasty decisions? I say we stay out of the studio altogether, and let's see how long we can live without each other."

Troy didn't speak.

Aubrey stubbed out his cigarette and waved his hand to dissipate the smoke. "Sorry about Hilary. You wanna talk about it?"

"Later. I'm going to rest up a little before the sound check."

Aubrey closed the door behind him with a click. Troy pulled a drawstring and the curtains traversed. Only a thin slice of light projected onto the far wall, dust particles dancing inside it in slow motion. He lay down on the bed with a pillow over his eyes, replaying the events of the last twenty-four hours, and for the first time in many years, he began to pray. For forgiveness. For something like life after death. He remembered when he was five years old, and his mother had taken him to the county fair. It was without doubt the best day of his life. He ate cotton candy for the first time, saw a woman with a beard, and watched a man wrestle an alligator in the mud. He was just tall enough to ride the roller coaster, and when it was over, he hugged his mother tight and said, "Mommy, that was fun. Let's never do it again."

11. Backstage Impasse

Troy was eating some Chinese take-out from a carton, sweet and sour chicken, as Chance, the band's official chauffeur, drove him from the hotel to the arena.

"I stopped by Mr. Trueblood's flat a couple hours ago, just to be sure I could find the address," Chance said in what remained of his Leeds accent. "I happened to see him taking out the rubbish and introduced myself. Quite the convivial chap, isn't he?"

Chance was Chauncey Phillip Anderson III. A dozen tours ago when a limo hadn't arrived at the prescribed time in Pittsburgh, Chance happened to pull up in his cab and Fen put him on the payroll as a full-time driver. Almost sixty now, Chance was a fun-loving, insouciant Brit who fell in love with the States as a young man after WWII and never left. He was affable, well educated, and still referred to the band as "his boys." He also looked the part, attired in the customary gray chauffeur's cap over a short crop of silver hair, black driving gloves, white shirt, black bow tie, and impeccable manners to compliment his contagious smile. Although everyone privately agreed that keeping a full-time driver was not pragmatic, he was good for morale.

"What did the kid say?"

"Oh, nothing much really. He was very complimentary of

you, of course. But he was supremely polite, which I certainly admire." Chance checked the rear-view mirror and whipped around a dallying pickup truck. "The lad was with a delightful young woman, a Miss Lani. Quite fetching I must say."

"Really? What did she look like?"

"Black hair, blue eyes, and very exotic skin. She was rather demure, though she did happen to mention, inadvertently I think, that she was moving back to her island at the end of the year. Her father's health is waning. Young Jasper appeared to be caught rather off-guard by the remark. By the way, might I inquire as to the whereabouts of Miss Hilary this afternoon?"

"I don't know." Troy polished off the sweet and sour. "Miss Hilary and I decided to go our separate ways."

Chance glanced at Troy. He turned his attention back to the road. He eyed Troy again. "I'm sorry to hear that, mate." At the stoplight he removed his glasses and cleaned them with a handkerchief. Chance and Hil had established an enduring friendship in the form of a book club in which they were the only members, reading at least a novel a week. "May I ask when you had this row?"

"Today," Troy said. "Just a few hours ago."

"Might I be so bold as to ask what happened?"

"I'm not sure," Troy said staring blankly out the window. "It was her idea, not mine. I can't think about it now, Chance. I've got a show to do."

"I understand. So where are the rest of my boys? Why does no one take the Big Ride any longer?"

"I'm here, that's all I know." Troy wiped his mouth off with a napkin and stretched out, legs crossed, head reclined against the headrest, eyes closed.

"This gas shortage is tough enough on us limo jockeys. The last thing we need is dissension within the ranks. Don't you fellows miss the screaming girls running alongside the car? The sexual frivolities in the back seat? You have a reputation to uphold as rock superstars. Teen idols and the like."

Troy was quiet, so Chance drove.

They were gliding along in the stillness of the desert when Chance yelled, "Whoa, bloody hell!"

Troy's head popped up like it was spring-loaded in a jack-in-the-box. A rusted-out pickup veered wildly from an exit ramp, ricocheted off a concrete retaining wall, and came careening toward the limo. Chance slammed on the brakes. Troy's right knee was thrust forward, smashing into the dashboard. The truck swerved just in front of them and skipped down an embankment, rolled over twice, and crashed into a giant saguaro. The limo skidded across the pavement. Chance turned the steering wheel as hard as he could into the fishtail, and the hulking battleship laid a figure-eight of hot rubber until it slid onto the shoulder. One of the rear tires was blown out by a fat barrel cactus. The Big Ride finally came to rest near a stand of timothy trees, a blanket of dust lifting toward the heavens.

Chance and Troy collected their wits. Steam hissed angrily under the hood like dragon smoke.

"You all right, son?" Chance said. He shoved the gearshift into park and set the emergency brake.

"Doesn't anyone in this town know how to drive?" Troy clutched his knee. "Last night I almost got killed going back to the ranch. What the fuck is the problem with people? We'll all be lucky just to get out of this desert alive."

"It's like this everywhere, lad. I see it every day." Chance was breathing heavily. "No one has proper regard for his fellow motorists."

They got out of the limo. Troy tried to flex his knee.

Chance descended off into the gully to check on the truck, also engulfed in a billowing cloud of dust. He stumbled over a tumbleweed, then stepped more gingerly around rocks and desert vegetation to the accordion-like front end of the vehicle. He returned to the limo.

"Is he alive?"

"He is, the drunk bugger. There's an empty bottle of gin in his lap." Chance tried to start the Big Ride's ignition but it wouldn't turn over. "The gentleman is in need of immediate medical attention, as are you. I'm going for help."

"You're gonna walk?"

"Hitch, hopefully. I shall return, as General MacArthur might say. Please don't leave the crash site."

Troy massaged his knee as he watched Chance disappear into the distance. So much for the sound check. Nils would erupt. Troy lowered himself into the sand and against a rock. He closed his eyes. It would be the first show Hilary had missed in three years. He should've asked her to marry him, he thought. He should've asked if she wanted a baby.

It was over an hour before sirens were audible, whining in from the city. A procession of ambulances, tow trucks, and squad cars arrived in a flurry with Chance's face illuminated by flashing red lights.

"Sorry," Chance called out huffing and puffing, his shirt soaked with sweat. "I had to walk several miles before I finally managed to fetch a ride."

Troy tried to stretch his knee. "Nils is gonna flip. My knee is swelling up like a water balloon. I'm not sure how I'm gonna go on tonight."

Within seconds, the medics were loading the drunk truck driver onto a stretcher and hoisting him into an ambulance. A policeman was asking Troy some questions for his accident report when a second officer approached.

"Hey, hold the phone. You know who this is Officer Russell? We got us a real-live rock star in our presence. This here's Troy Archer of the Unknowns," the exuberant cop said. "I saw your picture in the paper this morning. Hey, how 'bout an auto-graph?"

It was one of those moments Troy genuinely hated his job. He signed the back of the officer's ticket book.

"Who?" asked the first cop.

"The singer of the Unknowns. You never heard of the Un-knowns? Only the best rock 'n' roll outfit in the whole U S of A."

"Is the other guy gonna make it?" Troy asked.

"Drunks always make it," said the first cop. "It's the people they hit who usually don't."

* * *

They had been waiting in University Hospital's ER for twenty minutes when a starched-white nurse arrived to wheel Troy into x-ray.

"Chance, call Nils." Troy pointed to a pay phone. "If he yells, yell right back. Tell him I'll be there by show time." He checked his watch. "And send a car over to Jasper Trueblood's. I prom-ised him a limo." His voice trailed off as he was rolled away in a wheelchair.

Troy was treated, given a shot of cortisone, crutches, a pre-scription for painkillers, and an ice pack taped to his knee. There was a severe contusion and some strained ligaments but nothing requiring a cast. The doctor advised him not to put pressure on the leg for a couple of days.

"Sounds good, Doc," Troy said. "Right after the second en-core."

Troy and Chance ended up catching a cab to the show, ar-riving just after eight o'clock. The opening act was about to go on. They pulled into the stage entrance of the Tucson Perform-ing Arts Facility amidst jugglers juggling, scalpers scalping, and Hare Krishnas chanting off-key. Troy was led through the stage door by beefy security guards as they pushed past paparazzi and

157

reporters. He was a little wobbly on his crutches though his steroid-enhanced knee felt surprisingly stable. He heard the audience bellow out its boisterous applause as the opening act took the stage, and a silhouette rushed toward him. It was Nils, predictably manic.

"Troy. Are you alive?" Nils asked. He was the best dressed person in the entire arena in a powder blue seersucker suit and a yellow silk tie.

"I banged up my knee a little, that's all. Luckily our team had Chance and the Big Ride."

Nils pressed his palms together as if in prayer. His facial expressions changed like strata cooling in the ocean after a lava flow, one layer at a time until it metamorphosed into smooth black obsidian. Finally he said, "Thank you, God." He squeezed Troy's shoulder, careful not to knock him over on his crutches. "Did the other guy survive?"

"Drunks always survive," Troy said, quoting the cop. "No one knows where the hell they're going. The whole world is a runaway train."

Nils bobbed his head up and down as if his neck was attempting to pump this new information into his cerebral cortex. "Thank God you're all right. We have a doctor on the premises if you need one."

"C'est la vie," Troy said flatly.

"We've got a major fucking problem to deal with." Nils ushered Troy aside and addressed him in a low and serious tone. "I don't know what happened at your little pool party this afternoon, but Fen didn't show up for the sound check and right now he's downstairs sulking in the dressing room like a spoiled teenager. He says he won't go on."

"He'll go on," Troy said.

"I don't care what his problem is, Troy. We've got three lousy dates left on this tour, and there's no reason why we can't all cooperate for one more goddamn week. Everything was hunky-dory in Albuquerque, and now it's completely fucked up again. I heard all about Fen's legal bullshit and frankly, I couldn't care less. Right now I have a job to do. We have signed contracts and legal obligations. Talk some sense into him, Troy. Tell him I won't let this ship sink on my watch. We're supposed to be fucking professionals."

"All right, Nils, enough with the lecture. Fendleman'll go on. If he weren't going on, he wouldn't be in the arena. I'll drag him out there by his hair caveman-style if I have to."

They headed for the dressing room through the conglomeration of roadies who were babysitting amps, speakers, light standards, girders, and suspension beams. Backstage was the usual coterie of tour staff, security, promoters, wives, girlfriends, friends, and friends of friends. Nils, running interference as a human shield, led Troy through the commotion and just as they were about to duck into a heavily guarded staircase, Troy caught a glimpse of Jasper Trueblood, blissful and grinning ear-to-ear. He was pointing out someone in the crowd to a young woman with black hair. They were sitting on aluminum folding chairs, holding hands, laughing.

"Nils, I'll be back in two minutes."

Despite Nils' protests, Troy hobbled through the gauntlet of backstage onlookers and hangers-on until he reached Jasper, who looked mildly euphoric and decidedly unlike the pugilist he had encountered in that restroom fewer than twenty-four hours before.

Troy whispered, "Jasper."

Jasper stood up and Troy hugged him. A circle of faces watched, including Lani's.

"Somebody said you and Chance drove off a cliff."

"No such luck. I'm glad to see you made it. Remember that guy who almost steamrolled us last night?"

Jasper nodded. "Yeah."

"Maybe it was the same guy. Nobody knows how to drive anymore. It's an epidemic."

"I'm glad you're OK," Jasper said. "Troy, this is Lani Sablan. Lani, Troy Archer."

Troy gazed deep into her twinkling periwinkle eyes. He wanted Miss Lani Sablan to know that Jasper Trueblood was his guest of honor. "It's a pleasure to meet you. Jasper has excellent taste. He's said a lot of nice things about you."

She blushed as Troy kissed her hand. Behind her left ear was a fragrant white plumeria with a yellow center. Left ear—close to the heart, indicating she was spoken for.

"Stick around after the show. You two are riding with me."

Before Jasper could say anything else, Nils hustled Troy off through the serpentine hallways and shadowy catacombs that led to the dressing room.

The house lights went up after the opening act concluded its set, and the next warm-up act prepared to take the stage. Beach balls bounced in the crowd, and Frisbees sailed through a haze of marijuana smoke.

Downstairs, under the pulsating vibrations of the audience clapping and stomping their feet, Nils' face sported an odd smirk. "You want me to come in there and kick some ass?"

"No," Troy said. "Stay here. Keep everyone out."

The dressing room was a concrete bunker with mint green cinder block walls, comfortable old furniture, fluorescent lights, and a buffet table. The entrails of the Unknowns, Fendleman and Toon, were brooding at opposite ends. Aubrey paged through a magazine and talked to someone on the phone about chord progressions. The wardrobe trunks were opened up but no one was dressed yet. Aubrey wore jeans and sandals, no shirt. Fen was dressed in black from shirt to shoes. Toon was hardly dressed at all, sitting at a table in white boxer shorts with hearts in the pattern and an undershirt with shoulder straps.

Aubrey hung up the phone. "Are you still alive?"

"More or less." Troy had already decided to limp onstage with or without the rest of them. He related the story of the accident as he sorted through wardrobe for something to wear.

"What are you doing?" Aubrey asked.

"I'm bakin' a fuckin' cake, Aubrey. What does it look like I'm doin'?" Troy said.

"Didn't Nils tell you?" Aubrey said. "These guys won't go on."

Troyed pulled on his one-piece Spandex costume without looking at them, then began to apply his makeup. "First of all, if they won't go on, why are they here?" he said as he stared into the vanity mirror, which was outlined in small lightbulbs. "And second, if they won't go on, they won't go on. It's a free country. I'm goin' on with or without 'em."

Fen pointed at Toon. "Give me one good reason why I should go out there with this heathen. He tried to kill me today, and he's on drugs even as we speak. Give me one good fucking reason," he shouted.

"Cincinnati," Troy said.

The room settled into an eerie silence. Troy was referring to the eleven people who had been trampled to death at a Who concert just five months before. A human stampede. Rock 'n' roll wasn't worth dying for. "I won't be held responsible for people getting killed because you two are unable to make nice together in the sandbox. If I have to get the goddamn crew to play the instruments, I'm goin' out there." Toon seemed to be melting, but Fen wasn't giving in.

"I steadfastly refuse," Fen said.

"You *steadfastly refuse?* Well then let me tell you something, you prima donna son of a bitch. I *steadfastly* declare war on your ass! I'll tell the crowd right up front the shit you're pullin', and you better hope we don't end up with blood on our hands."

"I'm too old and too talented to put up with him anymore. I can find a dozen drummers just as good as he is out of the trade magazines."

"Yeah, but how many can sink a Cadillac into a swimming pool on the first try?" Toon taunted.

"Fuck you," Fendleman said.

"Come kiss daddy in his new Caddy," Toon said.

Fen's face reddened.

"Enough!" Troy jumped in. "Fen, do what you have to do but I'm warning you, don't underestimate me."

"You're *warning* me?" Fen was nearly foaming at the mouth. He hurled a coffee mug and it smashed into the far wall. "I hate this shit. I'm a fucking slave to my own music. All right, here's my best offer, so take it or leave it. I'll go on tonight, but this is it. The farewell performance. Period. Fuck the rest of the tour. He said he was going to be sober and he's not. That was the deal. Shit, just look at him."

Toon was chopping up an anthill-sized pile of sparkling pinkish Peruvian cocaine with a straight razor, cutting the lines into letters: u-n-k-n-o-w-n-s. He snorted the first three letters through a hundred dollar bill and deep into his sinus cavities. He picked out a two-carat rock, inspected it, and tucked under his lower lip like a chaw of tobacco. His eyes were so dilated they were almost entirely black.

"It's not just the coke," Fen said. "Tell Troy what you're drinking."

Troy continued to get dressed.

Toon raised a glass, which contained an ominous green concoction. "What, this little thing?"

"Tell Troy what's in it."

"No alcohol, you can be sure of that," Toon said smugly.

"Tell him."

"Well, if you must know, this is a new party drink I made up all by myself called the Cactus Cocktail." Toon took a sip and grimaced. "It can be mixed to taste of course, but I prefer to start with fifteen medium-sized, well-cleaned peyote buttons, a quart of whole milk, shaved ice, two scoops of your favorite ice cream, and throw it all in a blender. Delicious. The next thing you know, you want to go for a swim, but you don't want to get out of the car to do it." Toon began laughing so hard that he doubled over and when he came up for air his face was crimson.

"Why. Larry?" Troy asked. "You haven't done this shit for a long time."

Just as Toon's grin dissolved there was a knock at the door. Nils stuck his head in. "Thirty minutes to show time."

"Close the fucking door," Troy shouted.

Nils made a hasty exit.

Relief washed over Troy as everyone joined him at the wardrobe trunks and got dressed, avoiding direct eye contact.

Finally Toon broke the calm. "So Fen, tell everyone about Lord Loophole."

Fen made a noise like air being let out of a balloon. "You know, when I was doing blow every day, I thought I was just a recreational user, too. But if you ingest it by the wheelbarrowful, that's not recreational, that's suicidal. I said from the beginning I wouldn't do this tour if you were using."

"You're boring the shit out of everyone again," Toon said. "Tell them about your new lawyer, Fen."

Fendleman continued unabated, "And I happen to know there's no way you could do this tour if you weren't using. You're hooked, man. An addict. You trick-fuck yourself into thinking it's just a glass of wine here or a line of nose candy there, but sooner or later you always end up like this. Wired."

Toon stood up. "You're such a sanctimonious piece of shit. The first time I used dope on this entire tour was three days ago when I found out you were planning to sabotage the band." He returned to his seat, sniffling from all the coke draining through his sinuses. "Now, Fen," Toon said in an even tone, "tell 'em what you're up to or I swear to God I'm gonna come over there and break your fucking arm."

No one moved. Fendleman blushed. "It's true," he said abashedly. "The time has come. I'm out."

"And what exactly does that mean?" Troy said.

"It means I intend to protect myself, and my music."

Troy surprised even himself by briskly taking Fen by the shoulders and sitting him down. "The Unknowns have always been a democracy. It takes a three-fourths majority to make any major decisions, it always has. I say we take a vote."

Fendleman laughed. "Forget it. You're lucky I'm going on tonight."

"What's with this lawyer bullshit, Fen?" Troy said. "We have lawyers. Why do we need more fucking lawyers? Why not just finish the tour and take a break like we always do. That way there's no lawsuits, no muss, no fuss. We take some time off and after twelve months, if you still want to dissolve the partnership, we'll draw up the papers. I mean, what's the rush? All we have left is one in San Diego and two in L.A. It's been a long tour. Nerves are frayed. We just need some time to decompress." It occurred to Troy that he had said the same words to Hilary just a few hours earlier.

Fen was resolute.

"Look," Troy said, "can't we just keep all the suits out of it for now? I'm not up for all the meetings and affidavits and documents in triplicate. We'll be together one more week. That's all. Hell, half our shit's already in San Diego."

Fen's eyes were glazed over in a kind of trance. "Tonight's it."

"Why burn bridges? A lot can change in a year. Toon only went on this binge because of you."

Toon was in the corner, snorting what was left of the U-N-K-N-O-W-N-S.

164

"Nothing's changed in fifteen years," Fen said, "except the hotels are shittier and the promoters can't insure us. I'm sorry about Hilary. She told me you two broke up. But business is business."

"Leave Hilary out of this." Troy had the sudden urge to kick Fen in the nuts.

"Tonight's it. I'm sorry," Fen said. "That's my compromise. That's the best I can do."

Aubrey and Toon were staring, waiting for one final miracle from Troy's bag of tricks. "What do you mean you're going to protect yourself?"

"I wrote every single that ever hit the charts. I'm not going to walk away from my life's work and let you three run around dive bars doing my material. I wrote it. It's mine."

Toon shook his head and proceeded to snort the final S. He licked his index finger, wiped it along the table top, and dabbed it along his gums. Aubrey looked like he was about to start bawling.

"You can't just waltz in, hire some prick lawyer, and expect to break a contract," Troy said. "Are you really that naïve? Who in the hell do you think you're dealing with here? You and I started this group. You think you've got the stage presence or vocal range to make your songs hits? And believe me, I could find fifteen lead guitars in the trades just as fast as you could find fifteen drummers. You never were any great shakes on the axe, motherfucker. You're lucky you found somebody to sing your goddamn songs."

Fendleman smiled. In a friendlier, almost conciliatory voice he offered, "After the incident in the pool today, I swore to myself I'd never play onstage with the Unknowns again. But you've got a point about Cincinnati. So I'll concede tonight but this is it. The rest of the tour is canceled, and I don't give a fuck who sues us. As for all the rest of it, we'll let the courts decide."

"You'll lose," Troy said.

"Maybe," Fen replied.

Aubrey stood and pointed at Fen, his finger shaking. "You can't stop us from going on the road." His eyes were wet with rage. "We'll change the name of the band. We'll do whatever we have to do."

Fen threw his arms in the air. "I won't let you replace me with some studio musician and run around playing my songs as if they were yours. I wrote them, I own the rights, they're a part of me." Fen patted his chest with his hand.

Tears trickled down Aubrey's cheeks. Toon seemed shaken, too, despite being as wide-eyed as a salamander. Even though Troy thought he should've seen this coming, he was still astonished that it was really over, just as he had been with Hilary.

"Aren't you going to say anything, Troy?" Aubrey asked.

Troy had to sit down. "I feel lightheaded. It always happens when lawyers get involved." He rubbed his bum knee.

"I'm sorry, but you had to know we couldn't go on forever. And Larry, it's not even you," Fen said. "It's me. You have every right to live your life at a hundred miles an hour with the top down. And I hope everything works out. But musically I'm headed in a different direction. I'm interested in power ballads and—"

Toon interrupted. "You want synthesizers. Synthesizers make synthetic music. It's artificial. We're artificial enough. We've been over this a million fucking times. We're a guitar band. Enough with all the overdubbing and post-production bullshit. Let's get back to basics."

Aubrey pleaded, "We're not a guitar band, we're rock 'n' roll, man. Hell, we can bring in an electric piano, a brass section, maybe some black gospel singers to do backup vocals. Why do we have to be so stagnant? We could do lots of things. The Stones were onto all this shit ages ago. If it's good enough for

Mick-fucking-Jagger, it sure as hell ought to be good enough for us."

"I'm so sick of talking about synthesizers," Troy said.

"Me, too," Fen said. "It's time to move on."

Troy walked over, sat down, and draped an arm around his old friend's shoulder. "We've always been democratic, Fen. Please. Just placate me for old times' sake."

Fen started to complain but Troy placed a finger to his lips. "Shhh. So, Fen wants a divorce and Aubrey wants to stay together. Larry, what's your vote?"

"If Fendleman wants out, we can't hold a gun to his head," Toon said. "So why take a vote?"

"In or out?" Troy repeated.

"I abstain," Toon said, sniffling.

"No abstentions."

"OK, then I'm out."

Aubrey's eyes flashed. "Why?"

"Because we used to be cool, Aubrey. We were counterculture and anti-establishment. We were anti-everything. Now what are we? The whole world revolves around the bottom line, and nothing's commercial enough to suit the record label. We used to represent rebellion. All we represent now is the fucking Pepsi generation."

Aubrey turned toward Troy. "How do you vote?"

Troy had hoped to convince Fen to reconsider by showing the unanimous support of the other three, but Toon was right. They couldn't force Fendleman to do anything, and Troy no longer had the energy to be the lone oracle. "I'm sorry, Aubrey. I just don't think it's gonna work anymore," Troy said.

Aubrey hid his face in his hands and began to weep.

Troy felt like hell. "I'm sorry."

"Fuck you all," Aubrey grunted from behind his hands.

Several minutes of shell-shocked silence were interrupted by

Nils' knock on the door.

"Five minutes 'til show time." Nils slammed the door behind him.

"We should tell him what's happening," Toon said.

"Wait 'til after the show," Troy said.

The building's foundation began to rumble with the restless foot-stomping of the audience.

Toon pulled on his shoes. "If this is our last show, I say we give 'em somethin' to remember. I say we play until security throws us out of the joint just like in the old days."

The Unknowns did not engage in their long-held tradition of joining hands for a final rally cry just before taking the stage. Troy smelled an air of impending doom as thick as burning hair and promised himself if he could just get through this night without bloodshed, he was going indulge in that nervous breakdown he'd been promising himself.

12. The Unknowns Face the Music

A frenzied phalanx of anxious fans energized the darkened auditorium as the ceremonial trumpet erupted into the fanfare used to introduce horse races, "Call to the Post." It one of Troy's ideas from years earlier when he had attended the Preakness at Pimlico. The ritual produced a heightened sense of expectation in the audience, a kind of audio foreplay. Tonight's crowd wasn't bad, but with a paid attendance of just over twelve thousand, it was far from a sell-out.

Flash pots exploded and mushroom clouds puffed their way to the ceiling as the audience gasped. The fog machine belched a thick, vaporous haze that rolled across the stage. The spotlight splashed on Toon, standing above his drums, beating his chest with drumsticks. He tossed the sticks into the floor seats where small pockets of humanity converged. The rest of the band maneuvered through the shadows, and Troy noticeably limped. A blast of light flooded the auditorium and prisms of color bounced all over the building, lasers ricocheting like a battle between rainbows.

Not a soul was seated as the Unknowns kicked into their opening number, heads and necks craning to get a better view in the mezzanine section while the chairs on floor level were moved forward in herd-like fashion ever closer to the stage. Fans waved their hands in the air and stood on their chairs. Women climbed onto the shoulders of their boyfriends and husbands.

The first song was a thrashing old relic off the debut record, their first hit, featuring an up-tempo beat and hot licks on guitar. During the second chorus, in the midst of the feedback and old dive-bomber riffs, Fendleman became enraged at some technical snafu and kicked an amp. He motioned toward it with the neck of his Stratocaster and the lead technician slithered out from the wings on his hands and knees. Troy hated when shows started like this. The tech adjusted Fen's amp until it was back at full throttle, then slid offstage in reverse. The song reached its crescendo, screeched to an abrupt halt, and the audience erupted into a riotous ovation. The sustained applause went all through Troy, triggering nerve endings and raising goose bumps on his arms. Would he miss this? Hell yes, he thought. Who wouldn't?

"Hello, Tucson," Troy shouted into the mic. He was wearing his Spandex and top hat. He didn't like to talk much early in the show, preferring instead to build momentum through the music. Toon was clad in his familiar gym shorts, tennis shoes, wristbands, headband, bare chest. The typically recalcitrant Aubrey wore red pants, red suspenders, and seemed a bit fidgety as he doctored a guitar string. Fen looked dapper as usual in his white linen suit and sunglasses. People in the audience shouted out names of songs and other unintelligible comments, which Troy had learned to ignore. He happened to see Jasper and his girlfriend on the side of the stage and pointed the mic in their direction. They waved enthusiastically. Troy had sung the hits hundreds of times in concert, especially the early ones. The band didn't really play to the audience anymore as much as they played to each other. Occasionally, just to spark his interest in a particular tune, Troy would mentally dedicate it to someone, usually Hilary, his Calliope, the Greek muse of music and eloquence. Tonight, however, Calliope was missing in action. He sang the song for Jasper Trueblood and his island girlfriend.

Troy threw the microphone high in the air, spun around twice, and caught it on the fly as the band ripped into the first verse of the next number. His knee was feeling much better. They did a couple more classics and launched into the title track from their latest release, "Love Is a Many Splintered Thing." It was an immense production number that required all twelve hundred lights plus five-color effects, trusses, hydraulics, and chain lifts. The better the lighting, the less Troy could see of the audience, and this configuration was absolutely blinding. By the end of each tour, annoying details resulting from bad studio decisions became glaringly obvious. For example, Troy regretted the plodding tempo of this song, especially the chorus.

Everything was running smoothly, and they did a half dozen more songs without additional technical problems. "Ladies and gentlemen," Troy announced, "I'd like to introduce your players this evening."

The audience howled.

"On drums, the greatest percussionist in rock 'n' roll history. He's hell when he's well and he's seldom sick. The vivacious . . . the loquacious . . . Lar-ry Tooooon."

Toon pounded away on every piece of equipment he had then stood up with arms raised high and proceeded to smash both sticks down on the cymbals. He took a deep, theatrical bow and tossed more drumsticks into the audience.

Troy continued. "On lead guitar, Mis-ter John Fen-dle-man."

Fen laid down some space licks and waved. The crowd cheered.

"And on bass guitar, rock 'n' roll icon and your master of disaster, Mis-ter . . . Au-brey . . . Har-mon."

Aubrey's face was pale, eyes glassy, and rather than the perfunctory bow or wave he did something he hadn't done in fifteen years, something so astonishing, so audacious, so completely out of character that even the crew took notice from the wings. The notoriously stoic and laconic bass player took the microphone in hand and for the first time in the band's history, directly addressed the audience.

"I'd like to make an announcement," Aubrey said, his voice cracking.

Troy could see he was fragile, with the pallor of someone who's just woken up from a horrible nightmare.

"Tonight, you are a part of history," Aubrey said. A hush settled over the crowd. "This is the last live performance the Unknowns will ever do."

Lovely, Troy thought. Here we go.

There was a smattering of applause. No one seemed to fully comprehend what was transpiring, like Aubrey was speaking in tongues. He continued, "And I'd like to say one more thing."

Troy shuddered.

"Without you," Aubrey said, "there would have been no us." He unplugged his vintage Fender and handed it to a delirious patron in the front row. He took a step backward and began to applaud the audience.

Fen and Toon looked at Troy, who shrugged. All three of them chimed in and clapped along. The crowd burst into a prolonged ovation that lasted several minutes. Apparently, Aubrey had to say a final farewell. The gathering roar rocked the arena.

Troy smiled when he heard Nils shout from the wings, "What in the living fuck is he talking about?"

The band wailed through another string of dusty hits and after one particular number Aubrey had helped to write, Troy saw Aubrey babbling to himself and kicking his mic stand. "Hey," Troy said, wiping his brow with the back of his hand. "What're ya doing?"

Inexplicably, Aubrey started smashing another guitar into

everything in sight including some extremely sensitive sound equipment. Shards and shrapnel sprayed as Troy tried to stop him, but Aubrey pushed away and continued his onslaught. By the time the roadies corralled him, he had destroyed so much equipment that the show couldn't continue. Fans bellowed wildly. Aubrey collapsed in the arms of the crew. They carried him backstage while the fans clamored for more.

Troy checked his watch. They hadn't played long enough to satisfy the contract, but it was going to have to do. So much for legal obligations. He stood center-stage blowing kisses. The crowd reacted in kind. So this is it, he thought, capturing the moment and committing it to memory. This is how it all ends.

Larry Toon returned to the percussion platform and dumped over his congas, bongos, bass drum, snare drum, tom toms, and with great panache his Chinese gongs. He kicked his kick drums and anything else that remained standing. A cymbal wobbled across the stage. Breathing heavily, he took a final bow, unloaded his last dozen drumsticks into the audience, and disappeared. The faithful cheered on with their lighters and matches waving in the air until the house lights came on. Towering velvet curtains traversed the stage. The show was over. There would be no encore.

Backstage was bedlam. People were shouting orders and rushing into each other, trying to clear a path for Aubrey, who was being wheeled out on a stretcher to an open area to receive care from an in-house medic. Nils instructed the security guards to keep the press and everyone else at bay. Troy, Fen, and Toon stared with towels draped over their shoulders and sweat dripping down their foreheads. The medic strapped an oxygen mask over Aubrey's mouth and checked his vital signs.

Toon leaned over to Troy. "Shouldn't we get him to a real hospital? I don't want some fucking rent-a-doctor working on him," he said audibly enough for the medic to hear.

"Yes," the man said, undaunted, "we're taking him over to University Hospital. Your friend's suffering from dehydration. We need to get some fluids in his system."

"I'm going with you," Troy said.

"Me, too," said Toon.

Fendleman looked at them. There was an awkward silence. "I'll call the hospital later to see what's what," Fen said, "but it seems like everything's under control."

Troy nodded. Toon turned away.

"Larry," Fen said.

Toon shifted back around and did not make eye contact.

Fen extended his hand, and Toon paused then shook it half-heartedly. Fen shook Troy's hand as well. No more was said but it was clear that this was it. The last act. Fen headed off downstairs to the dressing room.

"Don't forget your thirty pieces of silver," Toon muttered under his breath.

As the medic and some of the crew guided the stretcher toward the loading dock where an ambulance waited, Troy heard Jasper call out, "Hey Troy, is he OK?"

Troy hobbled over to Jasper. His knee was throbbing again. "I think so. We're taking him to University Hospital for some tests. I wanted to connect with you and Lani for the post-party, but I have to go with Aubrey. Can we do it another time?"

"Sure," Jasper said holding Lani's hand. "Another time."

"Chance should be around here somewhere to give you a ride home."

"Go take care of Aubrey. We'll be fine."

Troy remembered he had to find Jasper a job, and for the first time it occurred to him that the demise of the band meant Chance was unemployed as well as other people he hadn't even considered.

Jasper stammered, "Thanks again for tonight, for . . . everything."

Troy looked into his eyes. "Thank you." He hugged Jasper Trueblood hard enough that Jasper's rib cage ached.

* * *

The concert hall was nearly empty as the crew broke down the stage with robot-like precision. Jasper and Lani were ready to leave, but there was no sign of Chance. As they searched for him in the parking lot near the stage entrance, Jasper wondered if a cab would take him and Lani all the way back to campus for four dollars, which was all he had. "Well, what d'ya think?"

"I think we should walk," Lani said.

"Really?" Jasper asked. "We could catch a cab. I've got four bucks."

She waved him off. "Walking won't take more than an hour. Come on, Jazz. It'll be fun. It's not even midnight."

So they hiked through downtown, which was practically deserted, Jasper shuffling along and gabbing about the concert, Lani listening with her purse slung over her shoulder. After a few blocks, Lani said, "Wait a sec." She stopped and stepped out of her black pumps, reached up under her skirt with both hands and shimmied her panty hose down over her hips and thighs, removing them. Jasper's pulse leapfrogged as her hands disappeared up under her blouse and unfastened her bra. She contorted and squirmed free like a female Houdini wriggling out of a straightjacket. She wedged the hose and bra into her purse. "There," she said, carrying her pumps and walking barefoot. "Much better."

They talked more about the concert and school and Lani's ailing father. Jasper didn't even mind when she reminisced about her old boyfriend. Tonight, Jasper felt like he was standing on top of a mountain and owned everything he could see.

"Daddy's already had two heart operations. He's seventy, now. He looks old, and he never looked old until I saw him last Christmas. That scared me. Mom needs me back home, but I'm afraid to watch him die."

Jasper stopped walking and took a breath then walked some more. "I'd hate to see you leave Lani but if you do, I understand why. Maybe better than anyone else on Earth. Do what you have to do. Years from now, you'll be glad you did. I hate to be so blunt, but the only thing worse than watching my mother die would have been not watching my mother die."

"I've heard you go on and on about your mom, but you hardly ever talk about your father. What's happening with him these days? You said he called you?"

Jasper laughed. "I had completely severed all ties with him until two days ago. I even changed my name but he finally tracked me down."

"Jasper Trueblood isn't your real name?"

"No."

Lani stopped and smiled. "Seriously? What is it?"

"Don't laugh." Jasper extended his hand. "Junior McPherson. I still cringe when I hear that name. I feel like a fugitive on the lam."

"Wow!" she exclaimed. "You're not kidding! Junior McPherson is a perfectly delightful name. How come you changed it?"

"Let's save this conversation for another time, OK? Tonight's too perfect to get started on the old man. But I promise that someday if you really want to, we'll dissect every brutal detail."

"Well, I think you should un-sever the ties with him. You only get one dad in this life. You should talk to him."

"That's what Troy said."

"Really?"

"Yeah. There's something very important I want to ask you." They stopped walking and kissed on the street corner. Jasper held Lani's hands in his. "Have I ever told you how much I love your hands? Of all your physical attributes, I have to say I love your hands as much as any of them. They look like a surgeon's or a pianist's."

Lani glimpsed at her hands with a smile. "Can I tell you a secret?" she whispered her warm breath in his ear. "You smell just like my first boyfriend. Like wet stones in the morning. I love that smell."

Jasper decided to walk barefoot too, figuring he already smelled like wet stones so why not? They strolled through campus down Campbell Avenue and past University Hospital.

"That's where they took Aubrey," Jasper said.

"Do you want to stop in? Maybe we can see if he's all right."

"No, we'd probably just be in the way. Tell me more about your first boyfriend."

"Well, it was in the eighth grade, and his name was Jerome Telro. The kids called him Jerry, but I always called him Jerome. I think about him sometimes. The first boy I ever let kiss me. I remember the day I fell for him, too. Our history teacher, Mr. Bosch, asked the class if anyone wanted to be president of the United States. The girls mostly giggled and all the boys said 'no' except for Jerome. Not only did he want to be president, he had a campaign strategy. He was going to be a hero in the next war that came along, then a lawyer, then a governor, and then the president. He told Mr. Bosch that he figured it was about a fifty-fifty proposition. Some of the kids laughed but Mr. Bosch didn't and neither did I."

"Cool," Jasper said. "Whatever happened to him?"

"I don't know," she said. "But you smell just like him. Hey poet," she said, "do Prufrock for me? Please? You don't have to do the whole thing, just a little. Pretty please?"

Jasper kicked into his serious old-time poet voice, making dramatic hand gestures as they walked.

"Oh, do not ask, 'What is it?'
Let us go and make our visit.

177

In the room the women come and go
Talking of Michelangelo."

As Jasper continued to recite Eliot, Lani leaned into him at her favorite lines. When they finally reached her sorority house, he found himself wishing they could walk off like this forever, hand-in-hand into the moonlit desert.

"I love that poem," Lani said. "I love that poem with my whole heart. Hey, Jasper."

"Yeah?" Even if she wanted the date to end, he was thinking, it was still the single greatest night in recorded human history, and no one could ever take it away from him.

"You wanna come inside? There's some white wine left in the fridge."

"Well, if you insist."

They sneaked through the sorority house so as not to rouse the sisters. Lani led him to the kitchen, held a finger up to her lips, and tiptoed with wine and glasses down a dark hall and up some stairs. As they crept along, she motioned toward a door. "Judy," she mouthed quietly, her best friend.

Jasper nodded and they kept walking.

She opened the door to her room. Jasper had been there before, but not since her roommate had dropped out of school. It was so tranquil, unlike anything Jasper was used to or could imagine. Lani lit candles and killed the overhead light. She turned the radio on low. They drank the wine, talked quietly,, then began to kiss on her bed. Lani rubbed her hand between his legs and Jasper sighed.

"Can I make a confession?" he asked.

"Sure," she whispered.

"This is not something a guy usually feels very comfortable—"

"Go ahead, Jazz. Tell me anything."

He took a deep breath. "I'm actually rather shy with the opposite sex when it gets right down to it and . . . I've had a few casual girlfriends, a few physical encounters but I've never actually—"

All the blue in Lani's eyes gleamed at once. "Gone all the way?"

"Yes." Jasper looked to see if she was going to laugh and when she didn't he said, "This is gonna sound corny, but I've always wanted to save the first time for someone special, you know? Someone . . . really special. But never in a million years would I have ever have guessed it would be with someone as special as you."

Lani seemed to like this. A lot. Her eyes welled with tears and she smiled. She leaned in and kissed his forehead, nose, lips, and then Jasper could feel her tongue against his. She intermittently bit his earlobe and neck and disrobed in the flickering candle-light until the only thing she was wearing was the flower behind her ear. Jasper wrapped his arms around her waist and kissed each breast. Lani moaned a little. Then she tenderly whispered words he would remember for the rest of his life.

"Take off your clothes and lay back, haole boy. I'm gonna show you how it's done."

And she did.

When it was all over and Lani Sablan from the island of Guam had drifted off to sleep in his arms, Jasper thought about how surreal it had all been. He wanted to commit every detail to memory: the way her hair fell around her neck when she moved, the oblong shadows cast on the wall by the candlelight, the way her tiny moans blended in with the radio in the background.

Lani slept heavily now with a sheet loosely cocooned over the two of them. Although he was careful not to awaken her, Jasper wasn't at all sleepy. In fact, he would have loved nothing better than to run a full marathon door-to-door and sing his torch song for Lani Sablan, like some love-crazed somnambulist to all the fine denizens of the greater metropolitan area. He could smell her perfume. He could feel her heartbeat and her breath on his neck. Long after Lani Sablan had returned to the island of Guam to tend to her ailing father, Jasper would remember this as the night he realized how many poems there were left to write.

PART IV: MONDAY

13. Deja Voodoo

Lani kissed Jasper's ear, waking him from a deep sleep. He rubbed his eyes and saw that she was already dressed in white open-toed sandals, red culottes, white tank top, and a ponytail bouncing behind her head.

"Hey, sleepyhead, I gotta skedaddle. Judy and I have a midterm this morning."

He smiled. "So it wasn't a dream."

She smiled back. "Oh, it was real all right. You know, you really surprised me last night."

"I did? In a good way?"

"In a very good way. Listen, I'm late, so let's talk later. Can we drop you off at the loft?"

No, if it was all right, Jasper would let himself out the back door and walk home. Lani bent over to kiss him again, and he snatched her arm and pulled her on top of him. She screamed and giggled.

"Not now, silly," she said. "Judy's waiting in the car."

Jasper's line of vision locked on hers. "So I did OK?"

Lani wrestled out of his grasp and climbed off the bed,

181

smoothing her outfit. "Put it this way. If last night really was your first time, either you're a damn fast learner or I'm a damn good teacher."

He smiled. "Maybe both."

She took two steps and paused. "So was it? Your first time I mean? Or is that just a line you use?"

"It was my first time, you really did deflower me, and I meant every word I said. I'd have never guessed that it would be with someone as special as you."

Lani looked at him the same way she had the night before. She came back and kissed him on the lips one more time. "Call me."

Jasper heard the door close and the clip-clop of flip-flops descending the stairs. He rolled over and pulled the sheet up around him. A small oscillating fan circulated a welcome breeze as he curled up, then recalled the previous evening frame by glorious frame. An unexpected bonus was that he harbored no illusions that Lani was in love with him. He still wasn't fantasizing about that pig farm in Nebraska just yet. While they were in bed together, he had fiercely fought the temptation to say *I love you* a dozen times. Now he was glad he hadn't. Men probably told her that all the time. And he suspected she may not have gone to the concert if it hadn't been for the limo and backstage amenities. But even if last night was nothing more than an ephemeral slice of serendipity pie, he didn't care. He wanted to savor every bite.

Jasper walked to his loft in no hurry to be anywhere since he was officially unemployed. He could afford to be without work for about a week, so he figured he had a day or two in which he would defrost the refrigerator, vacuum the apartment, write some poems. He passed by University Hospital and wondered about the Unknowns. Troy had promised to help him find a job, but considering all that had happened with Aubrey, he doubted he'd ever hear from Troy Archer again. But Jasper would never forget Troy, and felt privileged to have attended what appeared to be the band's grand finale. He guessed it was going to hit a hundred degrees by noon as he was sweating by the time he reached home, not even ten a.m. As he climbed up the steps to his apartment, his heart stopped. Someone was sitting on the top step.

"Surprise."

"Jesus, Bud. You scared the shit out of me."

"Sorry," Bud said as he smoked a joint. He stood up and blew a trail of smoke skyward. Next to him was a black valise. "How was your evening with Miss Lani?" He offered Jasper the joint.

Jasper, shaken by the ambush, took a hit and noticed Bud's suitcase. "It was the best night of my entire life. I couldn't have scripted it any better myself."

"That's it? No details? Well, I guess you're not the kiss-and-tell type, huh?" Bud said. "I respect that in a man."

"Come in, have a seat." Jasper unlocked the door and shoved piles of clothes and papers under furniture. He handed Bud an ashtray. Why was Bud here? Maybe Aubrey had lapsed into a coma. "Is Aubrey all right?"

"He's already been released. He'll be back to his old self in no time," Bud said. "How did you end up getting home last night?"

"Lani and I walked," said Jasper. "It wasn't that far."

Bud sat in the white wicker rocker, suitcase by his side. "Troy asked me to come by and make sure you made it home in one piece. I been sittin' on those steps for the better part of an hour."

"I ended up spending the night at Lani's. Can I get you anything? I'm no match for your venison stew, but I've got some iced tea."

"No thanks, I'm good." Bud took a quick look around. "I like your place. It's very cozy."

"It won't be mine for long if I don't find a new job." Jasper gestured toward the suitcase. "Goin' somewhere?"

"I am." Bud sat back in the rocker and crossed his legs. He crushed the joint out in the ashtray. "You can have the rest of that."

"Thanks. Business or pleasure?"

"Business, mostly."

"Where ya goin'?"

Bud's scratched his muttonchops. "Little place in southern Illinois, maybe you've heard of it. Belleville, home of Jimmy Connors, the tennis player. Thought you might like to join me."

Jasper broke out laughing. "Yeah, right." But when Bud didn't laugh and it was clear that he was serious, Jasper shook his head. "No way, Jose. No way in fucking hell I'm goin' back there."

"Look at me," Bud said.

Jasper looked.

Bud leaned forward so his face was close to Jasper's. "Troy broke up with Hilary and the Unknowns in a single day. He's a mess. It's gonna be a while before he gets his shit together enough to face his demons, but that's what he aims to do. And you know who he says inspired him? You. He says you inspired him to change his life. He wants to reciprocate. He's very generous that way. He's paying for every dime of this."

"For every dime of what?" Jasper said. "You mean goin' back to Belleville? Like today? Like right now? Forget it. I'm not ready to see my old man yet. I could barely talk to him on the phone."

"I know and I tend to agree with you. I told Troy he was crazy, that it was too soon, but he says you'll never be ready. He says you can't prepare for something like this, you just have to do it."

"This is total bullshit," Jasper said. "I thought you guys were my friends. I'm not ready to face my old man. Come on, help me find a job, that's what I really need."

Bud readjusted his cowboy hat.

"When I saw there was someone at the top of the steps, I had the eeriest feeling it was my father. Look, I want to go back eventually, but you don't understand. I'm not just afraid to confront him, I'm afraid to confront Junior McPherson. I don't know if I could take all my friends calling me 'Junior' again."

"You don't have to see anyone but your old man. Here's the proposal. We fly into St. Louis, rent a car, and drive directly to Belleville, home of Jimmy Connors. You go straight up to the house, knock on the door, look him in the eye, and hear what he has to say. That's it. If you want to respond, fine, but if you don't want to, that's fine, too. Just hear him out. The whole thing may only take ten minutes. I'll be your wheelman, sitting in the car, reading the newspaper, waiting to make our escape. When you're finished, we'll go over to St. Louis, have a couple steaks, crash at a nice hotel, and fly back to Tucson the next morning. As for finding a job, that's the least of your worries. I'll make a few phone calls and see what I can wrestle up for you. If nothing else, I'll put you to work on the ranch."

Jasper shook his head.

"Troy's right, you know. This won't get any better. It's going to haunt your ass until it manifests itself as ulcers and tumors and all kinds of shit. Trust me, it'll get exponentially worse. It won't go away."

Jasper had to admit he'd seen plenty evidence of that.

"Troy told me all about your conversation. Your mother died of cancer. You skipped town and changed your name. How's that working out for you so far?" Bud asked.

"Like shit."

"Give this a shot. What's the worst that could happen?"

Jasper didn't have to think long. "The worst that could happen is that someone could be maimed or killed. Look, I'm grateful to you and Troy. But I just can't. I talked to my father three days ago for the first time in a year. It's too soon to see him. It's too . . .soon."

There was silence. Finally, "Well, you can't say I didn't try."

185

Another uncomfortable quiet settled over the room. Jasper realized Bud was right; it was never going to be easy, not now, not a decade from now. And what if his old man was dying just like Lani's. Seeing him again was an intimidating proposition, but perhaps an opportunity to bury Junior McPherson once and for all. He had an inkling that if he did it, if he faced Robert McPherson right here and now, today, before the clock struck midnight, somehow his life might correct itself, like a dislocated shoulder popped back into place.

"You'd go with me?"

Bud nodded. "Every step of the way."

"Why would Troy do this for me?"

"You saved his ass in that bar, and you didn't do it because he was a rock star. You did it because his ass needed saving. He also feels guilty about what happened at your store."

"Yeah. I didn't believe him at first."

"Well, he was telling the truth."

Jasper exhaled deeply. What the old man would look like? Sound like? Was he still so disconsolate that he was barely alive, or had he managed to retrofit himself back into the tyrannical dictator of yesteryear? Everyone was becoming someone else, ever since Doris had died. Jasper needed some sense of closure because he was mentally, emotionally, and spiritually spent. Add to that he was too broke to return for a visit anytime soon, and too fragile to return for good. "Shit, OK," he heard himself say. He couldn't believe it. He was actually going to do it. "I'm in. The less I think about it, the easier it'll be. Now that my old man's tracked me down, he's probably on his way out here. We might pass him on a plane flying in the opposite direction. Should I call first?"

"No," Bud said. "Never relinquish the element of surprise."

What Jasper regretted most was depriving himself of the afterglow of having spent the night with Lani Sablan from the island of Guam. He would call her from the road. "I feel like I've just agreed to become the first human parachutist. I wish I had something stronger to drink than tea."

Before he packed, Jasper gave Bud a quick tour of the apartment, an abbreviated version of Bud's tour of the ranch. "The place came furnished. The only thing I actually own is that." he said, pointing to the shiny guitar-shaped clock that had been carved from a rare redwood, two weeks' pay.

Bud pursed his lips and nodded.

"Maybe you could make it run counterclockwise for me. I thought that was pretty cool the way you had all those clocks going backwards. It would make a great conversation piece." Jasper all jitters and nervous energy.

The phone rang and Jasper answered it. After a long pause he said, "Hold on for a second," and covered the mouthpiece with the palm of his hand. "Bud, it's Tony, my boss at Thyme Market. He's willing to give me another chance. He wants to know if I can come in starting tomorrow morning."

"How much was he paying you?"

"Four-fifty an hour."

"No dice," Bud whispered. "I'll get you ten bucks an hour, minimum."

Jasper swallowed hard and told Tony he intended to pursue other options. Tony told Jasper to call back within twenty-four hours if he changed his mind. Within twenty-four hours, everything might be a mere whisper of what it was right now.

* * *

As Flight 321 touched down with a screech, Jasper was startled awake.

"You look pale," Bud said.

Jasper rubbed his eyes. "I just dreamt I was in a fistfight with the old man, but I couldn't hit him because I didn't have any arms. I kept swinging but there was nothing but air."

Bud smiled.

"What do you think it means?"

"It means subconsciously you don't want to hurt him, but consciously you want to knock him out cold."

Jasper could see blurry waves of heat rising off the tarmac. His stomach rumbled. They rented a car and drove out of Lambert Airport on a mission that felt like a covert military operation. It was agreed that Bud would drive directly over to Belleville, drop Jasper off, and wait for him at the bowling alley down the street.

"I don't even know your last name," Jasper said.

"Black. Bud Black."

Jasper turned the air conditioner on high and fiddled with the radio until he found KSHE, the rock station he was raised on. They passed downtown and all the comfortable old haunts: the sand-blasted red brick buildings, churches, saloons, and the Gateway Arch, a.k.a. the world's largest croquet wicket. He had forgotten the beauty of the skyline, the skyscrapers, the hours spent at Busch Stadium sneaking down from general admission into box seats, hanging out after the game by the statue of Stan Musial, begging players for autographs. As an infant, Jasper's first words were: *mama, dada, Stan the Man.* It was all so familiar and yet so foreign.

Crossing the Mississippi, Jasper noted that the water level seemed especially low. Apparently it'd been a dry spring. Bud, who'd grown up with Troy just upriver in Alton, agreed. He'd never seen the water this low or this muddy. A road sign read: THE PEOPLE OF ILLINOIS WELCOME YOU.

They drove through the squalor of East St. Louis, one of the highest homicide rates per capita in North America and a dangerous place to be especially after dark with its burned-out storefronts and steel bars fortifying pawn shop windows. Jasper's father had grown up there. Pawn your weapon on Monday morning, buy it back on Friday night.

They finally reached West Main Street in Belleville, and Jasper felt a sense of doom. Beyond deja vu, it was more like deja voodoo. Memories about his mother loomed like vultures in trees on every street corner. They drove past his old high school, grade school, and the basketball courts where he had developed a deadly jump shot in his refuge from the old man's temper. The lush lawns and brick homes stood in stark contrast to the cactus, sand, and adobe of the desert. Each dwelling and edifice had a story to tell, and most had secrets to conceal. There wasn't a tavern in the entire town that he couldn't walk into and find someone to buy him a beer. Junior McPherson was rising in his bloodstream.

At twilight, the rental car coasted into Jasper's empty driveway at 235 Magellan Drive. The lawn was in an advanced state of neglect. Weeds had waged a full-court press, and dandelion tendrils floated on the evening breeze in a miniature ballet of insurrection. The hedges seemed hell-bent on consuming the house whole. The maple trees were dead, the foundation cracked. Rolled-up newspapers littered the sidewalk. Shingles were peeling off the roof.

After a moment, Bud said, "Inhale through your nose and exhale through your mouth. You have nothing to fear but fear itself."

"FDR?"

"That's right. Be strong. Don't let him smell your fear. I know this is painful, but pain is just the body's way of eliminating weakness. You can do it. Look him in the eye and hear what the fucker has to say." Bud stuck out his chin and pointed to it. "Let him hit you right in the kisser. Show him that you can take anything he can dish out. And no matter how long it takes, I'll be down at that bowling alley waiting for you. Look for the guy rolling the three-hundred game." Bud grinned from behind his sunglasses.

Jasper peered at himself in the rear-view mirror, hair tousled from sleeping on the plane, eyes decidedly bloodshot. He wanted to be back in bed with Lani, the fan swiping away at them, rustling her hair.

"You don't have to say a word," Bud said. "Let him do all the talking."

"Why are you doing this? Troy feels some obligation, but why you?"

"Because," Bud said, "it's the American way to root for the underdog."

"Gee, thanks." Jasper was especially cognizant of the state of the lawn. This was certainly not the finely manicured yard of the Robert McPherson he knew. He thought about Bud and Vietnam and overcoming hysterical blindness. It inspired him just enough to open the car door and step out of the vehicle. "Time to storm the Bastille. Wish me luck."

"Remember, he called you." Bud pulled away and Jasper was on his own, deep behind enemy lines.

He marched up the sidewalk and found the spare house key hidden in where it always was, under the welcome mat, which was so well-worn it read simply: E L C O. He picked the key up but, on second thought, replaced it under the mat. He knocked on the door. The mailbox overflowed.

Across the street at St. Martin's Catholic Church and its adjacent playground, a group of boys played kickball. When Jasper was in high school, his father, wearing only boxer shorts, had chased him through the churchyard. Jasper didn't remember what family felony he'd committed, but some of his friends had witnessed the incident though never mentioned it, which made the spectacle worse.

He knocked on the door a little more deliberately and rang

the doorbell. Maybe he'd find the old man with a shotgun in his mouth and his brains blown all over the wall. He should've made Bud wait. He walked around to the garage to look for the car, but the windows were covered. Maybe the old man was working a swing shift. Impatient, he unlocked the front door with the spare key and poked his head inside.

"Anybody ho . . . ?" his voice trailed off. The living room was in shambles, and the dining room was annihilated, reduced to a skeleton of its former self. Sections of floorboards were missing, and the walls had gaping holes the size of fists. He could see straight down into the basement from the kitchen. Clothes, canned goods, trash, frames without pictures, and countless miscellaneous items were strewn everywhere. He turned on a light and cockroaches scurried. Everything was filthy and smelled like rotting garbage. The gentle geometry of spider webs stretched out in every corner, eternal resting grounds to a multitude of dead insects in varying stages of decomposition. It was amazing to think this was the same house he'd grown up in, that all this could've happened in less than a year. Jasper was a deep-sea diver swimming through the wreckage of a vessel on which he'd once sailed. He walked cautiously, guardedly, praying he wouldn't find his father in pieces.

Descending the fourteen stairs to see what if anything remained of his bedroom, the third step still creaked, which was all it had taken to awaken his mother late at night if he tried to slip in after curfew. She'd had a highly developed sense of maternal radar.

His old room was in relatively good shape. Despite being coated in a filmy gauze of dust, the posters and St. Louis Cardinal pennants were still hanging on the walls, and his desk, chair, and beat-up old dresser hadn't moved. Everything was right where Junior McPherson had left it. Jasper said the name aloud, "Junior McPherson." Spooky, he thought.

He meandered around the rest of the basement and as it had been upstairs, there was extensive devastation: garlands of diaphanous cobwebs suspended from the ceiling, structural damage to the walls. Even the foundation had been violated. In one corner, there was a jackhammer resting against a support beam and beneath it, chunks of concrete had been excavated down to the bare dirt. Was he digging a grave? A tunnel to China? Two thirty-five Magellan Drive was a shell. If its condition reflected Robert McPherson's state of mind, maybe this unannounced visit wasn't such a good idea.

The garage had been his father's sanctuary. When he was growing up, Jasper tried to avoid it as much as possible. It was particularly unsettling being back in this dank, musty part of the house. Tools of all shapes and sizes were hung on walls and scattered on the floor. An oak barrel of nails was dumped over onto the oil-stained cement. Old peanut butter jars were nailed through the lid to the overhead support beams, each jar containing different-sized screws, nuts, and bolts. Next to the garage door was the lawn mower and an assortment of rusted garden tools.

On a homemade table was Robert McPherson's collection of war memorabilia. He had been in the Navy at the tail-end of World War II, and it occurred to Jasper for the first time that his father had spoken of being on Guam back in the days when he was a sailor in the Pacific theater. Over the years, his father had accumulated an assortment of pistols and rifles, a bayonet, grenades, old uniforms, news clippings, photographs, and a glass case that displayed various ribbons and medals. Jasper didn't know how much action his father had actually seen.

Near the back of the table was an old cloth gym bag which he'd never seen before. Inside there were dozens of letters, mostly correspondence between his parents. While Robert was fighting overseas, Jasper's mother worked for Ma Bell. Jasper reached inside an envelope postmarked December 12, 1944, written in flowery cursive penmanship, doodlings of arrow-pierced hearts decorating the marginalia.

Dearest Love of Mine,

Received three of your letters today, each more of a boost than the one before. The days and nights seem to be getting longer without you, although I keep telling myself the day will come, God willing, that this separation ends and our life together can finally begin. I look at the man in the moon and send him messages for you. Look at him tonight when you're lonely and know I'm looking at him, too.

Thanks for sending my cardigans and those delightful pictures of you and your girlfriends at the lake. The boys in the barracks are calling you, "Legs McPherson." I told them you were an athlete and they seem to have no trouble believing it. Please send me the lyrics to our songs, especially Sinatra and Cole Porter. Your halibut recipe sounds mouthwatering. I can almost taste it from here.

I love you with all my heart, Honey. I don't know how I'd get through this without you. Promise me not to worry so much. You're right that the battlefield changes many men, but it won't change me. Ike is going to win this thing before you can say "mares eat oats and does eat oats and little lambs eat ivy." I pray this will be my last Christmas away from home. Always remember my darling, I love 'em big and I love 'em small, but I love my Doris best of all!

In My Thoughts Always,
Your Loving Husband

Jasper folded the faded yellow letter into thirds and returned it to its tattered envelope. He felt guilty for having read it and sickened by its irony. He heard the front door and then the squeak of the third step. He zipped the gym bag and returned it to the exact spot he'd found it. When he stood up and turned around, he was facing a .38 snub-nosed revolver.

"Hands in the air!" Robert McPherson screamed. "Now!"

Jasper raised his hands, heart pounding, arms shaking. "Don't shoot me. It's Junior. Your son."

His father lowered the gun and raised his hand to his forehead, shading his eyes to get a better view. "Junior? Is that you?"

"Yes," Jasper said, hoping this admission wouldn't prove to be fatal. "It's me."

Robert McPherson turned on the fluorescent light and approached cautiously. His hair was gray, his steps measured. He wore horned-rimmed glasses, which Jasper had never seen and which obscured the familiar scar on his eyebrow. There was still a white spot on his right forearm where the word *Doris* used to be.

"Well I'll be damned, it really is you. Thank you, Jesus." He used the pistol to make the sign of the cross. "For thine is the kingdom, the power, and the glory for now and forever." He reached out and embraced Jasper who was relieved to be alive. His heart reverberated inside his ribcage.

When the cold barrel of the gun inadvertently touched the back of his neck, Jasper pushed away. He should've called first.

"Happy irthday, son. I didn't want you to see the place like this. I've been redecorating. Let me look at you." He turned Jasper around. "You look like you've dropped a few pounds."

"You look like you've gained a few," Jasper snapped back. "Maybe you should lay off the Tootsie Rolls." He was starting to feel like Junior McPherson again and decided that this droll exchange of witty repartee was over. This trip was strictly business. He glanced at his watch and set a one-hour time limit. That way he had a goal, an ending to look forward to. "I can't stay long. I've got to get back to Tucson," he said.

Robert McPherson looked down at the gun. "Sorry to scare the life out of you like that. I got robbed a couple months ago, and I saw the light on so I thought . . . I go to prayer meetings

194

on Monday and Thursday nights over at St. Ignatius. I'd love to take you with me some night. Pentecostal. Anyway, I'm usually not home until much later, but tonight I decided to leave early. Something told me to head home. So when I pulled in the driveway and saw the lights on, I thought to myself, they've cased the place. I sure as hell never expected to see you. You're a sight for sore eyes, Junior, you really are. I've been absolutely beside myself trying to find you."

"If you're afraid of getting robbed, why is the key still under the doormat?"

"Everything's the way it was when your mother. . . left us. I haven't changed anything. If they want it, they can have it. There's nothing left of value anyway. It's all just a façade. Like the body is a façade for the soul."

Relying on Bud's advice, Jasper peered defiantly into the old man's eyes. "Look, you called me. If you've got something to say, say it."

These words appeared to deflate Robert McPherson. He stared, sighed dramatically, and shook his head. Jasper hoped he wouldn't cry as he had before on the phone.

"Have it your way," Robert McPherson said. "Come on upstairs. I have something to show you."

Jasper skipped over the infamous third step from the top. He missed his mother now more than ever, but he wouldn't want her to witness this. The obliteration of her home was blasphemous. She was lucky not to be around to see it. He resolved not to allow the old man to browbeat or humiliate him. If he had to, Jasper would physically defend himself. He knew not to let the gun out of his sight.

14. No One Is a Stranger to You

Robert McPherson turned on the rest of the lights upstairs. Though he wouldn't have imagined it possible, Jasper could see that 235 Magellan Drive was even more draconian than his initial reconnaissance suggested. He used to scrub these kitchen walls with soap and water in exchange for a modest allowance, which he generally spent on concert tickets. Now the walls were filthy, holes pock-marked the plaster, and the gossamer architecture of even more spider webs and cobwebs coalescing in corners. Doris McPherson, a woman who loved clean walls, would have been appalled.

They stopped at a room over the garage which, in another lifetime, had been designated as storage for towels and linens. It was now padlocked. Robert McPherson searched his pockets for his keys, the gun still pointed toward the floor. "I know what you must be thinking," he said. "How could anyone live like this?"

Jasper resisted the temptation to make snide comments about the post-Armageddon motif. "How you live is your business."

"When the house got robbed, I was vulnerable. I'm either at work or church, so I'm never here to protect all this shit, pardon my language, Lord. Fortunately they didn't get much. I don't have anything that anyone would want." Robert McPherson inhaled and exhaled through his nose. "I sleep here, that's all. It's the strangest thing. I can't live here, but I can't leave either. I'm a sitting duck for thieves." He waggled the pistol. "I carry this as a precaution, in case they come while I'm home. Maybe I should just put up a sign on the porch with my daily schedule." He smirked and unlocked the door.

The cramped room had been transformed into sleeping quarters and was, in direct contrast to the rest of the premises, immaculate. This was the Robert McPherson Jasper remembered: underwear and socks stacked in an open footlocker, shoes shined and lined up on the floor, the bed made with military corners and just begging for a quarter to be bounced off it. There were also papers and envelopes organized on a small wooden desk. Order. Discipline. Control.

The expanse of one wall displayed framed photographs, mostly old black-and-whites, a shrine of sorts to Doris McPherson. Dozens of pictures were thumb-tacked together that featured his mother from early teens up until her fortieth birthday, when the relationship between his parents fell into the vortex of its downward spiral. Interspersed like afterthoughts were photos of Jasper in his previous incarnation as Junior McPherson.

He couldn't stop looking at his mother.

"Those," his father motioned toward the baby pictures, "when we first got you, were the happiest days of my life. Your mother's, too. When I came home from work, you used to wave your arms up in the air, a signal for me to pick you up and hold you above my head. You'd laugh so hard your face would turn red. It scared your mother silly. Poor doting Doris, always afraid you were going to break. You were the happiest little baby I ever laid eyes on, kiddo. Top drawer. Those were the days."

His father had aged dramatically. In less than a year, his complexion was the color of oysters, the corners of his eyes had new wrinkles, and he had lots more gray hair. He had aged more in a year than Jimmy Carter had in four.

"Can I get you something to drink?" his father asked removing his necktie. "A beer? You're legal now."

Jasper had always wanted to drink beer with his father, talk sports, talk politics, play pool, do the things other guys did with their dads. "No thanks," he said. He sat on a lawn chair, next to the old TV. The eyes of Jesus from a Sacred Heart painting seemed to bore into him. Forty-eight minutes to go.

Robert McPherson set the revolver on the desk. "Son, whether you believe it or not, I love you and I always have. Your mother and I have already had this conversation with you once, when you were five years old, but I guess it didn't take so let's try again."

Jasper didn't respond.

"There's something different about you," Robert McPherson said. "You seem harder. More confident. Like you've grown up all of a sudden. I think that desert has made a man out of you, Junior."

"That desert has made Jasper Trueblood out of me."

Robert McPherson lowered his head and pushed his glasses up. He mumbled something, then said, "I guess the only thing to do is to begin at the beginning. See that one?" He pointed to a photo of Doris McPherson in her youth, dapper in a mink stole and black mittens, standing in snow. "Your mother and I met in forty-two, just a couple months before that was taken. We were married in forty-four, two weeks before I left for the Navy. If anything happened to me, I wanted to make sure she got the benefits, so we got hitched before I shipped out. She wanted to have a baby more than anything, but it didn't happen before I left for war."

Jasper cringed, not eager to hear about Robert and Doris' sex life.

"A fertility specialist checked us out. He said there was nothing wrong physically, we just had to keep trying. But that wasn't easy for your mother. Patience was never her strong suit. She wanted a baby and she wanted one right then. The more we tried, the more frustrated we got, and it went on like that forever. By fifty-eight, after all those years of trying, we decided, well, *she* decided, that it was time to look into adoption. We went to Catholic Charities and after a year of haggling with lawyers and legal maneuvering," Robert McPherson looked straight into Jasper's eyes, "we got you."

Jasper snorted. "So what are you saying? I'm adopted?" He laughed, but then in a sober tone said, "Is that what you're saying?" This was what the old man had meant on the phone: *there are things you should know about your life.* Skeletons were spilling out of the closet all at once. It was like some bad soap opera, and he was playing the lead. "I don't fucking believe you."

"I'm afraid I can prove it." Robert McPherson pushed off the bed and went to the locker. He hauled out a cardboard box and a large manila envelope from which he extracted an official-looking certificate, embossed by a raised seal. "Here."

Scrolled at the top were the words: ADOPTION DECREE. The type was badly faded, names and signatures nearly illegible. Jasper skimmed over a second document titled: AMENDED BIRTH RECORD. Both were from the state of Illinois. As he read and reread their contents, it became evident that his entire life had been one meticulously orchestrated lie. He hadn't cried since before his mother's funeral. He couldn't even remember the last time he cried, but tears filled his eyes. "You're l-lying." Jasper's voice cracked. "It's a hoax."

"No son, it's true. When you disappeared, I realized I had a responsibility to inform you of your birthright. It was the proper thing to do. That's why I hired the detective. Who knows how much longer I'll be around? I needed to tell you these things before it was too late. When Doris died and they put me in that fucking nut house over in St. Louis, pardon my language, Lord, one of the shrinks actually made some sense. We were talking about you, and she said that I should come clean, that someday you might need medical records or your kids might want to look up their family tree. Who knows? In any case, she's the one who convinced me to tell you. I'm sorry it took so long."

This would be an apropos time to grab the pistol and drop this prick in a pool of blood, Jasper thought. He stood, feeling the heat of his own face. He believed he could take the old man in hand-to-hand combat, and his right fist tightened. He shifted his weight back and forth. "What kind of a sick motherfucker would lie to his own kid for twenty-one years?"

"There's more to it than that. Sit down, Junior. I'll tell you the rest."

"My name is not *Junior*," he shouted, continuing to stand, facing the other direction with wet eyes fixed on the Sacred Heart. He breathed heavily through his nose, both fists now clenched.

"The week before you started kindergarten, your mother and I explained all this to you. I guess you were too young to understand, but you were such a precocious little fella. We consulted a child psychologist, and so we'd all agreed that five was the right age. We sat you down in the living room, and Doris explained how mommy and daddy wanted a baby so God allowed another woman to bring you into the world for us. Doris asked if you understood. You nodded, but I could see your little mind at work. You looked at Doris and said, 'Mom, where's my real mom?' Doris spent the rest of the day locked in the bedroom crying her eyes out. I slept on the couch that night." His father smiled and just as quickly that smile dissolved. "You never mentioned it, and we wondered if you had blocked it out for some reason. Maybe you thought it was just another bedtime story. I wanted to talk to you about it when you were older, but Doris was beside herself. I just couldn't put her through it again."

"So I'll ask the question again," Jasper said at a lower decibel. "Where's my real mom?"

Robert McPherson pointed at Jasper. "I don't know where your biological mother is, the court records are sealed. But your real mother is sitting at the right hand of Jesus Christ even as we speak." He pointed at the painting of the Sacred Heart. "Don't forget that. No mother ever loved a son more than Doris loved you."

Jasper tossed the documents back on the bed. "This is bullshit. She would never do this to me. *You* would, but she wouldn't."

His father pulled a thin book out of the manila envelope. "Here."

The well-worn satin cover featured frolicking bunny rabbits twirling blue ribbons that read: MY BABY BOOK. Inside were illustrations of birds and lambs, a stork with a baby bundle in its beak, flowers, puppies, balloons, and birthday cakes, as well as Jasper's personal history. There was a section for his birth announcement, a gift tally from the baby shower, height and weight chart, and a graph depicting baby's first crawl, first step, first words. Also noted in minute detail were baby's favorite food, color, song, all inscribed by Doris McPherson's unmistakably loop-happy calligraphy.

To Our Son Junior,

Mommy & Daddy waited for you for so very long. It wasn't God's will that Mommy carry a baby in her tummy like most mothers. Mommy & Daddy prayed that God would send us a little boy just like you some other way. So one day a woman who couldn't take care of you but carried you in her tummy gave you to Mommy & Daddy to be their little boy. From the moment we saw you, we knew God had answered our prayers. You were ours to love forever. Mommy & Daddy hope that as you grow older, you'll come to realize how much you mean to us.

At 14 months you started waving to Daddy when he left for work. You always got so tickled whenever Daddy would walk in the door. Around 16 mos. you knew your two stuffed dogs by name, Morgan and Snowball, & often got them & kissed them when Mommy would ask you to.

Loved your cars and balls. At 18 mos. you fed yourself real well & all the time. You said quite a few words & gave almost every word a try. At 22 mos. you could count to five & loved to write with a pencil on anything you could get your hands on. You recited your ABC's at 27 mos. Stuffed your pants with Kleenex in case you had an "accident." 32 mos. & you say just about anything now & get into everything. You are a very active child & we can't keep you down. Play baseball with Mommy in the backyard like a gold glover.

40 mos. & you won't go to bed without Mommy & Daddy going with you. So we do, until you fall asleep. At 48 mos. you love to hold a conversation with anyone. No one is a stranger to you. Always ask Mommy to tell you a story before you go to sleep every nite. Play outside most of the day. Like to watch cartoons on TV each morning. Told us you'd rather wait until you're older to go to church with us because you don't like to sit still for so long. So maybe when you're older you'll get more sense in your head.

That was all. Jasper closed the book, aghast. The entries stopped just before, *Mom, where's my real mom?*

"After all the paperwork went through for your adoption," Robert McPherson said, "the most amazing thing happened. Doris finally got pregnant. The doctors said the psychological barriers had been broken, if you believe in that sort of thing. So after more than a decade of trying, I finally knocked the old girl up. Well, to be truthful, I wanted to call off the adoption. I mean, we were finally going to have one of our own, right? But she wouldn't hear of it. I can still hear her telling the attorney on the phone, *that's my baby, mister, and don't you forget it.*

"Exactly three months to the day after we picked you up, Doris had a miscarriage. A bad one. There would be no more pregnancies. Of course, this made her love you even more, if that's possible. You became her whole life. If I was tough on you growing up, it was because I didn't want you to be soft. I was afraid she was going to spoil you. I'm not an educated man, but I know the world's a rough place. I didn't want you to think anyone was going to give you something for nothing." Robert McPherson picked up his Bible from the nightstand and held it in his hands. "I was the last person on Earth who should've been a parent, I admit that. I'm too selfish. I had the G.I. Bill waiting for me and I could have gone to college, but I married your mother instead and went to work. I was a lousy father. Just look at you. I hardly recognize my own son." He reached out but Jasper backed away.

Jasper bit his lip. He'd heard enough. "You know, I read your phony love letters stashed away in the garage. 'Look at the moon and know it's the same moon I'm looking at.' Whatever happened to all that?" Jasper pointed at the painting of the Sacred Heart. "Look at your God and tell me it's OK to lie for twenty-one years to someone you supposedly love. Your God is cool with that? Does your God tell you to torture me my entire life and treat me like shit? To whip me in the bathtub with a leather belt because you think I'm a pussy for taking a bath instead of a fucking three-minute military shower? You're like one of those killers on death row who runs to Jesus just before they pull the switch. Well, maybe Jesus can forgive you, but I can't. Did you know there's scientific proof that stress causes cancer?"

His father laid the Bible down, closed his eyes, and made the sign of the cross. Then he was still. "I deserve this. The only thing keeping me going is the knowledge that Jesus Christ is my personal Lord and Savior, and the hope that someday soon I'll be taken away from this cesspool and reunited with Doris in the kingdom of Heaven."

What was left to say to someone waiting to die? Jasper needed a long, hot shower to wash away this fiction. "I feel sick."

"Can I get you something?" Robert McPherson asked as he dabbed his eyes with a handkerchief.

"You know, since we're being so brutally honest here, maybe you could answer a question for me." He checked his watch. Eighteen minutes to go.

Robert McPherson was now holding a rosary.

"Let's say I was adopted. Let's say everything is just as you've described. That would explain a lot. It would explain why we have so little in common and why you called me a *bastard* all the time. You felt disconnected from me, like I wasn't really yours. I can see that now. And I can see why it would be difficult to get close to a child that wasn't your own flesh and blood. I mean, that's just human nature. I would've probably felt the same way."

Robert McPherson interrupted. "But—"

"No," Jasper raised his hand in the air, "please let me finish. What I can't figure out is why you treated her so horribly even when you knew she was dying. She was your wife, man. She had cancer. How could you do that to your own wife? And please don't say you never hit her," he added, "because if you do I swear I'll take that gun and shoot you in the face."

Robert McPherson dropped his rosary on the bed and rubbed his eyes. He took a long breath and let out a whimper. "I was afraid." He blew his nose into a handkerchief. "I was terrified."

"Of what?"

"Of everything. Of this. Of being left alone without her."

Jasper was unable to muster much empathy or sympathy as his father retreated into himself. "Why couldn't you do something nice for her? Why couldn't you take her on a vacation or some goddamn thing? She was your fucking wife."

"I was a fool." His father straightened up, seemed to recapture what remained of his composure. "Now, let me ask you a question. You have a girlfriend out there in Arizona?"

Jasper didn't respond.

"Ever have a fight with her? A quarrel of some kind? Well, multiply that times thirty-four years of marriage and then come talk to me. It ain't as easy as it seems, Junior. As for you, I made a lot of mistakes. We didn't know things like they do today. My mother didn't tell me she loved me, but she didn't have to. She worked from sunrise to sundown six days a week to take care of us. That's how I knew she loved me. That's how you showed love in those days. And my old man?"

Jasper cut in. "Your old man was a no-good drunk who ran out on the family during the Great Depression. When you were seven you ironed your own shirts and hauled ashes all day for a dime, which you gave to your mother. I know all this. You're not answering my question. Why did you treat her like shit even when you knew she was dying?"

"Hey, I'll take the heat for my mistakes. I'm not going to blame it all on my parents like they do today—everyone singing the blues cause mommy didn't breast-feed 'em. I'm just saying I wasn't prepared for fatherhood. I was a dumb sailor doing anything in the world I could think of to make your mother happy. You're right. Guilty as charged. I was shit as a father and not much better as a husband. But you weren't always the perfect child, either. Put yourself in my position. I come home from a long day at work just to walk in the door and have your mother tell me you had to be spanked, which for some reason was always my responsibility. I didn't want to paddle you. I didn't want to dole out the discipline. I just wanted to come home and eat dinner, but your mother was a demanding woman."

Jasper sat back down in the lawn chair. He noted that Troy had intuited all this.

"We agreed to raise you together, as a team, consulting on everything, but eventually she took over the child-rearing duties. I was relegated to fixing things and being the hatchet man. I resented the hell out of that." Robert McPherson untied his shoes and placed them under the bed.

Jasper remembered telling Troy about the fake spanking.

"I was trapped. I was nothing more than a paycheck around here. When your mother was diagnosed with cancer, I wanted to run like hell," Robert McPherson laughed. "I wanted to run and never look back. I was never more afraid in my life. Not even in the war. I'd become a coward, and that's probably why I tried so hard to make a man out of you. But you're wrong about one thing. I loved you just as much as Doris did. The day we got you, I felt like my life had truly begun. Those first years were the best ever for Doris and me. I took her for granted. We could have had so much more. I asked God why He took her instead of me. I begged Him to take me, too, but one night after I'd been reading the Scriptures and praying for four or five hours, I saw Jesus and He said, 'Robert, this is not your time.' That's when I realized I had to keep going. I had to find a way to keep pushing on."

Jasper rubbed his face. Twelve minutes.

"I swear I heard those words as clear as can be. Robert, this is not your time. I don't expect you to believe this, and frankly I don't care if you do or not," Robert McPherson was laying on the bed, eyes fixated on the ceiling. He pointed to a spot. "But an image of Jesus Christ appeared to me right there. Praise the Lord. Right there on those ceiling tiles."

Jasper looked up.

"I don't think about tomorrow. I don't think about next week. Just today. Baby steps." Robert McPherson held out a holy card with angels on the front.

Jasper turned it over:

In memory of our dearly departed
DORIS LYNN MCPHERSON
Born: October 20, 1930
Died: December 2, 1978
from her loving family

"Keep it," Robert McPherson said. "I have more. Keep it all." He stashed everything back into the manila envelope. "There's all sorts of keepsakes in here." He set it on the floor next to Jasper's lawn chair. "Your first drawings, old report cards, family pictures . . . all kinds of mementos."

Jasper wanted to feel compassion, understanding, tenderness—something, but just couldn't manage it. The discussion was over and more than anything, he wanted out of 235 Magellan Drive. As for the adoption bombshell, he knew it would take time to assimilate. Troy and Bud had been right. About everything. This had been a trip worth taking. He felt lighter, cleaner, a snake that had shed its skin. Four minutes left. He grabbed the manila envelope. "Listen, I gotta run," he said.

Robert McPherson wiped his eyes one last time. "I love you. You can change your name, but you'll always be my son."

Jasper faced the door but he did not step toward the threshold.

"It doesn't take much to make a baby," his father said, "but it takes a lifetime to take care of one."

Jasper waited. His last name, Trueblood, took on a whole new timbre.

"Perhaps," Robert McPherson rose from the bed, "if we can't be father and son, we could try being friends."

There was a long pause. "I don't know," Jasper said. "Maybe in time. I'm not Junior McPherson anymore. I'm not exactly sure who I am, but I'm not Junior McPherson." He would not hug Robert nor shake his hand. As a kid in school, Jasper always resented being tricked by classmates, being the butt of practical jokes. Now, he thought, it seemed his entire life had been a game of deception played by conniving adults in a court of law. A shell game called *adoption*. "I'll contact you when I'm ready. I have to leave."

Robert McPherson nodded.

Jasper made his way out of 235 Magellan Drive without further eye contact, thinking he'd never return, not for all the mud in the Mississippi River. He walked out the front door into the nightfall, careful not to turn around lest he be reduced to a pillar of salt. *No one is a stranger to you.* Ironic, Jasper thought. His life was populated by nothing but strangers. He was a stranger to himself.

As Jasper headed toward the bowling alley, he passed by the churchyard. The light was on in the rectory window, and he approached St. Martin's Catholic Church where fourteen years before he had dazzled Doris McPherson by becoming the first altar boy in his second grade class. He knocked on the rectory door, expecting the pastor, Father Ross, but instead, a woman answered. She was elderly and portly, gray hair in a bun, wearing an apron and an oven mitt on one hand. "May I help you?"

"Oh, hi. Uh, yes. My name is—" Jasper swallowed hard, "—Junior McPherson. I'm headed out of town tomorrow, and I was just wondering if Father Ross might be available for a minute or two. It wouldn't take long."

The woman had a creamy complexion and rosy cheeks, like Mrs. Claus. He guessed she was a maid, not knowing for sure if priests had maids.

"Certainly," she said. "Let me get him for you." She scurried off to fetch the good reverend, and Jasper supposed she'd seen her fair share of distressed parishioners pounding on the door with baskets full of despair. Doris McPherson had been a regular customer.

"Well, I'll be. *Junior McPherson*," Father Ross said with a big grin and teeth slightly yellowed from too many Winstons. He wore house slippers and the customary black suit, black shirt, but no collar. He still had that Norman Rockwell smile, an abundance of freckles speckling his cheeks, and all that bright red hair. Unlike Robert McPherson, Father Ross looked younger than Jasper remembered. "Come in, come in," he said welcoming Jasper with a hearty handshake.

"This is Sister Marie. She was sent here last spring. The diocese also gave us a new associate pastor since you've been gone. Father Roundtree."

Jasper had never seen a nun out of her habit and wondered if this were even legal. He politely took Sister Marie's meaty paw in his. "Pleasure to meet you." Nuns still gave him the creeps, even the nice ones.

"Sister Marie was just about to take some oatmeal cookies out of the oven. Why don't you join us?"

"No thanks," Jasper said. The thought of food was repulsive. He patted his stomach. "Trying to watch my weight."

"Yeah, you're looking very good. All right then. Sister, please show Junior to the den. I have someone on the phone. Give me a minute and I'll be right with you."

The accommodating Sister Marie escorted Jasper to the den, which was decorated in cozy earth tones and lots of red leather furniture, bookshelves, and a fireplace glowing with embers. Jasper had been in this room before, many moons ago, and was still astonished at how civilian it felt. Take away the crucifix and portraits of the pope and bishop, and it could have belonged to anyone.

Father Ross had been the associate pastor when Jasper attended St. Martin's Elementary School, and he was well known for the brevity of his sermons and leniency in the confessional. He also played third base on the church softball team and drank beer after the games with the other men. The only thing that distinguished Father Ross from any regular parishioner was his collar.

"It's good to see you, Junior. Have a seat. I heard you disappeared for awhile."

"I went to college in Arizona."

"What brings you back to town? Have you seen your dad?"

Jasper cleared his throat and leaned back in the chair. "Actually, I just came from there."

"How is he?" Father Ross lit a cigarette and set it in a large glass ashtray.

"Not great. Do you ever see him?"

"I haven't spoken with Bob recently, but occasionally I'll see him in the middle of the week, hiding in a back pew during seven o'clock Mass. I used to see him out working in the yard occasionally, but not lately. He's a sick man, Junior."

"Yeah," Jasper said. "He's become some sorta religious zealot. It's hard to talk to him. You should see the house."

"He's using religion as a crutch," Father Ross said. "Using the church to prop him up. The good Lord helps those who help themselves. Your father needs to be in therapy in order to deal with your mother's death. He needs professional help. God gives us all tools, Junior, but prayer must be accompanied by action. God can move mountains but you have to bring a shovel."

"Can I ask you a question? On the subject of my mother?"

"Sure," the priest said, exhaling a plume of bluish-white smoke.

"Do you keep baptismal records as far back as nineteen fifty-nine? I was christened by Monsignor Collins."

"Sure we do. The diocese office has them."

"Would my file contain a copy of my birth certificate? Anything relative to my actual birth?"

"Why do you ask?"

"Well, this is from a man who sees Jesus on his bedroom ceiling, so I don't know if it's a hallucination or what, but my father claims I was adopted."

"No need to dig out any files for that, Junior," Father Ross took another drag. "I know for a fact that you're adopted. Monsignor Collins discussed it with me after one of your mother's visits. I remember it quite distinctly."

Jasper leaned back in his chair, raking his fingers through his hair.

"I'm sorry. I just assumed you knew."

"Yes," Jasper said. "One would assume that, wouldn't one?"

"Can I get you something to drink? I've got some root beer in the refrigerator."

"No thanks. I really can't stay."

"So how are you doing, Junior? Since Doris died, I mean."

"Well, I thought I was holding up pretty well until this adoption thing blindsided me. The old man just told me, not more than five minutes ago. I feel like someone just knocked the wind out of me, and that someone was my mother. How could she do this? How could she hide something like this for all these years? He said they told me when I was little, but I don't remember any of it."

"I don't know what your parents' reasons were, Junior, but I do know one thing. Doris loved you with her whole heart and soul. In fact, she loved you as much as any mother has ever loved any child, I'm convinced of that. She was a good Catholic and a devoted member of this parish, but all human beings make mistakes. It doesn't change how much she loved you or how well she raised you. After you're finished being angry with her, you be sure to remember that, all right?"

Jasper sighed. "You know, maybe I do have time for one quick drink. Got anything stronger than root beer?"

15. Counterclockwise In Kansas City

A few days after Jasper and Bud returned to the ranch from Belleville, Illinois—home of Jimmy Connors—Jasper cleaned out his apartment and left the keys on the kitchen table. He was going to work on the ranch, and Bud offered him ten dollars an hour to start. The labor would be physically demanding but in addition to his increase in salary, there were perks that, as Bud put it, Thyme Market couldn't touch. Jasper would live rent-free in the guesthouse out back with the other ranch hands, participate in the evening meal as long as he was willing to take his weekly turn in the kitchen, swim in the pool, use the spa, and Bud would even fix the blown piston on his motorcycle.

"All I ask," Bud said, "is an honest day's work for an honest day's pay."

Jasper would work forty hours a week, eight hours a day, and one weekend day per month. There would be no one looking over his shoulder. He'd receive thirty paid minutes for lunch, but could also take more time as needed. Water breaks were always encouraged.

"Is Troy around?"

"No," Bud said. "He went on vacation. I'm not really sure where."

Jasper started his new job and Bud had been right—it was exhausting. Shoveling manure and clearing stones with a pickax and wheelbarrow were Jasper's most stimulating tasks. The job gave him lots of time to think, too much time. He'd was fixated on his spurious birth and Robert McPherson's devious ambush. Does a five-year-old forget a declarative statement that ends with a response like: *Mom, where's my real mom?* He searched his memory but there was no recollection of the kindergarten-era conversation. It was like amnesia due to severe head trauma. Between the physical and mental fatigue, he could barely stand up in the shower by day's end. He was hunched over, his skeleton stuck in Phase Three of the evolutionary chart.

Jasper's other preoccupation, Lani, called the night she left for Guam and he hadn't heard from her since. Two weeks later he had mailed her a letter, but no reply. Did she ever think about him or the night they spent together? He hoped her father was well. Come hell or high water, as Robert McPherson would say, Jasper would meet up again with Lani Sablan from the island of Guam.

The physical exertion of work on the ranch provided one unanticipated benefit; his belly was tight. He'd shed those final pounds, and he got a good tan in the process, all a young person could really ask of any job. He was inclined to go bar hopping and show off his new physique, but could scarcely scrape up enough energy at the end of the day, the result of too many desert rocks built into too many desert stone walls. It was the first time he had saved any money.

He mostly stayed to himself in the guest house, writing maudlin poems that dripped angst and self-pity, reading, watching TV, and occasionally playing poker with the other guys. He visited the main house once a day with the other hired hands for the evening meal and never saw Troy, who was off doing whatever it was that jet-set rock stars did when they weren't busy being jet-set rock stars. Besides Bud, Jasper's best friend was Betty, the maid, a sweet woman in her sixties who snorted when she laughed and cooked fabulous Italian dinners. In addition to an apple and banana in the morning, the evening meal was usually the only food he ever ate. He was more or less on a stress diet, a regimen of rumination and anxiety.

Doris McPherson had deceived him, not conceived him. And when she used to say he had her eyes, she'd been lying. "WHO—AM—I?" Jasper would bellow into the canyons on lonely weekend journeys. Sometimes his echoes were broken.

During his exiles into the Santa Catalinas, he spent hours spinning elaborate plot twists around his biological mother, speculating on who she might be. Before meeting Troy Archer, he'd have hoped for someone like Liz Taylor or Barbara Streisand, but now he understood that even acclaimed celebrities, affluent and powerful, had as many headaches as anyone else, maybe more. He prayed for only one thing: that she hadn't been damaged soul who'd been raped or molested. That would be too much. In football terms, that would be piling on. Pregnancy, labor, and childbirth were tough enough. He tried to imagine the anguish required to carry a baby full-term, endure the hell of delivery, and then walk away. That would have to change you in a permanent sort of way. He really wanted to find this woman and thank her, and he intended to keep looking no matter how long it took. As for the flip side, a biological father, Jasper never gave it a second thought. One Robert McPherson was enough.

* * *

It was an early morning in December, several months after the Unknowns' controversial final performance, and Troy was back from his solo vacation to Cabo San Lucas, his first excursion without Hilary Hightower in three years. He was laying in bed and reading the new John Lennon interview in *Playboy*, getting a feel for what his own interview in the magazine might look like when it would be released the following summer. Troy'd been doing a lot of reading—Hilary would have been proud. Lennon's voice and wit were unmistakable as he discussed his childhood, Yoko, their son, and his new album. And certainly no indepth discourse with John Lennon would be complete without a full appraisal of the Beatles' breakup.

The day after twelve thousand fans had witnessed the live implosion of the Unknowns, Bobby Lee had called to get Troy's perspective on the band's public demise and a reaction to the front page headline in the *Tucson Citizen*: "Unknowns Unravel On-Stage." Troy had talked to Bobby Lee on the phone for over an hour, but now he couldn't seem to remember two words of the conversation. He'd have to wait and see it in print.

Suddenly, with a quick tap-tap on the door, Bud rushed into the bedroom. "Troy, let me see that magazine." He was all revved up and winded from sprinting up the stairs. "You'll, never, believe, what's, happened, Troy," he said breathlessly. Bud paged forward to the interview and the pictures of Lennon. "Somebody killed John Lennon."

Troy laughed. "Yeah right, Bud. Who killed him? You?"

Bud turned on the TV. It was on every major channel.

They sat on the bed and stared at the screen. The night before, John Lennon had been shot five times in the chest with hollow-point bullets. The TV coverage was reporting live from the scene of the crime at the Dakota Hotel on the Upper West Side of Manhattan, where weeping fans smoked marijuana, lit candles, sang old Beatles songs, and openly grieved with looks of pure dolor. John Lennon was dead. The words sounded surreal. *The* John Lennon was dead. Strangers embraced strangers, inconsolable. Even the reporters seemed shaken. For over an hour, Bud and Troy watched in spellbound silence, motionless, barely breathing.

"I can't watch this anymore," Bud said finally. He tossed the *Playboy* back on the bed.

Troy re-read the interview. Although he had never directly crossed paths with any of the Beatles, he was as influenced by their music and message as everyone else. Especially John. And in the interview, when John mentioned his strained relationship with his son Julian and Yoko's estrangement from her daughter Kyoko, shivers ran through Troy. He couldn't stop thinking about Gretchen. The last paragraph of the Lennon interview read like a rally cry from the other side.

PLAYBOY: "What is the Eighties' dream to you, John?"

LENNON: Well, you make your own dream. That's the Beatles' story, isn't it? That's Yoko's story. That's what I'm saying now. Produce your own dream. If you want to save Peru, go save Peru. It's quite possible to do anything, but not to put it on the leaders and the parking meters. Don't expect Jimmy Carter or Ronald Reagan or John Lennon or Yoko Ono or Bob Dylan or Jesus Christ to come and do it for you. You have to do it yourself. That's what the great masters and mistresses have been saying ever since time began. They can point the way, leave signposts and little instructions in various books that are now called holy and worshiped for the cover of the book and not for what it says, but the instructions are there for all to see, always have been and always will be. There's nothing new under the sun. All the roads lead to Rome. And people cannot provide it for you. *I can't wake you up. You can wake you up. I can't cure you. You can cure you."*

PLAYBOY: "What is it that keeps people from accepting that message?"

LENNON: "It's fear of the unknown. The unknown is what it

is. And to be frightened of it is what sends everybody scurrying around chasing dreams, illusions, wars, peace, love, hate, all that . . . it's all illusion. Unknown is what what it is. Accept that it's unknown and it's plain sailing. Everything is unknown . . . then you're ahead of the game. That's what it is. Right?"

That was it, the end of the interview. Troy keep repeating the words:

I can't wake you up. You can wake you up.

I can't cure you. You can cure you.

Accept that it's unknown. Everything is unknown.

These words rumbled around in Troy's head like dice in a tumbler. He didn't know what to do, but he knew he had to do something. So he put on his slumming clothes and spent the day at a park, attending a vigil that had been hastily organized by a local FM radio station. There were hundreds of other mourners, a live version of what Troy had seen on TV, and he remained on the fringes in order to maintain his anonymity. He wanted to be around other mourners, but he also wanted to be alone. Troy remembered a line by a writer he'd been reading, Aldous Huxley. *The martyrs go hand in hand into the arena; they are crucified alone.*

The radio broadcast was piped in over loudspeakers, one John Lennon song after another without commercial interruptions. Troy's knees buckled at the line: *imagine all the people, living for today.* He sat down on the grass. All of Lennon's lyrics had a surreal twist now. Everything meant more than it had before.

Two women sat under a palm tree, each with a small child in a stroller and a brown bag lunch. As they fed the children from jars of baby food, they took turns crying and consoling one another. For the first time since his parents died, Troy felt completely mortal. He had a finite amount of time left on the planet; he must use it judiciously. At that moment in that city park at that makeshift funeral for the late John Lennon, Troy Archer resolved he would proceed with caution but he would proceed nonetheless to locate Gretchen and make amends. Ask forgiveness. Whatever it might take, the full-court press was on.

* * *

Troy explained his plan to Bud, who was predictably apocalyptic but still agreed to locate a first-rate private investigator. In fact, he knew just the right character. Still, he warned Troy, "This is definitely selfish and potentially dangerous. It isn't just about Gretchen. What about her family? You could be seriously fucking up some innocent lives."

"I intend to be discreet. But I'm doing this with or without you, Bud."

"OK, but if this shit blows up in your face, don't blame me."

Two days later, Troy was seated at the dining room table with none other than Bud's old friend Leo "the Bloodhound" Squigg, retired FBI, who occasionally did a little freelance work to keep his hand in the game. Leo was a pleasant man, clean shaven, well-dressed, and a little hard of hearing. He spoke at the decibel level of a public address announcer. "I located a work address for our subject, one Mrs. Gretchen Alessandrelli."

Troy didn't expect the news this soon. He had scavenged Gretchen's social security number from some old tax documents stored in a gray lockbox. Already the Bloodhound had the scent and was hot on the trail.

Leo sipped a cold beer, "Get me a social and the whole thing's a cinch," he snapped his fingers. "Give me a couple more days to fly out there and set up photographic surveillance and I'll tell you what color her toothbrush is."

"No," Troy said. "I'll take it from here. Discretion is paramount. Fly where? Where are we flying? And how much do I owe you?"

Leo pointed his beer bottle at Bud. "I owe this cowboy for helpin' me build my deck last summer, so this one's on me."

"Nonsense," Bud said. "What's the fee?"

"I don't want your money," Leo said, "but my grandkids have been after me to take them horseback riding. Can I bring 'em out here for an hour or two?"

Troy nodded. "No problem, Leo. Horses, the pool, a four-star lunch. Anything you want. So, where is she? What'd'ya got for me?" Troy drummed his knuckles on the table. "Where's my ex-wife hiding out these days?"

Leo sipped his beer and set it on the table. "The former Mrs. Gretchen Archer is now Mrs. Gretchen Alessandrelli, and she's a bond trader in the financial district of downtown Kansas City, Missouri."

Troy smiled. "She grew up there."

"Kansas City is, if I'm not mistaken, the City of Fountains. It is also, arguably, the barbeque capital of the free world," Leo said. "Here." He handed Troy his business card with Gretchen's married name and work address written on the back. "The brokerage firm she works for occupies the seventeenth and eighteenth floors. If you want her home address—"

"No," Troy said. "This is good. This is plenty. I'll take it from here." He shook Leo's hand. "You're a genius, my friend, a bona fide genius. I'm gonna pack a suitcase right now." Troy could feel his heart tick-tocking like the beat of a metronome. He headed up the spiral staircase.

Leo helped himself to another beer.

"If you've got a minute, Leo, there's someone else I'd like you to meet," Bud said. "One of our ranch hands recently discovered he's adopted. He's been talkin' about searching for his biological mother."

"How old is he?"

"I don't know, twenty-one, maybe twenty-two. You ever done any work like that, Leo? Searched for someone's biological family?"

"Hell, Bud, I've done it all twice. When I was twenty-one I survived Pearl Harbor, when I was fifty-five I helped find Patty Hearst, and I did a whole bunch of crazy shit in-between. In fact, I'm so crazy I've even lived long enough to tell about it. It helps to be a little crazy, you know what I mean?"

* * *

The next day, Troy dispatched himself to Kansas City, Missouri, the City of Fountains, but without a hat or sunglasses. When one of the passengers in first-class noticed him and asked for an autograph, Troy realized that people recognized him mostly because of his hair. To remedy that, he instructed the cab driver to drop him off at a barber shop downtown, then asked the barber, an elderly gentleman, to buzz it. Buzz it all. The barber obliged and soon the Troy's locks fell and gathered in small blond piles on the white linoleum. Surprisingly and unlike Samson, he felt more powerful.

"Mind if I ask why you're cuttin' off all your hair, young feller?"

"Time for a change," Troy said. "Time for something more mature."

When the barber had finished trimming up the sideburns, Troy peered into the mirror, looking like one of those basketball players from the 1950s.

"Four bucks," the man said and rang up the cash register.

Troy handed him a twenty. "Keep the change."

The old man, a bit perplexed, said, "Thank you. Thank you very much."

Troy nodded, admiring his own reflection and rubbing his hands over his new crew cut. His next destination would be to buy a winter coat, for Kansas City, with its arctic wind chill, was as frigid as the North Pole, and Troy had actually been to the North Pole.

The barber directed him to a clothing store, where Troy

bought three pairs of jeans, three flannel shirts, socks, under-wear, work boots, a stocking cap, and a quilted parka. The new Troy Archer could easily have been mistaken for a logger from the Great Northwest. He secured a hotel room at the Imperial Arms because it was within walking distance to Gretchen's of-fice. Troy had sworn off driving.

"And how long are you planning to stay with us, sir?" the clerk asked.

"A week," Troy said, not really knowing. He paid in cash and signed the register *Jasper Trueblood*. He didn't want to leave a pa-per trail, though he wasn't exactly sure why.

Troy had bad dreams and didn't sleep very well on his first night in the Imperial Arms. At the dawn of Day Two, he began to implement his plan. First, he would rigorously do his daily ex-ercise regimen to help alleviate stress. Normally he'd jog outside but with the ice, traffic-blackened snow, and onerous exhaust fumes from downtown traffic, he decided to do calisthenics in his hotel room instead. He wanted Gretchen to see someone in control. Calm. Self-assured. Contrite. Not the asshole she'd been married to.

He ran in place, watching the reflection of his head bobbing up and down on the sliding glass patio doors. He did push-ups and sit-ups and jumping jacks until he could feel the burn, then he did some more. Soon he'd built up a healthy sweat, but his jangled nerves were far worse than the stage fright from any show he'd ever done, worse than Woodstock, worse than all the stadiums and concert halls put together. For months he had imagined how this moment might look. He'd lay in bed every night and concoct dialogues that always led to the same line of questioning.

Had she been pregnant?

After the workout, he headed downtown on foot toward her office and when he arrived, conducted a bit of surveillance on the skyscraper's steel-and-mirrored-glass motif to get a feel for the life of a bond trader extraordinaire in downtown Kansas City.

The strategy was to set up an appointment on the pretense of buying something. Troy didn't know anything about bonds but figured this was a way to get her alone, on her own turf, where she might feel less likely to scratch his eyes out. He sensed, now more strongly than ever, that he'd been led here by external forces, a combination of John Lennon and Jasper Trueblood, to kick-start his conscience. He should've done this long ago.

As he approached the massive quadruple-revolving-door entrance, he took a couple deep breaths and exhaled frosty plumes that were snatched away by the purposeful wind. He sat in the lobby and gazed at the Christmas décor, watching passers-by, wondering if any of them were Gretchen. Troy re-read Leo's card for the hundredth time: MRS. GRETCHEN ALESSANDRELLI. Great name, he thought. He folded up his newspaper, took the elevator up to seventeen, and read the roster on the wall: Kansas City Securities. Bud's warnings echoed in his head. His initial impulse was to make a mad dash for the airport. Please God, he prayed, don't let me fuck this up.

"Hi," he said to the receptionist, coolly playing the part of an eccentric millionaire logger. "I'm interested in purchasing some securities. Is Ms. Alessandrelli available by any chance?"

"I'll check. Do you have an appointment?" the girl behind a mahogany desk asked without making eye contact.

"No," he said, stocking cap in hand. "Do I need one?"

"Not necessarily, but I think she might be over at the Board of Trade this morning. Let me check. Your name, sir?"

"Jasper Trueblood."

"Just a minute." She picked up a phone but spoke too softly for Troy to eavesdrop. "I'm sorry, Mr. Trueblood, but she's at a risk management seminar until after lunch."

"Risk management. She's taking the seminar?"

"No, she's giving the seminar."

"Oh," Troy said.

"Would you like to see one of our other brokers or traders?"

"No, I can wait until she's available."

The receptionist finally looked at him, sized him up, and scheduled an appointment for three o'clock. Troy returned to the lobby where he restlessly rearranged himself in the uncomfortable chairs then took a walk downtown. He heard a Salvation Army volunteer ringing a bell and threw his contribution into the kettle. He purchased a glass of grapefruit juice and a bagel and later, back in the lobby, gum from a gumball machine. By 2:55, he was suitably panic-stricken.

"May I help you?" the receptionist asked.

"Yes," Troy said. "I had a three o'clock with Ms. Alessandrelli." He could feel his heart playing bass and time slow to a crawl.

"Oh yes, Mr. Trueblood. I'm sorry, Ms. Alessandrelli isn't back, but I expect her any minute."

"No problem, I don't mind waiting." And just as Troy went for a chair he recognized his ex-wife strut into the room. Mrs. Gretchen Alessandrelli, ex-wife and bond trading magnate. She emerged through the double doors all dashing in her girl curves and dressed in a pin-striped suit with black pumps. The consummate professional. Her hair was pinned up, a lighter shade of auburn than he remembered, and she carried a stack of manila folders. Troy averted his gaze.

"Ms. Alessandrelli," the receptionist said, "there's a Mr. Trueblood here to see you."

"Give me a minute. I have a quick phone call to make," she said in that still familiar husky voice. Troy did not look up from his magazine as she vanished into her office. He was close to levitating.

Ten minutes later the receptionist said, "Sir, Ms. Alessandrelli will see you now. It's the last office on your right."

Troy's hand felt strangely detached from his body as he knocked on her door, staring at the gold name plate: *Ms. Gretchen Alessandrelli*. He was damn proud of her even though he knew he had long since squandered the right to be.

She opened the door. He smelled a wisp of her perfume, a mix of vanilla and sandalwood. "Come in. I'm sorry that took so long. Please sit down and make yourself comfortable, Mr. Trueblood. I want you to feel at home. What can I help you with today?"

Troy sat down and made himself as comfortable as possible considering he was about to go into cardiac arrest. He waited until she was seated before he looked her directly in the eye. His fingertips tingled. She really did look amazing.

"I'd like to buy a hundred thousand dollars of useless paper." He could see her breathing stop when she recognized him.

She sat back in her chair. Her mouth was open and her eyes squinted as if he were sitting far away. "Troy Archer."

"Hi Gretchen," he said with a smile. "I hope you'll forgive me for barging in on you like this. I was in the neighborhood, as they say, and might I add, you look spectacular."

"Troy Archer. I never thought I'd see you again. For the longest time, I never wanted to see you again." She stood and circled him as if he were a dead mammal that had washed ashore. "What are you doing here? How did you find me?"

"Please don't call security and please don't shoot me. I just want five minutes, that's all."

"Let's step across the hall, over in the conference room." As Gretchen followed him out of her office, she turned a family photo face-down.

"You look wonderful," Troy said. "You really do."

"I didn't realize it until just now," she said, "but I'm still mad at you. How many years has it been?"

224

"I don't know," Troy said. "A long time. And see, that's why I'm here. To apologize for the way I treated you. I was a real shit back then, Gretchen, and it's taken me a long time to admit it. You have every reason to hate me, but I really need to say I'm sorry for all the lying and cheating. I behaved badly and I'm sorry. Losing you was a big mistake. Losing you was the biggest mistake I've ever made."

"It's a little late for apologies. I mean, did you think the world was just gonna save you a place in line?"

"Of course it's late. It's way too late. It's just that since the band broke up, I've had time to think about what an egomaniac I was, what a narcissist and hedonist, how I've never done anything for anybody in this world except myself. I guess because of what happened to my parents, I figured I didn't owe anything to anyone, including you. I don't expect you to forgive me. Really. If it were reversed, I probably wouldn't forgive you. But I just couldn't go to my grave without apologizing for my lies and infidelity. I was a real prick. You were the best thing that ever happened to me, Gretchen, and I never had the brains to realize it."

Gretchen's face softened. "You were a rock star. What did I expect? I don't know what the hell I was thinking." She stopped in mid-thought and looked at his hair. "Hey, are you dying or something?"

"No." Troy smiled. "For the first time in my life, I'm actually living. I'm trying to be authentic as opposed to the sanctimonious piece of shit I always was. I've practiced this conversation a million times, but it's I'm watching another person talking to you. An out-of-body experience."

Gretchen sneered. "You can't believe how angry I was at you for the longest time. It used to soothe my nerves to drift off to sleep at night and fantasize about ways of murdering you and making it look like an accident. God, I was so pissed at you Troy Scott Archer."

Troy hadn't heard his middle name used in vain since they were married. "I really am sorry."

"I was in therapy for four years."

Troy nodded. "You deserved a lot better than me, that's for damn sure."

"I heard about your band. I'm sorry you broke up. It's terrible what happened to John Lennon, too."

"Yeah." Troy stared at his shoes and watched one disconnected foot, without permission from his brain, begin to tap on the white pile carpet. "How are your parents?"

"Oh, they're fine. Retired and living at the Lake of the Ozarks. Daddy bought himself a bass boat. Mom does a lot of work for the church. You want some coffee or something?"

"No, but can I ask you something?"

Gretchen sat back in her chair as if to distance herself from what she was about to hear. She crossed her legs and folded her arms. She had the air of a baroness—someone who wielded considerable power and aimed to keep it.

"At the time you and I broke up, you had missed—how can I say this delicately?—a couple of menstrual cycles, and there was some question as to whether or not you may have been pregnant." He paused, surveying her brown doe eyes. "And I was just wondering, were you? Pregnant?" This was blunter than he had rehearsed.

Gretchen laughed. She leaned forward and slapped him so hard on the shoulder that she nearly knocked him off his perch. "Hell yes I was pregnant. Why do you think I was so pissed off? I miscarried in the twentieth week while the Unknowns were off touring Tokyo or Bangkok or God knows where. And for years I blamed you for the miscarriage. Then I got tired of being mad at you and at life and met my husband, Jeffrey. I guess it all worked out for the best. We've had twins since, Timmy and Jimmy. They're four. But you and me? No, we never had a baby.

Close, but no cigar."

Troy took a deep breath and then let it out. "Miscarried. Hmm. Sorry. I never knew that." He wanted to get a second opinion, call in expert witnesses, sue someone. "This may sound funny considering the disaster I was as a husband but as I drift off to sleep at night, as you're conniving ways to surreptitiously murder me, I often imagine a little stage play that goes something like this. I track you down and find out that we do, in fact, have a child. You graciously and generously agree to allow for me to meet with him or her, and in the final act, I'm able to salvage something of a reconciliation with my past. With you. But I have to confess, a miscarriage was never part of the plot. I guess if it had been, it wouldn't have been a very good fantasy, huh?"

Gretchen stood and poured herself a cup of coffee. "Like I said, Troy, you can't just disappear for a decade and expect the rest of the world to wait for you. Life went on without you. Life does that."

"I know, I know," he said. "I'm finally figuring that out."

"Are you sure you won't have some coffee?"

"No, I'm going to let you get back to work. I'm sorry about the miscarriage and for being such an asshole. I really hope you and the rest of the Alessandrellis have a great life. You seem happy, and that makes me happy."

Gretchen gave him a brief hug. "I accept your apology and thank you. Better late than never. So where are you living these days?"

"Here," Troy said impulsively, a reflex action. "I've moved to Kansas City."

They shook hands, parted company, and Troy walked back to his hotel. The adventure was over. Now what?

* * *

Troy brooded and moped around the hotel, resisting the tempta-

227

tion to purchase a fifth of hard liquor and get mind-numbingly loaded. He turned on the clock radio, but music was no longer his ally. He watched TV, did more calisthenics, read newspapers, and generally wasted time. He called Bud and recapped everything. Bud mentioned that Leo Squigg had been hired to track down the biological mother of Jasper Trueblood. Troy wished him luck. If anyone could find her, it was the Bloodhound, Leo Squigg.

Almost as disappointing as the revelation of Gretchen's miscarriage was that after all these years, Troy had lied to her again. He did not feel alive or like a real person for the first time, and on the last day of his week-long stay at the Imperial Arms he picked up the morning paper and flipped through the classifieds. An ad caught his eye that'd been running all week. He dialed the number.

"Crisis Hotline, may I help you?"

"Yes," Troy said and cleared his throat. "Uh, I'm calling about your ad in the paper. Are you still looking for volunteers?"

"We're always looking for volunteers, sir," a male voice said. "Are you over twenty-one?"

Troy smiled. "Yes."

"Excellent. Our volunteer coordinator is Phyllis Worrell. When would you like to come in for an interview?"

"How about today?"

"All right, let me check. Please hold." And then, "Phyllis has an opening at the end of the day. Can you be here at four?"

"Sure," Troy said. He wrote down the address.

"And your name, sir?"

"Jasper Trueblood."

* * *

Phyllis Worrell was the classic non-profit, save-the-world-one-person-at-a-time, type-A personality, intense at times, circumspect at others, and always doing six things at once. She was a redhead, dressed in a sequined green skirt with a winter-themed Christmas scene stitched in the center, and silver drop earrings with a tiny feather dangling from each. There was a pencil behind her ear and black reading glasses on top of her head. She shook Troy's hand firmly and they sat down.

"Before we get started, Jasper, I have some papers I need you to sign, forms to fill out, an application, and we'll need to see a driver's license or some other form of photo I.D."

Troy hadn't anticipated all this. He had no way to prove he was anyone other than Troy Archer. The whole world had become security-conscious. "Ms. Worrell?"

"Please call me Phyllis."

"Phyllis, I want to get off on the right foot with you, so I'm going to be completely candid. My name is not Jasper Trueblood."

Phyllis put on her glasses to get a better look at this imposter. "So what is it?"

"Troy Archer." He searched her eyes for any trace of recognition.

"Then why did you tell my assistant your name was Jasper Trueblood?" She removed the pencil from behind her ear as if to record the response.

"Do you listen to popular music, Phyllis? Rock 'n' roll?"

"No," she said. "And what does that have to do with the price of rice in Shanghai?"

"I retired last year from a rock 'n' roll outfit called the Unknowns. We were pretty big. In seventy-eight, we headlined right down the road at Arrowhead Stadium. In sixty-nine, we played Woodstock."

"And?"

"And, well, I just used another name because I didn't want any preferential treatment. I just wanna be like all your other volunteers. People tend to swoon over celebrities."

Phyllis removed her glasses and tapped her pencil on the desk a few times. "Troy Archer, let me explain something to you. I don't care if you're the King of Prussia. If you work here, you're on a level playing field with everyone else. Everyone gets treated the same. Period. Most of our volunteers are professionals with careers and families. We're severely understaffed, and I can assure you that we don't have time for star treatment. You don't get your own desk, you don't get your own phone. We share everything. So if it's all the same to you, let's dispense with the alias, shall we?"

Troy nodded. "It won't happen again." He decided that he absolutely adored Phyllis Worrell. She was a double scoop of serendipity, and he could easily imagine running right through a plate glass window for her.

After filling out the necessary forms and signing on the various dotted lines, he spoke with Phyllis again. This time she was smoking a thin cigarette as long as a ballpoint pen.

"So, do we have all our i's dotted and t's crossed?" she asked as she scanned each document.

"Yes," Troy said. "And no more alias."

"Very well then, let's do the interview. Here." She handed him a thirty-page training pamphlet. "Take this home and read it carefully. Bring it to work with you every day during training."

Troy paged through it.

"So when did you get out of the music business?"

"Last year."

"And how long have you lived in Kansas City?"

"I just got here a week ago. I grew up near St. Louis, and I've been looking for a place to settle down. I've always liked Kansas City."

"Where are you living?"

"I'm still in a hotel, but I'm looking for something more permanent."

"I see," Phyllis said. "I should tell you right now that we require our volunteers to commit to at least one continuous year of service. There's also a background check, a thorough screening process, and if you're accepted, an extensive forty-five hour training period. It's very costly to train new people, so we need you to commit for a minimum of twelve months after the training concludes. Is that something you're prepared to do?"

"Absolutely," Troy said. "Do people ever stay longer?"

"Some do." She pointed down the row of cubicles. "See Scooter, first guy on the right? He was just promoted to a paid position last month. He's been here four and half years. Anything's possible. So why the Crisis Center? What led you to volunteer?"

"I don't know, exactly. I think I'm pretty intuitive with people. That seems like a positive quality to have around here."

"Intuition is valuable," Phyllis said, "although I should add that for all serious calls, like a suicide, you'll have a script to go by and a supervisor listening on another line. Some people still refer to it as the 'Suicide Hotline' but we prefer 'Crisis Center'. It sounds less threatening and it's more accurate. Only about one call in ten is a suicide."

"Should I be writing this down?" Troy asked.

"No. I'll put you with Scooter tomorrow. You can take notes then. Read the manual tonight. We really need volunteers, so let's get the wheels in motion. I'll see what I can do to expedite the background check and accelerate the processing. Scooter will go over all of this with you again so just listen for now.

"Volunteers are required to work one four-hour shift per week, the maximum is two shifts. We avoid burnout by limiting the hours. There are two graveyard positions that are paid because it's virtually impossible to find volunteers to work in the middle of the night. We also ask that you work a minimum of one holiday per year."

"Is this your busiest time of year? Christmas?"

"It's busy right after Christmas," Phyllis said, "but we actually log more suicide calls when the weather warms up at the beginning of spring. We usually get about a hundred and fifty calls a day, but it's been up to two hundred since John Lennon got shot. Did you hear about that?"

Troy nodded. "Yeah."

"Yes," Phyllis said. "I suppose you would have." She went right back into her spiel. "As I said, there's a forty-five hour training period before you're on your own, and a paid mental health professional is always in the phone room to monitor any serious developments."

"Isn't everything serious?"

"Well, yes and no. We get a lot of repeaters, people who call every day just to have someone to talk to. They're usually homebound and could be suffering anything from chronic mental illness to your plain old garden variety loneliness. A case of the blues. They're only allowed to speak to a crisis rep for ten minutes per day. That's the bargain we make with those folks. We log every call, and some of the repeaters have a file as thick as your arm. They don't need to be rescued as much as reminded someone's out there."

Troy ingested it all, wishing he were taking notes.

"I don't want to throw too much more at you today. We'll save that for tomorrow. I'm assuming your background screening will check out, so consider tomorrow the beginning of your training." She shook Troy's hand.

"That's it?"

"That's it for now. Can you be back at nine o'clock in the morning?"

"Sure. Thank you, Phyllis," Troy said. "You won't regret this."

"Good." She rose from behind her cluttered desk. "Before you leave, would you like to see the phone room in action?"

"Love to," Troy said, a new career launched. He felt like christening a battleship with a bottle of champagne.

* * *

Scooter was one of the few paid employees at the Crisis Center, a squat, sawed-off shotgun of a man who smiled a lot and appeared to be in his early-to-mid-thirties. His voice had the quality of an anesthesiologist's steady reassurance just before he gives the shot. He sported a perfectly manicured beard and moustache and lived with his wife and three dogs across the Missouri-Kansas state line in a suburb Troy had never heard of.

"Phyllis told me who you are," Scooter said. "I'm a big fan of the Unknowns but don't worry, your secret's safe with me. I would never have recognized you without the hair."

"I like your beard," Troy said. "I'm thinking of growing one myself. Do you happen to know of any apartments nearby?"

"Sure. Right down the street and around the corner. Pricey but nice. If you'd like, we can walk over there at lunch and take a look-see."

Scooter never again mentioned Troy's celebrity nor did anyone else, It helped that the volunteers and staffers used first names only. Troy rented an apartment and for the first time ever, he needed nothing more than a little shoe leather to commute to work. All the lunatics out there with driver's licenses would be forced to find a new victim.

During training, Troy learned that the goal of the Crisis Center was to prevent harm to the caller and to prevent the caller from doing harm to others. The Center was equipped with phone numbers for counselors and mental health professionals, but referrals were not the Center's primary function. The objective was to create an action plan in order to address the caller's crisis.

Seven months passed, the happiest, most fulfilling of Troy's life. He had a new purpose and even though his co-workers all found out who he was eventually, he was never treated differently because of it. He anonymously donated money to purchase

233

a new telecommunications system, and soon all the phone reps had headsets instead of the old hand-held receivers. Qualified mostly by persistent insomnia, Troy was promoted to graveyard shift where he was able to work twenty hours a week instead of just eight and because graveyard was a paid position, he proudly brought home a paycheck of $319.37 every other week. Unlike royalties, this check felt earned. It was reassuring to know he could do something besides croon love songs for a living. He was making a difference in people's lives. When he came home from work one muggy morning in the middle of July to the summer sounds of birds chirping in trees and children playing in yards, he heard the phone ringing and hurried to unlock the door.

"Hello."

"Troy?"

"Yes?"

"It's Gretchen," said the husky voice. "Alessandrelli."

Troy hadn't seen her since his surprise visit in December. He sensed distress. His instincts had become finely tuned at the Crisis Center. "Are you all right? You sound strange."

"We have to talk."

"OK sure. Talk about what?" he said.

"Not on the phone."

"Gretchen, what is it? Are you all right?"

"OK, Troy, I lied to you. There was no miscarriage."

Troy didn't say anything.

"We did have a baby. You are, technically, a father. We did have a baby."

Troy sat on the floor. "Why didn't you tell me?"

"I didn't want to disrupt her life. Many years ago, I told her that you died from heart complications. She hasn't asked about you since."

"Her? A girl?"

"Yes." Gretchen started to cry. "Felicity. She'll be in fifth grade

234

this fall. I have to be frank, Troy, she's very active and has lots of interests. She knows she was legally adopted by Jeffrey and she loves him. He is her dad, she is his daughter. She's a daddy's girl through and through. I never explained much about you, who you were or what you did for a living, and like I said, she's never asked. She's an excellent student and plays on the volleyball team. She's in the glee club and feeds the homeless through our church. Felicity's a highly motivated young lady. She has a tendency to look toward the future, not dwell in the past."

Troy was in shock. "Felicity. I love that name," he said. "It's very poetic."

"I was vehemently opposed to this, but Jeffrey thinks it's a good idea. He convinced me that someday she'll want to know you. Pretty brave, considering he's the one with the most to lose here, wouldn't you say? I felt meeting you would be unfair to Felicity. My husband and I have had some pretty heated debates over this, and I refused to give in. Then I read your goddamn interview in *Playboy* magazine today," her voice cracked, "and how you said I was too good for you." There was a short pause and then Gretchen was crying again. "And that really touched me. So I did some research and found out about your job at the Crisis Center. I thought to myself, why not? I'd probably want to know you if I were in her shoes."

"Thank you, Gretchen." Silently and joyously, Troy felt tears in his eyes.

"But I want you to listen very carefully."

Troy sobered up. "I'm listening."

"I'm going to let you meet with Felicity, but it's got to be on my terms."

"Yes, of course. Anything you say."

"Jeffrey and I would like to speak with you first to establish some ground rules. If you're not busy tonight, perhaps we could get together for dinner. Then, if all goes well, we'll proceed from there. Are you okay with that?"

"Yes, I'm . . . Yes."

When all the arrangements had been made, Troy was too wired to sleep even though he'd been working all night. He spent the balance of the day writing down reasons he was grateful to be alive and repeating the name of his daughter over and over again. Felicity. Fe-li-ci-ty. He wrote the name in a notebook thirty-seven times. She was in the glee club—maybe they could sing a duet. He decided to call Bud and tell him the news. Troy felt like a helium balloon about to slip off a wrist and sail out of an amusement park.

16. Curtain Call

Troy called Bud and recounted the entire saga detail by detail. They speculated about the preliminary meeting planned for that evening with the Alessandrellis. Bud seemed cautiously supportive. He caught Troy up on what had been happening at the ranch. Because Troy had requested to remain incommunicado, a sizable stack of mail and messages had accumulated.

The most dramatic news was splashed on the front page of Jasper Trueblood. The last few months had been tough on him. Leo Squigg had run into countless false leads and dead-ends in an exhaustive search for Jasper's biological mother. To compound the typical troubles of dealing with old documents, the adoption agency had used a fictitious name and social security number. The woman listed as "mother" on the adoption decree was Victoria Lynn Carver of St. Louis, Missouri. Leo eventually found the obituary for Victoria Lynn Carver in the microfilm room of the St. Louis Public Library. She had died thirty years before Jasper was born. After countless roadblocks, detours, one threat, two bribes, and eighty-seven pro bono hours, Leo had finally honed in on Jasper's biological mother holed up in Seattle, Washington. Enter Ms. Constance Marie Suggs, waitress at an International House of Pancakes. Jasper was scheduled to fly there in the morning.

"I hope he isn't disappointed," Troy said.

"I warned him it could go either way," said Bud. "He said he wants to thank her for giving him a chance to live. I thought that sounded pretty noble."

Troy considered Jasper Trueblood a turning point. The two of them had nothing and everything in common. He trusted the kid's karma.

"Where's the get-together with Felicity's parents?"

"We're having dinner at a restaurant in Crown Center. Who knows, maybe afterwards I'll actually get to meet her."

"It's Friday night," Bud said. "She might have a date."

"She's ten years old, Bud."

"I don't know, they start pretty young these days."

Troy said sternly, "If she's one minute after curfew, I'm calling the cops, the morgue, and every hospital in town. Then she's grounded for a month."

They laughed.

"It's been a long time since I've heard this much enthusiasm from you," Bud said. "You sound like you're generating a lot of positive energy."

"The Crisis Center has made me think about someone besides myself for a change. I went to work at a leper colony and was the one who ended up getting healed. You can't change the way you think to change the way you live, you have to change the way you live to change the way you think."

"I like that," Bud said. "So how are you going to spend the rest of the day?"

"I don't know," Troy said. "I've been working all night and I should probably try to get some sleep, but I'm too jacked up. I might go buy a copy of *Playboy* and see what I said about Gretchen. Did you know it was out?"

"Yeah, I just read it the other day. The interview was good. The centerfold was better."

"Bud, I just want to say thanks. For being my best friend."

"Call me tomorrow, will ya?" Bud said. "I want to know how everything turns out. The suspense is killing me."

* * *

Because everything was within walking distance or accessible by mass transit, Troy had resolutely refused to buy a car so he walked up to the Crisis Center to borrow Scooter's motorcycle. It was a beat-up old Kawasaki, and Troy was thinking maybe he could give Felicity a ride. He contemplated for hours what she might look like, sound like, and whether or not she would resent him. He would take all his cues from Gretchen and her husband. He waited until he knew Scooter would be on an afternoon break and found him in Phyllis' office with a glass of lemonade.

"Hey," Scooter said, feet up on the desk. "Shouldn't you be in bed?"

"I came in to ask a favor," Troy said.

Scooter rubbed the side of the glass against his forehead and condensation dripped down his brow. "This place needs a new air conditioner. What's up?"

Reaching into his pants pocket, Troy pulled out a hundred dollar bill. "I need to borrow your bike for a few hours. Here's cab fare so you can get home."

Scooter pushed the cash away. "Keep your money. Why do you need the bike?"

Troy unspooled the litany of recent developments. "I could rent a car, but I didn't renew my driver's license, plus fifth grade girls dig motorcycles. If I get to meet my daughter tonight, maybe my ex will let me give her a ride around the block or something. Know what I mean? Please."

"The timing's off, Troy. The brakes are really shaky. Any other time I wouldn't think twice, but—"

"I'll be very careful, Scooter, I promise. Cross my heart and hope to die. *Pleeeease*?" Troy squeezed Scooter's shoulder, "Don't worry, I used to race dirt bikes."

"This is no dirt bike," Scooter said, "It won't win any races. It needs a lot of work."

"I won't be in a hurry to get anywhere. I'll stay in the slow lane like a grandma drivin' to church uphill."

Scooter handed over the key and yanked his helmet off the top shelf of the closet. "You have to wear this."

Troy made it two hundred. "Here, treat Mimi to dinner." Scooter tried to resist but Troy stuffed the bills in Scooter's shirt pocket. "Placate me. I feel like celebrating. I'll be at your place by noon tomorrow with the bike and a full status report. Get the barbeque grill and horseshoes ready." Troy shook Scooter's hand and then, although it was more demonstrative than he had ever been before, embraced him. "I don't know exactly why all this is happening, but I think it's because of this place." He looked around the room. "I'm gonna meet my daughter, man." The words were as magical as a lunar eclipse.

As evidence to the Alessandrellis of what a responsible cave-man he'd evolved into, Troy resolved not to be late. He show-ered, then dressed himself appropriately in a crisp white shirt, linen slacks, and navy suit coat. He peered into the bathroom mirror at his hair, still short, and wondered why he hadn't cut it all off a lot sooner. He shaved his beard, which had become even fuller than Scooter's, careful not to nick his chin and force him to show up at dinner with toilet tissue stuck to his face. I'll be fine, he thought. He began repeating his daughter's name over and over like a mantra, "FE-LI-CI-TY, FE-LI-CI-TY."

Dinner reservations were for six o'clock and even though the restaurant was only fifteen minutes away, Troy allowed an hour for rush hour traffic and to fill up the gas tank. He revved the engine. It sputtered and coughed and he guided it into the flow of traffic. Scooter was right; the bike needed a complete overhaul. He tooled down Southwest Trafficway choking on gas fumes and exhaust from a Metro bus. Though Scooter's brakes screeched a little, the real problem was definitely the timing. Troy knew more about riding motorcycles than fixing them, but he was sure that all the backfiring and misfiring indicated a need for new points and plugs. Maybe a whole new electrical system. Troy made a mental note to buy Scooter a new scooter.

He stayed in the right lane, the slow lane, cautious and faithfully obeying the speed limit, thinking about his new life. He smiled as he remembered Toon driving his Cadillac into the swimming pool at the El Cerrito Hotel. He made another mental note to have his will updated. Now that he had found Felicity, with Gretchen's permission, he would make her a beneficiary. And he would have to include Jasper Trueblood, too. Troy could still imagine Jasper's old motorcycle with the blown piston collecting dust back at the ranch. He hoped the kid's biological mother wouldn't cut the cord for a second time.

Without bothering to check its blind spot, a silver Mercedes nearly sideswiped Troy, and he was reminded of the accident with Chance and the near-accident with Jasper. Either Chance was right and no one in this country knew how to drive, or Troy was personally attracting these capricious, mentally defective motorists. He maintained a safe distance from a string of construction barrels along the side of the road. There were more orange barrels in Kansas City than all the rest of the state combined.

Troy proceeded with extreme caution, and he had resolved to apply that same conservative approach with Gretchen and her husband. Troy wanted to be compliant to whatever role they were willing to allow him to play. He couldn't believe this was actually going to happen. He was a mile away from the restaurant when a gold 1966 Mustang swerved into his lane, weaving erratically. Early happy hour, Troy thought. Here we go again. He could swear he was a magnet to these misanthropes. He glanced into his mirror and as he started to pull into the adjacent lane, a landscaping truck merged. Horns honked. Lawn mowers and weed eaters rattled around in the truck's flat bed. Troy tried to return to his lane but the Mustang was all over the road. The driver punched the brakes as the contour of the street curved downhill. The Mustang screeched off the median and spun diagonally across three lanes of traffic. Troy saw the sparks and, in dodging its path, lost control of the bike.

When it was inevitable that he was going down, Troy pushed away from the handlebars and braced into a hard tuck-and-roll at forty miles an hour. This is it, he thought. This is it. Fe-li-ci-ty. His body became a projectile, careening off the guardrail and ricocheting back into traffic like a stone skipping on an alpine lake. A taxi cab behind the landscaping truck locked up its brakes and skidded hard but couldn't stop in time.

* * *

The next morning, Bud had just gotten off the phone with Jasper, who reported that the Eagle had landed in Seattle and all systems were go. Jasper had checked into a hotel and would go meet his biological mother, Ms. Constance Marie Suggs, that afternoon. He sounded upbeat on the phone, light years away from 235 Magellan Drive.

The maid, Betty, handed Bud a phone message. CALL PHYLLIS WORRELL—URGENT!—(816) 555-HELP. "She called while you were in the shower. She wants you to call her immediately."

"What's wrong?" Bud said.

"I don't know."

Bud phoned the Crisis Center and Phyllis broke the news. Troy had been rushed to a hospital but was pronounced dead on arrival. Bud's fingers twitched and the telephone cord wiggled as she described the scene. He sat on the table as he held the receiver to his ear.

Through the sniffles Phyllis said, "Troy had borrowed that motorcycle from a co-worker. It took a while to figure out exactly who was in the accident. Troy didn't have any ID with him."

Bud swallowed hard.

"He just wanted to be treated like everyone else," she said. "I had my doubts at first, but he was one of the best phone reps we've ever had. You should hear his tapes. He had a real gift for listening and saying just the right thing. And sometimes, between calls late at night, he liked to sing, too. He really did have a lovely voice."

To hear Troy Archer referred to in the past tense was disorienting as moonshine. Bud thanked her. He promised to call back as soon as he could figure out what arrangements had to be made. There was much to do. He felt pains in strange places. No time to feel sorry, just like there had been no time to grieve Joey Duco. Things had to be done. Troops had to be moved. A perimeter had to be established.

While Betty was never enamored with Troy's rock 'n' roll entourage, she had always been quite fond of Troy. She was screaming and crying and so openly distraught that Bud finally told her to take a couple days off. He had to concentrate.

"He was part of my family," Betty said dabbing a cloth napkin to her eyes. "All you boys are."

As soon as she was gone and Bud was alone, he uncorked a bottle of twenty-five-year-old single malt scotch. The aroma gagged him so badly that his eyes watered. He hadn't touched booze since his second divorce, and took a quick swig before he could talk himself out of it. He slammed the bottle down on the dining room table.

"Troy is dead," he said aloud. "Troy Archer is dead." He repeated it several times as if memorizing the line for a play. What to do first? he thought. He called information in Kansas City and got the number for Alessandrelli, Jeffrey & Gretchen.

"Hello."

"Hi, Gretchen this is Bud Black calling from Tucson. I'm not sure if you remember me?"

"Of course, Troy's friend. You were the one who went to Vietnam. We just heard about Troy's accident on the news." Gretchen inhaled deeply and started to cry. "We're all in shock, Bud. He was supposed to meet us last night for dinner. When he didn't show up, we just assumed he got cold feet." There was an extended pause then more crying and sniffling, "I thought he might have stood us up. I thought he hadn't changed a bit."

"Did he ever get to meet Felicity?"

"No," Gretchen said in a whimper. "He never did." Her husband took the phone.

"Bud, this is Jeff Alessandrelli. We're all sick about what happened. We talked to Felicity and she's devastated. We all are. I was looking forward to meeting him, too."

"Thanks, Jeff. You would've liked Troy." He decided to stop there. "Tell Gretchen I'll call her about the funeral arrangements as soon as I figure out the logistics, hopefully in the next few hours. There are some personal effects of Troy's which, if it's OK with you, I'd like to give to Felicity."

"Yes, yes, of course, and please let us know if there's anything we can do. I mean that."

Now Bud he had to call the Kansas City police, the morgue, the mortuary, and fifty other people. He downed another scotch, this time from a shot glass. He hunted down Troy's last will and testament out of storage.

I, Troy Scott Archer, being of sound mind and body, do hereby bequeath all of my worldly possessions to Bud Sinclair Black Jr. If Bud Sinclair Black Jr. should be deceased or otherwise incapacitated at the time of my demise, my estate shall be auctioned off to the highest bidder and the entirety of proceeds donated to the Boys Club of America.

Bud had no idea.

There was a letter in the same envelope as the will.

To Whom It May Concern:

Please do not bury me. I wish to be cremated and have my ashes floated down the Mississippi River on a raft like Huck Finn. As the raft is launched, it should be set on fire and cast adrift. Please do this after nightfall, not only for aesthetic purposes but also to help avoid detection by local authorities because it is undoubtedly illegal. I'm gonna keep my fire lit from St. Louis 'til New Orleans. Since I can't thank you in this life, I hope to properly thank you in the next.

Sincerely,
Troy Scott Archer

That was exactly what Bud would do, have the body cremated and fly to St. Louis to fulfill his best friend's final request. He opened an address book and assiduously proceeded down the list, informing Troy's friends or leaving messages, each time starting with the words, "This is Bud Black, and I'm afraid I have some terrible news about Troy Archer." He dialed up Troy's distant relatives, his lawyer, accountant, and several media representatives. He called radio stations, record companies, *Rolling Stone*, and Bobby Lee at *Playboy*. He called Chance, Fen, Toon, Aubrey, Nils, and even Hilary, who was now a graduate student at Smith College. She seemed more shaken up than anybody. He called Phyllis Worrell back, got Scooter's number, and talked to him, too. Bud called everyone he could possibly think of with one exception. He forgot to call Jasper Trueblood.

Five hours later when Bud had made all the calls he had in him, he grabbed the scotch and headed for the drawing room. He sat up all night, observing the rattlesnakes and reminiscing until he became so despondent that he threw his glass across the room. Troy was dead. Troy Archer was dead. He got down on the floor and rested his eyes. There was so much to do.

* * *

Bud had been asleep for several hours on the drawing room floor when the dream kicked in, that all-too-familiar, virulent, sensory-laden dream cloaked in familiar themes of rage, revenge, and survival. There were jungle sounds, the stench of cordite, exotic birds in treetops, stealth and death everywhere. The dream started with him in fatigues, combat boots laced tight, camo face grease blackening everything from neck to forehead except for his eyes. Like most of the other GIs, Private First Class Bud Black preferred the Russian-made AK-47 over the military-issue M-16. Better accuracy at long distance. He took out two high-capacity banana clips, fifty rounds each, and secured them together with electrical tape. He loaded the clip into the weapon and selected the three-round-burst option on the selector switch.

Your mission is to exterminate the enemy with extreme prejudice. Breathe three times then take the shot. Fourteen kills in sixty seconds. Private Duco died before he heard the magazine report. What makes the grass grow, soldier? Blood, sir. Bright red blood. Kill. Kill. Kill. Do what you're trained to do. Two in the chest, one in the head, that's the way to make sure they're dead. Kill the enemy before he kills you. Kill. Kill. Kill.

Bud crawled on his belly to the foyer and his first shots blew apart the terrarium. Cacti and glass panels were obliterated and the skylight overhead came crashing to the floor in a torrent of glass. He continued to move quickly, in short bursts, always one step ahead of Charlie, crouching behind furniture with a feral eye. He shot out the communications system, the Eye-dentifier, and deployed in an easterly direction. He sprayed a round through each of the towering windows and a few more into the chandelier. Bullets ricocheted off the dance floor and each report reverberated around the room. The giant disco ball crashed to the floor and exploded in a glass-dust mushroom cloud. Out of ammo, he reloaded the other clip.

Kill. Kill. Kill.

His next target was the greenhouse spa where Bud heard the squawking white cockatoo and instinctively hit the floor. He fired several rounds in the bird's direction and the cage fell, the bird shrieking. Bud fired into the steamy waters of the Jacuzzi and then blew out all the windows and sliding glass doors. Wood splintered, windows shattered, bullets bounced and ricocheted everywhere. On to the drawing room.

He sprayed the library. He shot out the rattlesnake cage and in the crush of sand and rock that crashed to the floor, several snakes slithered away. He took a few cracks at the sad clown paintings and the clocks. The cuckoo clock cuckooed. Bud shot it. Water began to drip in Broken Plumbing Falls. He fired several rounds into it obliterating a family picture, sparks flashing off the stone hearth. He unloaded a few more rounds into the cheetah until he was sure the cat was dead. They were all dead now. He had killed them all dead.

Bud took cover behind a chair and fired the rest of his ammo into the aquarium. An explosion of tempered glass, dozens of tropical fish, sea horses, coral, the Chinese pagoda, and eleven hundred and ninety-two gallons of synthetic salt water flushed out onto the carpet in a tidal wave of aquatic bedlam. In seconds, Bud's underwater dominion was flopping around on the floor, gills flailing frantically for survival. He pulled the trigger again. The clip was empty.

The dream was over.

"Joey!" Bud shouted and woke himself up. He was soaked in perspiration and breathing so heavily his chest was convulsing. He could not see. He felt the floor with both hands. It was bone dry. It had all been a dream. An hysterical dream. Bud felt his way toward the window. He tore down the blinds and drapes but couldn't see anything. He managed to unlatch the window but could not distinguish daylight or geometric shapes or shadows or anything but complete darkness. "No!" he howled. "No!"

17. Let's Do It Again Sometime

She's going to lie, Jasper predicted, putting himself in the comfortable working shoes of Constance Marie Suggs. Amidst all the speculation and conjecture, he was most concerned she would deny everything. He had said her name aloud a thousand times, spelled it out on chairs with his finger, whispered it in his sleep. Constance Marie Suggs. If she denied it, he'd show her Leo Squigg's stockpile of evidence, which he kept in a briefcase that Bud had lent him.

Sitting on the bed in Room 1218 at the Cascade Village Inn in downtown Seattle, Jasper had already resolved on the flight that this would be his last adventure for a very long time. Everything had changed dramatically since he'd met Troy Archer and although there were no regrets, in many ways he missed his former Thoreau-like life of quiet desperation.

His strategy for the encounter with his birth mother was based on a sermon by the old high school wrestling coach, "Know your opponent." The Bloodhound had tracked Constance down in Seattle, where she was working as a waitress in a district called Lower Queen Anne. Leo had informed Jasper that Queen Anne was a hill.

Besides Constance's occupation, Jasper learned she'd been living in Seattle since 1961, according to records Leo had obtained from the Washington State Department of Motor Vehicles. In view of this, Jasper had conjured up the following scenario: she ran away after the birth and adoption to escape the shame of being pregnant and unmarried in 1959 and subsequently tried to reinvent herself just like he had by migrating to uncharted waters. He would catch her off-guard, he thought, from point-blank range. See if she blinked. Jasper felt the jitters all over.

He called a cab and waited impatiently on a wooden bench outside the hotel lobby. The flight was exhausting, the anticipation debilitating, and he just wanted it to be over. To kill time he reread the legalese accumulated in Leo's investigation and, in particular, a piece of bureaucratic red tape from the adoption agency entitled: NON-IDENTIFYING INFORMATION FOR THE ADOPTEE. It was, by state law, the only background data the agency was authorized to reveal.

The birth mother was diagnosed as having severe hyperthyroidism. She stated that she had good health, but had always been overweight. The birth mother's father died from "heart involvement." As far as the birth mother knew, there was no history of mental disorders in her family. The birth mother was described as refined and well-groomed. It was believed that the birth parents "kept company" for five years. The birth mother stated she had "given the matter [of adoption] a great deal of thought and considered it [adoption] best for the child's welfare."

Leo had warned Jasper that because the name had been changed on the adoption papers, any or all of this information might be fabricated. Nonetheless, Jasper found it intriguing. He loved the part about his birth mother being "well-groomed," like she was a cocker spaniel at the kennel club. He also suspected the hyperthyroidism was genuine. It would explain the weight war he'd been fighting his entire life or at least up until the time he started lugging boulders around for a living. Another favorite line was that they had "kept company" for five years. From the surface of it, Jasper surmised that all this was a euphemistic way of saying the guy who impregnated her didn't have the common courtesy to marry her. She was probably better off without him.

An orange taxi coasted up and a middle-aged man in a blue baseball hat yelled out, "You call for a cab?"

"Yes." Jasper got in the back seat and set the briefcase on his lap. The driver pulled out into traffic, blending into the stream of cars.

"Where to?"

"The International House of Pancakes in Lower Queen Anne. You know where that is?"

"Sure," said the cabbie. "It's just a couple miles from here. First time in Seattle?"

"Yeah."

"I figured. I saw you staring up at the Monorail." He momentarily checked out Jasper in the rearview.

"Nice city," Jasper said. "Everything looks like a picture postcard." There were mountains and lakes, the Puget Sound, and towering evergreens. Majestic Mt. Rainier, snowcapped even in the summertime, stood prominently on the horizon like God flexing His bicep. There seemed to be a multitude of Asian restaurants with exotic names. He had no idea it would be so visually arresting.

"I'm from the Midwest originally," he said. "Live in Tucson now. Hell, I thought it rained up here all the time but this is spectacular. In Tucson, it's about a hundred and ten in the shade these days."

The cabbie said, "The eastern half of our state is more like what you're used to."

"I guess I was expecting a bunch of umbrellas and duck hunters. I heard it rained three hundred days a year."

251

"It rains but I'm from Anchorage, and I'd rather get a little wet than have snow up to my knees for six months. You know what I mean?"

Jasper remembered the wind chill factor of those unforgiving Midwestern winters. His mother's graveside service. "So tell me about Seattle. What's it like?"

"What do you want to know?"

"Anything," Jasper said, grateful to be thinking about something besides Constance Marie Suggs.

"Well, I moved here in seventy-two and from what I've seen, Seattle's got a little bit of everything."

He rambled on for a while and as they concluded their polite exchange, the driver rolled into the parking lot of the International House of Pancakes. Jasper gave him a generous tip and received a business card in return.

"Thanks and enjoy your stay. You've got my number if you need me." The cabbie hit the gas and sped away in a haze of exhaust.

So, Jasper thought, the moment of truth. He kept reminding himself he just wanted to thank her, that's all. Like last year's pilgrimage to 235 Magellan Drive, he'd give it a one-hour time limit. Get in and get out. Essentially, the same plan Constance Marie Suggs had had on May 9, 1959.

The restaurant was the familiar A-frame construction with the standard blue roof and half a dozen cars in the parking lot. Jasper heard a honking noise overhead and saw a formation of geese fly by in the shape of a check mark. Seattle seemed so resplendent that he thought he might stay an extra day or two to do some sightseeing after his soiree. He took a deep breath, opened the glass door, and held his briefcase behind a sign that read: PLEASE WAIT TO BE SEATED.

A man who wore a white shirt and blue tie approached.

"Good afternoon. Smoking or non-smoking?"

"Is Constance working today?"

"Connie? Uh yeah, her station is over here." The man led him to the very last table and handed him a menu. "She'll be right with you."

"Thanks." He scanned the dining room. There were more customers than he'd anticipated for a Saturday afternoon, mostly senior citizens sipping coffee and making casual conversation.

He browsed through the menu, hoping Leo had all his facts straight, praying she wouldn't lie. No one came for a long time which, in an odd way, was reassuring. Soft music played in the background and a ceiling fan swirled rhythmically overhead. There were four kinds of syrup at every table as well as the perfunctory place mats, silverware, cloth napkins, and ketchup bottles you had to beat unmercifully with the palm of your hand.

A heavyset woman in a brown and plaid waitress uniform approached. Jasper intuitively knew it was her, even before he read her name tag: CONNIE. His body went kamikaze. Too late to retreat. Failure was not an option.

She was almost exactly as the adoption agency's bio had described her: plump around the hips, green eyes identical to Jasper's, and short brown hair done up in a flip with blonde highlights. Her makeup was tasteful and understated. Physically she was exactly as advertised: well-groomed.

"Hi there. You ready to order or do you still need a few more minutes?" she said with alacrity and set down a glass of ice water.

Jasper closed the menu for effect. He felt like he was about to rob his first bank. "May I ask you a question first?"

"Sure honey, shoot."

He focused deep into her eyes, searching for the telltale blink. "Does the day May ninth, nineteen fifty-nine, mean anything to you?"

First she laughed, probably thinking it was some kind of joke, a trick question perhaps. Then she paused. "What did you say?"

Jasper repeated the question, and Constance's ready smile dissolved, her facial expression completing a total metamorphosis in five seconds flat. He could sense her thinking, the procession of the mind's gears running the numbers: five—nine—fifty-nine. Finally, she became flushed around the cheeks and started to bite her lip. She stared at him intently and raised a hand to her cheek. "Really?"

"Hi. My name is Jasper Trueblood."

She inspected him up and down before finally whispering, "I don't believe it." Under the gravity of the moment, she sat down at the opposite side of the table.

Jasper popped open his briefcase and spread out the pertinent documents side-by-side.

Connie read each one, her face alternating between pleasure and pain, first shaking her head then nodding, then smiling, then stone-faced. As she handed everything back to Jasper, she appeared to be thoroughly deflated.

Jasper held out his hand and she shook it meekly. "Please let me assure you that I'm not looking for money or a relationship or anything like that, so don't get the wrong idea. I just came to say thanks. That's all. I wanted to thank you for giving me the chance to live."

She gazed at him for two full minutes, tried to speak several times, but stopped. Finally, with a distant smile, she pointed at him. "You're much taller than I remember."

"Ha," Jasper laughed. He recognized humor as a defense mechanism, a trait he had obviously inherited. "I'm potty-trained, too."

The guy in the blue tie stopped by the table. "Connie, I could really use some help when you get a chance. Marla's on break." He walked away.

"Your boss?"

"Yeah, Steve. He's upset because the dishwasher called in sick

254

again. How did you find me?"

"Through a private investigator. I flew in today from Tucson to meet you and then I'm flying back. I know it's a terrible intrusion and I'm sorry I didn't call in advance, but I wanted to be as discreet as possible. I don't want to create any problems. I'm just hopin' to get some basic information, that's all." He'd been practicing those lines for over a month and was relieved to have remembered them.

"I'm gonna tell Steve I have to leave. I clock out in an hour anyway, and Marla can skip her break. Then we can go over to my place and talk in peace. I'm sure you must have a million questions. Of course you do, that's why you're here. He'll rant and rave but what can he do? Not only am I his best waitress, I'm also his girlfriend."

"I'd be happy to wash dishes for an hour. Really. I don't want to get you in trouble."

"Oh, it's too late for that," she said.

Jasper wondered if that remark was intended as a salvo in his direction.

She smiled nervously. "Odd, isn't it? I was watching The Phil Donahue Show the other day, and he had on all these people who were searching for their real parents."

"Biological parents," Jasper corrected her.

She squinted, nodded.

"I've found the semantics can get tricky. It's best just to stick to first names. May I call you Connie?"

"Sure. Anyway, like I was saying, the day I watched that show on TV, I wondered what it'd be like to actually meet you after all these years, but never in my wildest dreams did I think you'd waltz right through the front door and sit in my station." She left the table without another word, and Jasper couldn't help but feel that Doris McPherson was watching this cosmic psychodrama from on high. He hoped she would understand. After some muffled shouts back in the kitchen, Connie emerged with her purse.

"Where are you parked?"

"I'm not," he said. "A taxi dropped me off. I'm staying at a ho-tel downtown."

"We can walk. It's good exercise."

So they marched up Queen Anne Hill, Jasper with his brief-case and Connie with her purse, not saying much of anything. At one point, she was several paces in front of him creating an awkward distance between them. Jasper wondered if this was intentional. There were flowers in almost every yard and lots of shrubs and trees. Seattle seemed like the perfect place to grow things. A seagull bobbed and dipped before resting on a light pole then squealed and flew away.

Connie lived at the very top of the hill, a few blocks from an immense tower, which Jasper presumed belonged to a radio sta-tion. There was a mailbox at the side of the road. Connie peeked inside and pulled out a few envelopes.

"Bills," she said. "Always bills."

These were the first words she'd spoken in six blocks. Jasper wondered if he had made a colossal mistake by coming.

"Do you have any flowers in your yard?" he ventured, choos-ing his words carefully, beginning to appreciate the full dimen-sion of his invasion.

"In the backyard, I'll show you. Nothing gives me more plea-sure than tending my garden. If you have any interest in botany or horticulture, it probably came from me."

Jasper smiled and nodded enthusiastically though he had no interest in either.

They took a flagstone path around the side of the house. A canopy of tall conifer trees cast cool, elongated shadows in the late afternoon sun.

"Wow," Jasper said.

Connie's garden was a botanical fireworks display. There was a fountain in one corner, a birdbath and shrubs in another, and he had never seen so many flowers and plants growing in one place. He wished he'd had the foresight to bring her a bouquet of something.

"How many different kinds of flowers do you have?"

Connie thought for a moment. "I don't know, but I love their names. Would you like to hear some?"

"Sure." Jasper was glad she was speaking again.

As she turned on the water sprinkler to give her thirsty friends a drink, she rattled off a list of names, directing his attention here and there, occasionally bending over to point or pull off a dead leaf. He wasn't really listening but did notice that a few of the names sounded very poetic.

"You're a damn good . . . oops, sorry, pardon my French," Jasper blushed. "You're a darn good gardener, Connie."

She smiled. "You don't have to apologize. What am I gonna do, send you to your room?"

They both laughed and things seemed to loosen up.

"This is very impressive."

"Want to see something else?" Connie asked. "Look." She motioned off into the distance to where the Space Needle hung just above the horizon. From their heightened perspective at the top of Queen Anne Hill, the Space Needle's stem was obscured by trees and high-rise buildings. "Flying saucer."

"Cool," Jasper said.

"They have telescopes up there that you can use for a quarter. People are probably spying on us even as we speak." She smiled and Jasper followed her into the house.

"I'm going to get changed. In the meantime, make yourself at home. See what you can find to drink in the fridge. I'll be right out." She turned on the TV and snatched up some bras and panties that had been hanging from a coat tree.

The modest ranch-style home was like Connie: well-groomed.

It was filled with comfy, tasteful furniture and plenty of thriving house plants. As Jasper gravitated toward some old photos on the wall, it occurred to him that his biological mother, Constance Marie Suggs, was naked in the next room. Life was getting to be more surreal than his poetry. He tried to concentrate on the pictures. These people might be blood relatives, he thought. He noticed she left the sound down on the TV. He did that too, watched the screen without the sound. He heard the shower running.

In minutes, Connie came out looking refreshed and invigorated, wearing a red jumpsuit and sandals, hair wet and combed back. "You didn't get anything to drink?"

"I'm fine. Really."

"I hope you'll stay for dinner."

Jasper was relieved. He'd been getting the impression she wanted him to vacate the premises. "How 'bout I take you out somewhere."

"Nonsense," she said. "It'll give me a chance to show off my cooking skills. I used to take classes. I specialize in angel-hair pasta with fresh salmon and roasted vegetables. Steve's palate is about as sophisticated as a chili dog, so it'll be nice to cook for someone who appreciates it. Are you allergic to anything?"

"No," he said. "I eat everything."

She touched her hip with her fingertip. "You can probably thank me for that."

Connie poured herself a glass of White Zinfandel. Jasper assured her that he really didn't care for any but she poured one anyway. He wasn't hungry either, but kept that to himself as she banged some pots and pans together in the kitchen.

"You know, I probably have just as many questions for you as you have for me," she said.

"Ask me anything you'd like," Jasper offered.

"All right. Well, for starters, what do you do for a living? Are you in school?"

"I dropped out," he admitted sheepishly. "But I'll be going back one of these days. I've actually saved some money. Got a job working on a ranch. I push rocks around and shovel manure for a living. Once I save enough, I'll go back and finish. Besides that, I mostly like to write poetry. That's my real passion. I want to be a poet someday."

"You know, I used to write poetry back when I was in school. I was pretty good at it, too. I'll have to resurrect it out of the basement and show you." After a pause she said, "Are you happy?"

"Am I happy?" Jasper laughed. "Am I happy? I don't know," he shrugged. "Nobody's ever asked me that before. But I think I have a pretty high I.Q." He slightly cringed as he had no idea why he'd said that.

Connie smiled. "Tell me everything about yourself. I want to know it all." She chopped up garlic, green onion, red pepper, carrots, and mushrooms, occasionally pushing her hair back from her forehead with her wrist.

Jasper started by opening his briefcase and extracting MY BABY BOOK. As he read, he saw Connie stop cooking to listen, and then resume. He recounted his return to 235 Magellan Drive and how Doris, his other mother, had explained the adoption when he was five but it didn't take. He told her about *Mom, where's my real mom?* He told her about changing his name, that it cost two hundred and fifteen dollars, and how he'd never gotten over the death of Doris McPherson and doubted he ever would.

"In time, it'll get easier," Connie said, "but it's something that changes you permanently. You'll never get over it completely. You're not supposed to. I feel the same way about Daddy."

Jasper didn't know whether to continue or not, but he was finding this very cathartic. "I always felt loved, don't get me wrong. But there was something that just didn't click in my family." He expounded upon the chasm between himself and Robert McPherson, how their brains were not the same color, and how disappointed he was in Doris McPherson.

"For a woman, parenthood can be a very touchy subject. She didn't tell you," Connie said, "because she didn't want to get her heart broken again."

Jasper wondered if that was what he was doing to Connie, breaking her heart again, but he couldn't stop and went on. He recounted his chance encounter with Troy Archer, Bud, the ranch, the killer sunsets, Lani of course, and guessing who he was for the last seven months. He told her things that he never dreamed he would, things he didn't even know himself until he blurted them out.

By the time Jasper had concluded his life story, they finished eating dinner and Connie was loading the dishwasher. The meal was extraordinary. Connie poured him another glass of wine. He had been talking so long that at times he forgot to whom he was speaking. The conversation was strikingly similar to the night he had met Troy and ate Bud's venison stew, soul-searching until dawn, figuring out life's secrets with a perfect stranger.

"So," Jasper said after they had moved into the living room and were seated across from one another on the couch, "that's me. I wouldn't necessarily say I'm happy, but I'm getting there. When I think I'm not making much progress, I remember that just a year ago, I was still denying the existence of Junior McPherson. So, enough about me. Your turn."

"I usually don't drink," Connie said. "I think I'm getting tipsy."

Jasper complimented her again on the cuisine. The TV was still on with the sound down.

"I'll tell you everything but be forewarned, some of this isn't going to be very pretty. Are you sure you can take it?"

Jasper nodded although he wasn't sure at all.

Connie stood up. "I have old photo albums I can show you with lots of family pictures like those," she pointed to the wall. "When I've had enough time to process all this, I'll send you a letter and explain everything in more detail. I'll even mail you a copy of the Suggs' family tree and coat-of-arms if you'd like. I have all that stuff packed away somewhere. But for now," she took another sip of wine and a deep breath. "I'll tell you how you came to be." She paced across the room. "I was born in nineteen thirty-seven on New Year's Day, Decatur, Illinois, to Walter and Claire Suggs. Youngest of three. My parents thought their baby-making days were long gone by the time I popped out of the oven, but with two boys already, they were happy to have a girl. And Daddy spoiled me rotten, just as I'm sure Doris spoiled you."

Jasper nodded.

"We moved around a lot. Daddy was a car salesman and not a very good one, so every two or three years we'd just pack up and move. By the time I was old enough for school, it was obvious that Daddy's little princess was just decoration on the cake. He spent every free hour with my brothers, playing baseball or building go-carts. Girls weren't meant to actually do anything he once told me, but support their family. That was Daddy. I loved him, but he could be a real mule. As for my mother," Connie rolled her eyes, finished her wine, poured some more. "Claire loved to say that my *sin* killed Daddy. He had a heart attack a few weeks after they found out I was pregnant, and Claire had the gall to insinuate that his death was all my fault. She told her best friend that I had disappointed him into an early grave. Keep in mind, we're talking about a man who already had two heart surgeries and a bum ticker for over twenty years. I don't think my mother ever got over being dethroned as Walter's little princess."

"I'm sorry," Jasper said.

"Don't be." Connie laughed giddily. She poured more wine. "I hope you don't think I'm a lush."

"I don't."

261

"That woman resented the hell out of me. And to make matters worse, I'm just like her in a lot of ways. Not mean-spirited mind you, but selfish. I didn't want to be left out socially just because we didn't have any money. I was always running around with my girlfriends, going to parties, meeting men. I had plenty of boyfriends, but I was never intimate with any of them. Nineteen fifty-eight was just a hop-skip-and-a-jump away from the days of the Scarlet Letter. Men could screw around and brag about it all they wanted, but a woman was finished if she got a reputation for being easy."

Jasper drank more wine.

"My parents ran my life. I did what I was told and tried to say something witty to the boys to compensate for this." She pinched a roll of fat around her middle. "After you were handed over to Catholic Charities, they sent me to Seattle to live with my aunt and uncle. Claire used to call me 'her little floozy.' My parents were very strict Catholics, and this was their worst nightmare come true. And I was so stupid because, silly me," Connie said, "I thought you couldn't get pregnant the first time. The only thing more profound than my ignorance was my arrogance. I thought I was one sharp cookie."

"I was the result of your first time?"

"Yes."

Jasper found solace in this revelation although he wasn't sure why.

Connie sat down and scrutinized him carefully. "We're being one hundred percent honest here, right?"

"Right."

"Then I'm going to tell you something that might sting a little, but it's important."

Oh God, Jasper thought. "OK."

"When I found out I was pregnant, I wanted to get an abortion. Even though it was illegal, I wasn't against it morally like

262

my parents. I just didn't know where to get one. We lived in a small town. Everyone knew everyone. My parents controlled me. Of course now, as I'm sitting here with you face-to-face, I'm glad I didn't. But back then I couldn't bear the thought of giving you away to a total stranger or, worse yet, to my mother, who would've poisoned your mind while I worked all day had I decided to keep you. I wasn't ready for a baby, but where was I supposed to get an abortion in nineteen fifty-eight without my parents finding out? I would've been disowned. The Suggs family wasn't perfect, but it was the only family I had. I was absolutely miserable. Once I got so depressed I beat my stomach with my fists to try to induce a miscarriage."

As Connie went on with the story, Jasper was thinking this wasn't at all the way he'd imagined it. Even the worst-case-scenario fantasy of his conception was that his biological mother had been a hooker who didn't believe in abortion. The possibility that she had actually wanted to terminate the pregnancy had never occurred to him.

"When it was decided that I would give you up for adoption, I realized it was the right thing to do. Why make you pay for my mistake? I couldn't subject you to Claire, so I figured the unselfish thing to do was to give you to someone who could provide the kind of life I couldn't. It was the hardest decision I've ever had to make."

Jasper exhaled heavily. "Tell me about my father."

"We *kept company*, as your documents say, for one night, not five years. Horace Hanley was his name. He was working the professional wrestling circuits in the Midwestern states."

"Really? I'm the son of a famous grappler?" Jasper loved wrestling.

"Yup. He was known as 'Manly Horace Hanley'. My girlfriends and I were having dinner at a nightclub. He was there with some fellas and, well, you know, one thing led to another.

We went back to his hotel and I let him pin me."

They both laughed.

"Do you know where he is these days?"

"He died in a freak accident a couple months before you were born. What a body that man had. Pretty smart, too. He'd been a championship wrestler in high school and college, but he didn't talk much about wrestling when I was with him. Liked to talk about everything else though: art, religion, politics. He was three states away before I found out I was pregnant. Wrote him a note but never got a reply. Don't know for sure if he ever received it."

"What kind of freak accident?"

"He used to make extra cash performing at exhibitions—carnivals, state fairs, that kind of thing. Horace would lie down on a bench and his assistant would put a chunk of quarry stone on his stomach and smash it in two with a sledge hammer. Apparently, one afternoon they were unable to track down any quarry stone, so Horace's assistant used a slab of granite instead. But when he hit it with the sledge hammer, a sliver splintered off and caught Horace in the jugular. From what I read in the newspaper, he bled to death in no time flat."

"Holy hell. How bizarre is that?"

"Horace was a large man, so I knew you were going to be a big baby. I hated my mother for making me leave all my friends, but it was for the best. They say you can't run away from your problems, but I did. Well, until today that is."

Jasper set his empty goblet down on the table.

"May ninth, nineteen fifty-nine, was and still is the worst day of my life. I never got to see you or hold you. I heard you cry but only for a few seconds. When I stepped off the bus in Seattle, I was determined to change my life. I could've changed my name like you did, but I went the opposite direction. I wanted to make something new of Connie Suggs. I wanted to prove to my mother that I was worthwhile, that I was valuable. Sounds terrible when I say it today, but my whole life revolved around proving that woman wrong. My Uncle Roy and Auntie Mim had lived here for thirty years. Their kids were grown and moved out, so they had plenty of room. Uncle Roy worked at Boeing driving rivets into airplanes, and Auntie Mim taught fourth grade. They allowed me to become a part of their family, and I'll never be able to repay them for that. I finally got to see how a real family's supposed to work. I still see Roy and Mim every Tuesday night for canasta."

"Did you ever get married or have any other kids?"

"No kids but I was married once. Duke. We've been divorced for years. It's a long story."

"Go ahead," Jasper said. "I'd like to hear it."

Connie stared silently into her empty wine glass and began to cry.

Shit, Jasper thought, should've left well enough alone. He scooted over and consoled her, arm around her shoulder. She dabbed at her eyes with a napkin.

"We don't have to talk about this," he said. "I didn't mean to pry."

"He's the reason I kept my last name, Suggs. He didn't even want me to have his name. Can you believe that?"

"What was his name?"

"It doesn't matter," Connie said red-faced. "I met him through Uncle Roy. Duke worked at Boeing and he'd been married before. He had a couple kids by that marriage, so he wanted to devote more time to them before we had any of our own. I was just so crazy to be with him that I agreed. The day we got married was absolutely joyous. Uncle Roy and Auntie Mim rented a hall with a band and a caterer. My brothers flew in. My mother declined to attend, so what else is new? I didn't care. I thought I had it made with Duke. He was a real go-getter and I liked that."

265

She laughed. "I had this notion that we were special, that we were going to make it where others had failed. The word I used to describe us was *quixotic*. He was my quixotic Don Quixote."

"What happened?"

"He left me."

"How come?" Jasper said, hoping it wouldn't make her cry again.

"He left me for the reason all men leave their wives in this country, for someone younger, prettier, and with bigger boobs. He left me for some bouncy Boeing secretary who wore short skirts and fawned over all his boring stories. She adored him just like I did. A few years later, he dumped her, too."

"Sorry," Jasper said.

"Eight years of marriage was over in the blink of an eye. He used to tell me he was playing golf. Duke liked sports so I thought, great, he's really taken to golf. What he was actually doing was playing house with his little Boeing honey. Flying her friendly skies. It went on for two years before I finally figured out there was never any grass or dirt on his golf shoes. One morning on a whim I followed him, and he drove right past the golf course and directly over to her place. Then it finally dawned on me why he never looked me in the eye when he told me his tee time or golf score. Turns out his handicap was me."

For the first time it occurred to Jasper that being female must be tough. Men could be such assholes.

"By the time the divorce went through, I was thirty-seven," Connie continued. "I ended up with a house that wasn't paid for and a broken spirit. I would've done anything for that man. I didn't date for a long time after that. When I started going out with Steve, my biological alarm clock had already run down. Seeing you reminds me how much I wanted a baby. Now it's too late. Steve doesn't want kids. I hadn't really given any of this much thought recently, at least until you dropped out of the clouds. You were right. It is an incredible intrusion."

"I should've called," Jasper said. Suddenly Connie seemed sullen, morose.

"I don't blame you but the thing is, when I signed the adoption papers, the court promised to protect my privacy. Those records were to remain sealed, and they said they absolutely guaranteed my confidentiality. Yet here you are, sitting in my living room. It wasn't until I watched that TV show that I seriously entertained the idea of you finding me. The courts assured that would never happen."

"Are you angry that I came?" Jasper said.

She shook her head. "No. I'm angry with all the men, lawyers and judges, who made promises they couldn't keep. That's the intrusion. There's no doubt about it, men lie and intrude. That's what they do, invade your privacy when it suits their needs."

Jasper was wondering if it was time to leave. "I can understand your resentment about the legal system but with all due respect, Connie," Jasper said, "I feel like I have a right to know where I came from. All these secrets are toxic. Whoever changed your name on the birth records to Victoria Lynn Carver is toxic. Whoever told you that I wouldn't be interested in knowing where I came from is toxic. There are some things in life that no one has the right to conceal regardless of the law. I don't blame you. You were young. You made a mistake. Heck, I've made more mistakes than I can count. But all these secret deals that are sealed with a wink and a nod behind closed doors? The parents and lawyers need to know they're playing with the lives of real people. We're not paper dolls. We're not cardboard cut-outs. They're making business transactions with peoples' lives like we're soybeans or pork bellies."

When Connie didn't say anything, Jasper knew he had gone too far. "I'm not blaming you or judging you, Connie. All I'm saying is . . . shit, I'm sorry, this is coming out all wrong. I'm losing sight of why I came here. I wanted to thank you for nine months of agony and for giving me the gift of life. That's all I really wanted to say."

Connie wiped her tear-streaked cheeks.

He held her smooth hands in his. "Thank you for May ninth, nineteen fifty-nine, and the nine months leading up to it. That's what I came to say. Now that I've said it, it's time to go."

"No, you can't." Connie checked her watch. "My God, look at the time. It's two in the morning. Please stay. You must. *Please.* This couch pulls out and it's very comfortable. Say you'll stay."

"I've intruded enough already. You said so yourself."

"I was just a little overwhelmed, that's all. Look, when do you have to fly back to Arizona?"

"Well, anytime really. I have an open-ended return flight."

"Perfect," Connie replied. "Forget the hotel. Spend a couple days with me. I'll show you Seattle. This reunion is going to take time. We can't do it all in one night."

What the hell, he thought. "Are you sure?"

Connie pulled him up from the couch and kissed him on the cheek. "You bet I'm sure. Wait until Steve hears I'm taking vacation days. He's going to have a cow. Spare pillows and blankets and everything else you need are in that closet."

They said their goodnights. Connie retreated to the bedroom and shut the door. Jasper stripped to his underwear and crashed on the couch. Now that it was over, he felt as though he had just accomplished something so monumental that it would take several days to digest. All he knew for sure was that he felt like he could breathe again.

* * *

It was six a.m. the following morning, and something collided into the screen door. Jasper bolted straight up on the couch, looking around in that foggy disorientation one experiences when waking on foreign turf. When he saw the empty wineglass on the table, it all came back to him. He put on his clothes and quietly opened the front door to find the Sunday paper on the front porch.

He decided to turn on the TV but without the sound, so as not to wake Connie. He sat on the couch, stretched, yawned, and when he looked up again at the TV, there was an image of Troy Archer. He raced over and turned up the volume. "We interrupt this program for a special news bulletin. Troy Archer, lead singer of the highly acclaimed American rock band the Unknowns, was the victim of a fatal motorcycle accident in Kansas City, Missouri, on Friday evening. Kansas City officials say Archer was forced off the road by a motorist who fell asleep at the wheel and lost control of his vehicle. Three other drivers were injured, and all are in critical condition this morning at the Truman Medical Center. Preliminary police reports indicate Archer was wearing a safety helmet, and no traces of drugs or alcohol were present at the scene. Once again, lead singer Troy Archer of the Unknowns, dead at age forty-one."

"Fuck!" Jasper shouted. He looked at the newspaper. Troy's picture and obituary were on the bottom of Page One. "No!"

Connie came rushing out of the bedroom, cinching up her bathrobe. "What's wrong? What happened?"

He cried on her shoulder. For the first time since Doris died, he cried. He handed her the newspaper. There it was in black and white: ROCK LEGEND PERISHES IN FATAL CRASH. He remembered the first night they met, how they'd almost been T-boned by some runaway Buick. Troy always said no one knew how to drive.

Jasper tried to call Bud, but no one answered at the ranch. He had to get back to Tucson.

"I'm sorry."

"It's all right," Connie said. "I understand."

"I enjoyed last night," Jasper said. "I'm sorry I showed up on your doorstep unannounced. That was wrong of me."

"It's OK," Connie hugged him. "Let's do it again sometime."

He broke down once more and cried, burying his face in his hands, and Connie held him and rocked him gently, the way she hadn't been allowed to on that day in May of 1959.

* * *

Upon Jasper's return to Tucson, Leo Squigg filled him in on all the fateful details regarding Troy's death and Bud's relapse into hysterical blindness. Bud had been committed to a Scottsdale hospital where he would be worked on by a new team of dream doctors. The ranch was put on the market because Bud had decided he would not be coming back. Jasper, Betty, and the ranch hands understood. Jasper stayed at Leo's that first night, but hadn't heard from him since. He expected to be contacted by someone in regard to Troy's funeral, but several days passed without notice. Whenever one of the Unknowns' songs hit the airwaves, Jasper lapsed into melancholy.

He moved back to the heart of the city, into a studio apartment just two blocks from his old place. It didn't have a second-story sundeck or romantic view, but it cost less. Best of all, he didn't have to look for a job. Tony was willing to rehire him at Thyme Market. The salary wasn't nearly as much as he'd made on the ranch, but at least Jasper wouldn't be walking all bent over like the Hunchback of Notre Dame. Plus, he got to talk to people again. Tony still hadn't mentioned the incident about the back door nor had he entrusted Jasper with the keys. Jasper had only been back at the market three days when a familiar customer sauntered in.

"Mildred Landish," Jasper said, holding the door open. "Remember me?"

Old Mrs. Outlandish squinted at him and smiled. "I remember you, Jason."

"No, Jasper. That's Jas-per. How's everything? How's your son?"

"You made me hurry all the time," she said.

Jasper laughed, "Not anymore. Now I see you're the first customer in the store."

She smiled. "I beat everyone."

"Good for you, Mildred." He reached up to the top shelf and helped her with some cans of cat food. There had been many of these tiny reunions with customers but none more satisfying than this one. Just as she was about to leave, Jasper said, "Hey, Mildred."

She turned around.

"Remember that time when you told me that I should taste things? Just in case people ask what they taste like? Remember that?"

She smiled. "No."

"Well I just wanted you to know that I'm very fond of both the mixed grill and the savory salmon."

Mildred shooed him away with her hand. "Jasper, you poco loco." She grinned. "Adios."

The morning progressed uneventfully with delivery men and housewives and when it wasn't busy, Jasper loaded his pricing gun and slapped stickers on the new stock. When it was time for lunch, Tony's wife Pam took over the register and marked Jasper's tab for one carton of milk, a bag of chips, and a ham sandwich on rye—no more free handouts. He went outside to eat at one of the wooden picnic tables on the side of the building and pulled a poem he'd been working on from his back pocket, something new about Troy Archer and the idea of having to go backward to go forward. The working title was "Counterclockwise."

the womb of the desert is secluded
behind the organ pipe cactus & palo verde tree
if you look very closely
you will find a clock there

& whether you are a king, a tycoon
or rock 'n' roll superstar
a time will come when you will be inclined
to embrace this clock

crawl back inside the womb
to the warmth, the nourishment, the oxygen
knowing the only way to go forward
is to go backward

because tomorrow has already happened
yesterday never was
the tomb & the womb are synonymous
unless you can stop that clock

if only momentarily
for a day or two at a time
& only then can all be new again
even the moon

can belong to you & you alone

Just as Jasper finished reading the poem, he saw someone wearing an army jacket going through trash cans in the alley. It was King Rat! Jasper stuffed his lunch back into the brown bag and rushed out to greet him.

"Hey, I got somethin' for you."

King Rat returned a lid to a trash can with a loud metal clang and hurried away.

"No," Jasper insisted, running to catch up. "I'm not gonna hurt you. Here." He opened the bag and the King stopped abruptly. "It's nothin' special, just some lunch."

King Rat nervously sucked on his fingertips but did not retreat in fear.

"What's your name?"

King Rat looked at him then turned away.

"My name's Jasper. What's yours?"

No answer.

"That's all right. Here." He took out the carton of milk, opened it, and handed it to him along with the brown bag. King Rat held both items in his hands motionless as if awaiting further instructions. "Take care, brother," Jasper said.

King Rat sat on a trash can and ate the ham sandwich. He reached into the bag and held up the poem Jasper had inadvertently left there. King Rat unfolded it, looked it over on both sides then stashed it into his army jacket.

At quitting time, the night clerk took over the register but before Jasper could get out the door, he saw none other than Bud Black strolling up the sidewalk with a cane. He was wearing sunglasses and being led by a German shepherd to the front of the store. Leo was there too, sweating profusely through his banana-colored suit.

"Bud," Jasper hugged him. "Man, I've been so worried about you. Long time no hear. How are ya doin'?"

"Fine." Bud tapped his cane against the pavement and his dog sat down. "I'm gonna beat this thing just like I beat it before."

Jasper shook Leo's hand.

"I hope you understand about selling off the ranch," Bud said. "I couldn't bear to live there anymore."

Jasper said he did.

"Leo tells me Seattle went pretty well."

"It did. I liked Connie a lot. And if it weren't for you and Troy, I would've never even known about her much less met her."

"Hey," Leo jumped in, "What about me? I found her."

"Especially you, Leo." Jasper petted the German shepherd behind the ear then stopped, not knowing if it was permitted.

"I need your help," Bud said, his sunglasses aimed slightly over Jasper's head. He showed Jasper the letter he had found with Troy's will, the one requesting cremation and the ashes to be launched down the old Mississippi.

Jasper read it and gave it back. "That seems eccentric even for Troy. Why would he request this?"

"Troy used to say if you can't sing the blues, you can't sing rock 'n' roll. I'm not sure, but I think it's some final tribute to the blues. St. Louis to New Orleans? What else could it be?"

"Beats me," Jasper said. "Are you gonna do it?"

"That's why I'm here. I want you to go with me. Leo's got a sick wife, and I need someone to escort me back to St. Louis. I was going to wait 'til I could see again, but my doctors believe it's important to do it now, as part of my therapy. So do you mind if I borrow your eyes?"

Jasper could hardly say no after all Bud and Troy had done for him. "Hell, man, it'd be a privilege. I'm off in less than an hour, and I don't have to work for the next two days."

"Perfect. We're leaving tonight," Bud said. "By the way, here's some mail for you." He handed over a few letters and smiled behind his shades. "I'd read that top one first if I were you. I'm going to get some coffee and wait for you to get off work. Come on, Leo." They headed to the coffee shop across the street led by the dog.

The letter Bud referred to was postmarked Guam, USA. It was from Lani, written a month earlier. Jasper speed-read it. She missed him. She missed him every day, especially his poetry. And she signed it: *Love, Lani.* "Yeah," he yelled out and pumped his fist. "Ya-hoo!"

* * *

Jasper, Bud, and the dog piled into Leo's van. "We've got plenty of time before the flight," Bud said. "Let's grab a quick bite at the Palomino. Good news from Guam?"

Jasper was euphoric. "Her father's doing much better. She's coming back to finish school in January."

They stopped by Jasper's studio apartment. He threw a few clothes into a gym bag and in no time, they were eating veal Oscar. By midnight, Jasper and Bud had flown to St. Louis and registered at Stouffer's Riverfront Inn in order to fulfill Troy Archer's final will and testament. Bud brought just one suitcase, which contained the materials they would need to do the job, including the silver urn with Troy's ashes.

Early the next morning, Jasper led Bud by the arm down to the riverfront where they walked along the banks of the muddy Mississippi. Several hundred yards upstream, barges and tugs maneuvered through the ruddy currents as well as a few small pleasure craft. The day would be hot and humid. The river smelled dank like someone's flooded basement. Jasper noticed the water level was substantially higher than it had on their previous pilgrimage a year before.

They found a clearing at the river's edge, and Jasper gathered small logs to make the raft. Bud had come equipped with twine, rope, and a handsaw. In less than an hour, Jasper had constructed a crude sailing vessel about the size of a storm door. He was immensely proud of it and Bud, in charge of quality control, felt the craft with his hands: the logs, the knots . . . everything.

"Good," Bud said. "I think this is what he had in mind."

"There are some weeds up here," Jasper said. "I'll stash it and mark the spot with some rocks until tonight."

"Excellent."

They spent the rest of the day in the hotel room relaxing, and Jasper watched TV while Bud listened. Room service arrived and Jasper drank champagne toasts to Troy. Bud, who was back on the wagon, sipped sparkling cider and told stories about Troy as he twirled his cane like a baton. Jasper was impressed by how much Troy Archer had meant to Bud, that a man could be so close to another man. Sometimes it seemed he was reminiscing about a departed spouse.

Later, just after dark, the sacred ceremony began. Jasper carefully retraced his steps along the river while Bud held onto his elbow with one hand and carried the funeral items with the other. Jasper occasionally slipped and wobbled, unstable from too many toasts, but the smell of the night air and the lapping movement of the river was beginning to sober him up. The moon coated the sky with a milky rinse and lightning bugs sporadically illuminated the trail. Occasionally, Jasper felt Bud grip his arm a little tighter to balance himself. Other than a random car horn honking in the distance and their own breathing, the only sound came from the lick of the gurgling Mississippi and the call of countless insects. There was a sense of solemnity in the air.

"Right here, Bud. This is it. Stay put while I get the raft." He lugged the crude vessel out of the underbrush and dragged it down to the bank, wiping the sweat off his brow with his sleeve.

"Let's take inventory."

Jasper read off the items like he might with a delivery driver at Thyme Market. "We have one silver urn, one can of charcoal lighter, a box of wooden matches, rope, twine, and a microphone."

"The microphone was my idea."

"Nice touch," Jasper said. "The water's moving at a pretty good clip. Maybe I should roll up my pants legs and walk out into the drink a few yards to launch this baby. That way I can get the raft into the current."

"Just be careful," Bud said.

Jasper secured the urn and the microphone to the raft with the twine, crisscrossing it under and over the logs until it was snug. Bud felt it with his hands to make sure the knots were secure. Jasper doused the logs with lighter fluid and let them soak in for a while. The silver urn, about the size of a milk carton, had an ornamental lid that had been secured with tape. Troy's ashes weren't gray like a cigarette's but more of a fine white powder with pieces of bone fragment mixed in.

"Tell me what you see," Bud said.

"It's a nice night. The stars are out. The moon's bright and reflecting off the shoals and boils in the river. I can see whirlpools and small eddies swirling around. All in all, everything's pretty peaceful except for the mosquitoes. As long as the cops don't show up, we're flying under the radar."

"Beautiful," Bud said. "First, the eulogy." He addressed Jasper, his flock of one. Bud had explained that Troy was very specific about his funeral. He did not want fanfare or tributes, not even a public memorial or wake. All he wanted was this, to have his ashes floated down Old Man River. "Suddenly I feel like a man of the cloth."

Jasper hadn't been to a funeral since Doris McPherson's. Despite the champagne, he felt the sanctity of the moment and removed his baseball cap.

"Dearly beloved, those with us in the flesh and those with us in spirit, welcome. We are here today to commemorate the life of one Troy Scott Archer. Despite his persona, Troy was a private man. We are here not to celebrate the spectacle of his celebrity but to pay our final respects to a man who had a deep and abiding faith in humanity."

Jasper steadied himself.

"To his millions of fans, to the people around the world who loved him, he was a legend, a musical icon. But if Troy were here today, he'd be the first to tell you that fame didn't define him in the least. Troy's immense capacity for love and compassion is what set him apart from the rest of the world. Troy Archer loved life. He embraced life's sojourn into the unknown, and he even named his band after that journey."

"He liked adventure," Jasper said.

"Yes. Troy Scott Archer cherished the adventure of life. He relished his time on this Earth. I've never met an individual who cared more for humanity. He was always trying to find himself, and now finally I hope he has."

Jasper made the sign of the cross.

"To his daughter, Felicity, discovering you was probably the single most exhilarating experience of his abbreviated life. I'm sure you would've loved him just like we all did. And Jasper Trueblood."

Jasper straightened up.

"You were the turning point in his life."

"I was?"

"You sure were. Meeting you played a significant role in helping him to adjust to life after the band. His time at the Kansas City Crisis Center was the most satisfying period of his life. You inspired him."

"I did?"

"Yes," Bud said. "He said that more than once. Troy saw a lot of himself in you, from back when he was your age. Your courage to tackle family history really moved him."

Jasper was honored. "Wow." His eyes started to water.

"As for myself, what can I say? I've lost my best friend. But I tell ya' what, someday I'm gonna get my sight back and . . ." Bud hesitated, "and whenever I feel despair start to extrapolate in my bones and I feel like I can't go on, I'm gonna think about Troy Archer. I'm gonna remember how he was there for me after Nam, after my first divorce, after my second divorce—everything. I miss you, my friend." He paused. "OK, it's time."

Jasper led Bud through the marsh to the raft. The rush of the river became increasingly audible.

"Jasper, any last words?"

"Yes," He reached down and scooped up a fistful of mud from the bank.

"What are you doing? Describe it."

"I'm putting a little terra firma on the raft. I was an altar boy at a lot of funerals. They always did this. They did this for my mother."

He dropped a glop of Mother Earth on the corner of the raft and wiped his hand on his pants. "Remember man that you are dust and unto dust you shall return." And for the first time throughout the entire ordeal, Jasper saw Bud choke up and cry behind his dark glasses, his face framed by the moonlit sky.

They were silent for a moment then Jasper led Bud to the edge of the river. "Stand here." He dragged the crude ship to the lip of the water through the reeds and cattails. "As you can probably smell, I'm dousing the raft with more lighter fluid. Now I'm slipping off my socks and shoes and rolling up my pants. The trick will be not to drop the matches into the drink. Now I'm walking the raft out into the river." The water was colder than he expected. "Man, this lighter fluid stinks. OK, there. The raft's in the water. I'm about to light the match. You ready, captain?"

"Yeah. Let's do it."

The raft was visibly bobbing up and down, and Jasper had to stand in front of it so it didn't drift away while he lit the match. He walked out farther than he'd meant to and felt the water's nascent pull as his pants got wet up to the thigh. He remembered the first night he met Troy in the restroom of the Blue Parrot and how the redheaded man with the knife had peed in his pants. Jasper smiled.

"I'm lighting the match."

He was excited to see the raft might actually work as the urn and microphone seemed to be firmly cradled in its bosom. With the river fighting against him, he lit the wooden match, tossed it onboard, and stepped back from the brackish current. The raft instantly engulfed in flames. Jasper felt the swoosh of heat across his face as the funeral pyre ignited and rambled down the Mississippi, brightening the bank. "Wow! There it goes. Holy shit!"

"What's happening?"

"The whole thing went up like a bonfire, and it's cruisin' downstream. The flames are rolling right along. Wow," Jasper said, "that's about the coolest thing I've ever seen, Bud. We did it." Jasper stared. "We really did it."

"How far down is it now?"

"Pretty far. Fifty, sixty feet maybe. Jesus, it's burnin' like a son of a bitch. It's rockin' and rollin' right along. Mark Twain would be so proud. See ya on the other side," Jasper said as Troy's funeral pyre floated away down the river and into the night. Next stop, New Orleans. "Rest in peace."

"Now he's singin' where the catfish crawl," Bud said.

"We better get outa here before the cops come."

"Look up in the sky. Do you see any shooting stars?"

"No," Jasper said. "I see a lot of stars but they're staying put."

"Good. Hototo is my spirit guide. He says shooting stars are souls being sent back by the Creator because they haven't achieved enlightenment. The older I get, the more I think he might be right. We're not humans trying to experience the spirit world, we're spirits trying to experience the human world. Anyway, I hope Troy gets to stay."

"Amen, brother," Jasper said.

As the vessel worked its way into the night, they returned to the hotel, Bud's hand on Jasper's shoulder, the mud squishing under their footsteps, and the crickets cheering them on. When they reached the room, Bud went directly to bed. Jasper sat up and looked out over the lights of the city. At the river. At everything.

The next morning Bud was anxious to get back to Arizona and the dream doctors, inspired to continue his therapy.

"Since I don't know when I'll be back here again," Jasper said, "I was wondering if we could stop by my mother's grave for a couple minutes."

"Sure," Bud said. "You go right ahead. If it's all the same to you,

I think I'll wait here. Take the rental car and drive over there. You need some walkin' around money?"

"No thanks."

"You gonna stop by and see your old man?"

Jasper's head dropped. He hadn't talked to Robert McPherson since his maiden voyage to 235 Magellan Drive. "I don't know. Maybe."

"Take all the time you need. One thing blind people do very well is use the telephone. I have plenty of people to call, and there are flights leaving every few hours so don't hurry."

Jasper drove across the Eads Bridge with the air conditioner on full-blast and took a look down at the river. He crossed the state line, this time without the sense of foreboding he had experienced a year ago. An Unknowns song played on the FM radio. A cosmic coincidence? He smiled at his reflection in the rear-view mirror and sang along softly, tapping on the steering wheel. He could feel Troy in the car, not just hear his voice but actually feel his presence concealed in the glove compartment or stashed under the seat. There was a warmth, even with the air conditioner on.

It wasn't long before Jasper found the cemetery and the immense marble sign: MOUNT HOPE. The old joke back in high school was: *Mount Hope? Sure, where is she?* Sprinklers threw a steady spray over the vast stretches of green grass. It was still early. There was no one around.

Doris McPherson's burial site was just down the major thoroughfare and around the first bend. The grave was colonnaded by towering oak trees and seeing it all again from the road triggered an avalanche of icy funeral memories. After parking the rental car, Jasper walked around the trees and hedges until he located the old oak he had ferociously punched that cold December day. He gave the trunk a repentant little love tap. "I still think you'd make a nice coffee table."

He approached her plot. The headstone was a modest slab of marble, and the words engraved on it were the same as the flip side of his father's holy cards:

In memory of our dearly departed
DORIS LYNN MCPHERSON
Born: October 20, 1930
Died: December 2, 1978
from her loving family

He was not surprised to see a bouquet of slightly wilting chrysanthemums on his mother's grave. After witnessing the shrine on Robert McPherson's bedroom wall, Jasper expected no less. Careful not to walk directly on her grave, he sat under the forgiving oak. Priests had always instructed altar boys at funerals that stepping on a grave was highly disrespectful. He had read in a book one time, too, that if you ever chewed a blade grass from a cemetery, a drop of blood would drip from your lip.

"Hi, Mom," he said. "I'm not gonna make pope after all."

The sun was shining on his face and, ironically, the cemetery was full of life. Starlings and robins swooped among the hedgerows while crows cawed from the tops of far-off maples and sycamores. Butterflies fluttered through shadows and squirrels ran rampant, their tails upright like exclamation points scampering through the grass. The water sprinklers shut off with perfect synchronization.

"Finding Connie was something I had to do, but no one could ever take your place. You were the real deal all along. You know that. You were the real mom."

He sat under the tree for an hour, no longer idolizing and deifying her as he once had but seeing her as a human being. Doris McPherson was a person just like Troy Archer, just like himself. She laughed, cried, made mistakes, and fought to the end for her child. She taught Jasper how to love, how to be loved, and everything else he would need to survive.

"Someday, Mom," Jasper said aloud, "I want to be the same kind of parent to my kid that you were to me." He bent over, kissed the tombstone, and started to leave when down by the roadside he happened to see someone turn sharply and walk in the opposite direction.

Robert McPherson.

"Hey," Jasper shouted.

His father came to an abrupt halt, stopping nearly in mid-stride. He was holding a new bouquet for the grave. Red tulips. This sacred place would always serve as their common ground and for the first time in years, Jasper felt something akin to happiness. And it was at that very moment all the clocks in all the world stopped and real time kicked in. Life was finally moving clockwise again. Amazing, Jasper thought. Truly amazing.

"Hey!" he yelled out. "Wait up!"

Made in the USA
Middletown, DE
23 May 2015